I0604807

RISE OF THE STRONGEST SOVEREIGN

BOOK 3

RISE OF THE STRONGEST SOVEREIGN

BOOK 3

KAZ HUNTER

Podium

To Lucas.
May you find happiness in all things.

All rights reserved. No part of this publication may be reproduced, stored in a retrieval system, or transmitted in any form or by any means electronic, mechanical, photocopying, recording, or otherwise without prior written permission from Podium Publishing.

This is a work of fiction. Names, characters, places, and incidents are either products of the author's imagination or used fictitiously. Any resemblance to actual events, locales, or persons, living, dead, or undead, is entirely coincidental.

Copyright © 2024 by Kaz Hunter

Cover design by Xiaoraini

ISBN: 978-1-0394-5459-0

Published in 2024 by Podium Publishing
www.podiumaudio.com

RISE OF THE STRONGEST SOVEREIGN

BOOK 3

CHAPTER ONE

[Level: 25]

[Name: Jason Lee]

[Skills:]

[Monster Trainer: Tame a wild monster of an equal or lower power.]

[Pocket Dimension: Create a pocket dimension where you can store your unneeded monsters.]

[Rapid Heal: Heal a tamed monster! Warning: Overuse of this skill will have consequences.]

[Dual Leveling: A designated tamed monster will level up along with you! This will not decrease the XP that you receive. The monster may be in a pocket dimension at the time.]

[Interrogation: You may now speak to monsters you have not tamed, though they may not be willing to talk.]

[Random Strikes: You may now spontaneously tame a monster in the midst of combat. This is random and is not affected by any factors.]

[Brief Acquisition: Gain temporary control over a hostile mob. The duration of this will depend on the strength of the monster, as well as your level compared to its level. With this skill, you can tame monsters of a higher level than with your basic Monster Trainer skill.]

[Mirror Image: A tamed monster will temporarily generate an illusory image. This duplicate will not deal damage, nor can it be harmed. Illusion is controlled by target creature.]

[Bonus XP (passive): Earn extra XP per kill and level up faster!]

[Miniaturize: Shrink a target tamed creature down to a fraction of its size.]

Wham!

With a mighty thump, I slam into the interwoven mat of kraken tentacles. They bend under my weight, forming a bit of a trampoline, and I spring back up into the air. Over to the side, all the rat-people standing on the stairs of the apartment complex turn and look at me, and I give a small salute.

"I don't know who your boss is, but if you don't protect him, I'm going to cut his heart out."

It's a bit of an exaggeration, as I've never actually cut out the heart of a monster—it's a waste of time, really, since monster hearts don't actually give you any cool power-ups or anything—but the essence of the statement is true enough.

Of course, I'll do it anyway, whether or not they come after me, but I'm hoping that they'll rise to the challenge. In the corner of my vision, my chat screen goes wild with the display.

[ChaosRider: Yeah!!!! That's the way to do it, Jason!]

[IceQueen: Show those monsters up!]

[ShadowDancer: Do you think he can really take on all these things in his condition?]

"My condition is perfect." I perform a perfect flip, then dive down into the dungeon. Dark energy swirls around me, and I fall through into the opening chamber. I do my best to land with a perfect superhero stance; though, as the ground is a bit rough, I don't *quite* stick it.

"Ah, close enough." I stand up and rub my hands together, and Burnie flashes down to land on my shoulder. "Now, who's up for a bit of a scuffle?"

All around me, a great many beady rat eyes blink in surprise. There are dozens of the creatures, all wielding large flint knives and rusty swords. They certainly don't look like they're in any real shape to be fighting me. I draw out my Diamond Dagger as well as my Photonic Dagger, and they all hiss and take their stances.

And then all the rat-people from outside come diving back through the portal above me.

If they had come through one at a time, maybe I could have taken them. As it is, they all dive through in one giant pile, which lands on me with the force of a meteor. I'm driven to the ground, and the rest of them around the room run forward and start leaping onto the pile as well. The weight on my body grows more and more intense, and my chat window goes even wilder.

[RazorEdge: Ahhhhhhhhh! Is this the end of Jason?]

[DarkCynic: Nah, he'll pull through it well enough. He always does!]

[ShadowDancer: If I were under that pile, I know how I'd get out.]

[LunarEclipse: Hey, I can't see! Jason, you need to try to get to some light or something!]

"I'm . . . trying," I grunt. I can't see anything either, not really—nothing except the mass of tangled arms and legs flailing around me frantically. "Burnie? Little help here, please."

With that, an immense blast of flame, so hot that it burns blue instead of orange or red, erupts through the pile of rat-people. Now *that* makes them all jump back, and I'm able to climb to my feet. Ash and dead rats fall down around me, and I quickly take stock of my surroundings.

There are . . . oh, I'd say about fifty rat-people in total. Burnie settles down onto my shoulder, and the rat-people all hiss. The area is rocky, I should note, with a slope running up to the flickering portal above. Sort of like the entrance to an underground den, I'd say, though I don't see any exit that might allow us to go any deeper into the place. Oh well! That's fine by me.

"Let 'er rip, Burnie." I nod up at the Phoenix. "I'll take whatever you can't."

Burnie opens his beak and a great gout of flame explodes from his gullet. It washes over the rat-people, burning them to a crisp almost instantly. The fighters dive for cover, some into holes, some behind rocks, some behind other rats. Stone blackens and melts under the intense blast, and heat swirls around the openings of the small dens. By the time Burnie has turned a full circle and sent his scathing heat across the entire group, I estimate that there are less than a quarter of them left alive.

I'm sorry, Master, but I'm afraid I have to take a rest now, or I may overheat.

"You've earned it." I give him a nod. "Go back to your nest."

Burnie dips his beak and flashes back through to my pocket dimension, and I take my stance. With that, the last of the rat-people come roaring out, snarling and stabbing at me with their swords and weapons, and I rush forward to meet them.

Ting!

Scrrrrrrrrrape!

Snickt!

My blade blocks and parries the other weapons, and I stab down through the thin armor of the rat-people without discrimination. I cut down one, then the next, then the next, slowly working my way through the great horde of them. None can stand in my way, and within just a few moments, I've slain the last one. He falls to the ground with a gurgle, and I nod and slowly look around the dungeon.

"Well, that was even quicker than I thought it would be! Now, I think it's time to——"

CRACK!

I spin toward the noise, which comes from the opposite side of the dungeon as the portal. The ground rumbles, and a spiderweb of cracks spreads across the ground there. A smile blooms across my face, and I grip my daggers a bit tighter.

BLAM!

With a mighty roar, a rat king comes rumbling through. He stands at least ten feet tall and wields an enormous club. He snarls and thumps the ground, and then, without further preamble, charges forward toward me, lifting the weapon to smash me into bits.

Thankfully, I'm a bit faster than he is. I dive out of the way, and the club simply hits where I was standing. The shockwave makes me stumble, but not by much, and I throw both of my daggers into the exposed bits of the rat king's torso. They both sink in up to the hilt, and the rat king roars, but he's far from dead.

Time to try out my new dagger.

I quickly draw out the Dagger of Damage, which has yet to see any combat, and charge forward at the thing. He roars once more and lifts his club, and I drop to the ground and slide under him, driving the weapon into his thigh before yanking it back out.

[Damage Dealt: 1]

"One? That's hardly a paper cut." I jump back to my feet and spin back toward the thing. The description of the dagger says that it'll increase damage based on the number of times that the monster has been attacked. "Let's go again."

I run forward once more, and the rat king swings the club horizontally at me. This time I step back to dodge the thing, then lunge forward and land a cut along his arm.

[Damage Dealt: 2]

"Going up, going up." I nod, then leap in close and stab him three quick times in the gut. This time he at least seems to feel the damage, and staggers backward a bit.

[Damage Dealt: 4]

[Damage Dealt: 8]

[Damage Dealt: 16]

[GoldenShield: Ooh!!! I've seen sequences like this! It's going to get really big *really* fast!]

[LunarEclipse: Yeah! This is your most powerful weapon yet, Jason!]

[IceQueen: I'm not sure I get it.]

Frankly, I agree with IceQueen. Math has never been my strong suit, not by a long shot, but I decide to trust the sentiment of the chat. As the rat king snarls and charges forward once more, I prepare to deal as much damage as possible. I leap up to meet the thing and slash him across the arm, dealing thirty-two damage, when he spins like a top and whacks me with his tail.

Crack!

Oomph!

I'm blasted back into the wall, and the thing leaps forward, lifting the club over his head. It comes flashing down toward me, and I narrowly roll out of the way.

Blam!

The blast sends me rolling across the floor, and the rat king strides confidently toward my body. I groan and pull myself to my feet, then fling the dagger with all my might. It hits the rat king in the throat, and to my delight, the monster reels backward, stunned by the blow.

[Damage Dealt: 64]

That's as much as my sword can do on a good day. Now we're talking. I run toward the monster as fast as I can, but he lashes out with his club, doing his best to batter me into the ground. I jump up into the air, sailing nimbly over the thing, and slam into the rat king's belly. He gulps and staggers backward, and I jump upward and grab the blade, dragging it downward just as fast as I can. As I rip it out of his chest, I spin, then stab him in the gut, dealing two more blows.

[Damage Dealt: 128]

[Damage Dealt: 256]

Those two have the monster in pain, though he's still far from dead. I try to leap at him once more, but he spins to attack me with his tail. This time I'm able to anticipate it a bit better, but it's a powerful attack, and it *does* succeed in knocking me back. I gasp in a bit of pain, though nothing too bad, and he lunges at me with the club to flatten me like a pancake.

"Not . . . today!" I narrowly dodge as the thing brings the club smashing to the ground. If he can ever land a hit on me, I'll be feeling it for days, I'm quite certain of that. I stab him in the arm, and the monster screams.

[Damage Dealt: 512]

Now we're starting to get up into numbers that I can appreciate. The rat king, though, seems to sense the same thing, and suddenly changes his pattern of attack. He drops the club and scampers backward several feet, where he then seems to grow darker. His eyes grow black, and his claws lengthen. His body begins to emit a foul sort of stench—the smell of decay, of venom.

[ChaosRider: Now *that's* cool!]

[GoldenShield: Are you kidding? That's not cool, that's abominable!]

[Originalgoth: Someone's got a dictionary sitting next to their computer. I think he's cute.]

"And I think he's probably become venomous." I weigh my options, but I don't have many. The creature hisses and charges, and I gulp. If he hits me with a single claw, it's not going to go well for me. This thing looks like his venom is strong enough to drop a rhino, and while I've got a good bit of health, I have to admit that I don't like the idea of taking on something that's going to eat me up from the inside. I throw my dagger as hard as I can, and it hits the rat king in the shoulder, where it inflicts a long gash before falling to the ground.

[Damage Dealt: 1,024]

The rat king doesn't even seem to notice the damage, although a great deal of his skin does peel off, exposing the rotten skeleton. With that, he lunges forward, and I dive out of the way. Claws rake down my back, and a blistering pain shoots through me.

[Condition: Poisoned. You will begin to take 1 point of damage every 3 seconds for the next 24 hours.]

"I need someone to calculate how much that adds up to!" I grit my teeth and lunge forward, snatching up the dagger. The rat king lurches along just behind me as pain begins to radiate through my entire body. Desperately, I spin around and lift the dagger as the rat king throws himself upon me.

[Damage Dealt: 2,048]

With a great *scree*, the rat king is blasted backward by the force of the cut, even though it was little more than a scratch. With pain erupting up and down my back and through my arms and legs, I slowly rise, take the dagger firmly in my palm, and lunge forward. The rat king's dead eyes meet mine, and I bring the dagger crashing down.

[Damage Dealt: 4,096]

With one last blast, the rat king is torn clean in two, bones and rotten bits of his body splattering across the walls and floors. I take a shaky breath, then fall to my knees.

[LunarEclipse: I just ran the math! You'll take 20 points of damage per minute, or 1,200 points per hour, or 28,800 points over the course of the poisoning!]

"And how much health do I have?" I grit my teeth against the pain. "It's around five thousand, isn't it?"

No one answers, and I know I'm right. My health bar is down in the yellow, probably at about 60 percent, so somewhere around three thousand. That gives me less than three hours to find an antidote.

Somehow, I have a feeling that I'm just going to have to go deeper into the dungeon.

CHAPTER TWO

I open up my inventory and scan for healing items, but that's not something that I've really accumulated much of, except for a decent number of Pumped! products. I sigh in disappointment, then shrug and pull out a single Pumped! soft drink.

"This, at least, should let me heal up enough to make it down into the dungeon."

[Error: Rat King Venom is preventing you from healing.]

[ChaosRider: Wait, what???]

[FireStorm: That's not fair!!!]

[Originalgoth: I think that's totally fair. You're going down, kid.]

I try not to panic. I'm unable to heal, and I don't have a clue how big this dungeon is . . . It's not the biggest confidence booster I've ever had in my life. I swallow down my fear, though, and turn to face the darkness.

"This is just something to keep people moving through

the dungeon." I shrug and start striding into the tunnel. "Krak certainly told me plenty about the politics and designs of dungeons. That thing was put here by the boss to get people to come deeper inside and not just poke their heads in and then leave. We're going all the way to the bottom of this pit!"

[RazorEdge: Yeah! That's the Jason we know!]

[GoldenShield: You've got this, dude!]

[IceQueen: No one says "dude" anymore.]

[GoldenShield: I don't know what part of the world you're from, but everyone says "dude."]

The argument continues as I trek forward, and I ignore it. Instead, I tuck the Dagger of Damage into my inventory and take out my Photonic and Diamond Daggers once more. The scaling nature of the weapon is nice, but it's going to be mostly useful against bosses and mini-bosses. Right now, I'm likely to walk into a trap of sorts, something smaller and a bit more focused, which means that I need something that can deal a lot of damage very quickly. I keep my eyes peeled forward, knowing that I can't take much more damage and keep walking.

Suddenly, I glimpse a light ahead, and I start walking forward a bit faster. I feel the rock pressing in on all sides, and I find myself in a narrow crevice. I turn sideways to squeeze through and soon find myself sliding up to the exit.

There, the crevice overlooks a large room, obviously the next battle room of the dungeon. There's a well in the middle that glistens with a blueish light that's almost as bright as day. Something moves within the well, but I can't tell exactly what it is or if it's friend or foe. I hold my breath, looking about, then slowly step through.

"So, you have bested my little pet."

I freeze and look around, hoping that nothing jumps out at me. Suddenly, the form inside the well begins to rise up, and a lithe, dark shape clothed in black robes rises up out of the depths of the well. A moment later, it steps out and down onto the stone, and I find myself looking at a dark elf king. A crown of ebony sits upon his head, while his dark eyes seem to sparkle with mischief.

"And if I had to wager a guess, I'd say you have the antidote." I draw out my weapons and prepare to attack.

"Ah. Indeed, I do." The dark elf draws out a small vial that contains a glistening powder. "The essence of stardust. A powerful medicine that can be used to cure nearly any ailment, both from your world and from mine. If you can but defeat me, I will give it to you willingly."

"You mean that you'll be unable to stop me as I take it from your corpse." I flash a small, grim smile at him.

"Something like that." The elf returns my grim smile. "I . . . have somewhat less of a death wish than some of the dungeon bosses you may encounter. You may determine for yourself what you believe that to mean. For now . . ." He slowly turns to walk away. "I'm afraid that some more of my pets wish to meet you."

He raises his hands, and invisible chains wrap around my arms and legs. I grit my teeth and surge forward, but I'm held back as two doors open in the stone on the other side of the room. The king sweeps through, the doors close, and a rumble shakes the ground.

"Ho, hum, tum tum tum."

A powerfully low voice drifts through the air, and two more

doors open, one on either side of the room. A troll comes marching through each one, and they look at each other for a moment before turning to look at me. I should, at this point, note that my arms and legs are still being held rather tightly. The trolls hesitate a moment, then thump their chests and thunder across the ground, running for me with great delight upon their faces.

Now, before I continue, I should explain what these trolls look like. I've fought trolls before, and these are largely the same except for the fact that they're a good bit shorter and darker. Each one is probably only six or seven feet tall, a far cry from the others that I've seen in the past. Their skin is also laced with veins of something that looks like an ore of some sort, like coal or iron. I don't know, but I *do* know that they look quite hungry, and neither of them looks like they're going to want to share. They're both fighting to eat me before the other one does, and that means that I have mere seconds before troll teeth start sinking into my flesh.

Which, of course, just means that my success will look that much more epic.

I grit my teeth and strain against the chains. With all my might, I pull downward, and a loud *clang* echoes from above. Stone splinters and metal bends, and I rip my right arm free. Quickly, I swing it through the air, using the invisible chain rather like a whip. I can't see it, but there's a loud *whack* as it hits one of the trolls in the face. The other troll, though, doesn't seem to be hit, and it slams into me an instant later.

Now, there are two distinct effects from that impact. Three, really, I suppose. The first is that I'm torn free of the bonds. They break or dissolve back into whatever magic created them, or . . . something. The second is that my health drops down to about 40 percent. The third is that my body is plunged into even more pain than before. I fall to the ground, gasping in pain, then struggle to my feet as the trolls lumber and lunge at me again.

"I don't think so." I react reflexively and slam my Photonic Dagger into the stomach of the closest troll. It sinks in up to the hilt, and I turn it into a sword with a mental command. *That* makes the blade punch all the way up to its heart, and the troll bellows and staggers backward. I yank the blade back out, then as the second troll lunges at me, I throw my Diamond Dagger into its throat.

The troll howls in pain and staggers a bit, but not nearly as much as I might have liked. It does, though, give me a brief break, and I raise my sword and stab the first troll through the chest once more. With that, I snatch out my Dagger of Damage and, while the troll is held close, stab it as many times as I can.

[Damage Dealt: 1]

[Damage Dealt: 2]

[Damage Dealt: 4]

[Damage Dealt: 8]

[Damage Dealt: 16]

[Damage Dealt: 32]

The creature howls and starts to pull away, and I make one more stab at it, but it manages to yank itself backward. Quickly, I throw the dagger into its belly, dealing a solid and respectable sixty-four, then spin toward the second troll.

My Diamond Dagger still in its neck, it leaps upon me, battering me down to the ground. It lifts a foot and tries to stomp on my head, but I drop my weapons, reach up, and catch the foot a mere inch above my head.

[ChaosRider: Now that's the way to do it, eh, Jason?]

[IceQueen: YEAH!!! Now snap it in half!]

[ViperQueen: I doubt it's really that easy.]

"Watch . . . me." I take a deep breath, then twist the foot as hard as I can. The leg breaks at the knee, and everything from that point down to my hand turns into stone. I toss it to the side, where it smashes apart, and rise back to my feet. The troll staggers and stumbles into the first troll, who turns and smashes a fist into its face. The thing drops like a rock, smashing into rubble as it hits the ground. With that, I lunge forward, kicking the troll in the stomach as hard as I can.

WHAM!

The blast throws the troll backward into the wall, and I bend down, scoop up my sword, and lunge forward. A moment later, I've cut the thing down, and I quickly pick up all my weapons and start walking toward the doorway to follow the dark elf king.

Burble.

Bubbles rise up out of the depths of the well, and I turn and glance at it. More bubbles start to emerge, and the doors ahead of me slam shut.

"Any guesses on what's going to be coming out of there?"

[LunarEclipse: The dark elf king!]

[DarkCynic: A puppy!]

[IceQueen: A water troll!]

[GoldenShield: A legion of dark elf minions!]

[RazorEdge: Are we just going to let it slide that IceQueen thinks a *puppy* is going to come out?]

[IceQueen: I mean . . . like . . . a battle puppy.]

I'm forced to turn away from the chat as a great eruption of water sends a geyser almost to the ceiling of the cavern. As it comes crashing down, a great many rocks and such things come clattering to the floor along with it. Slowly, the water runs back into the well, and the rocks, now dry, rumble and pull themselves together to form a golem-troll-thing. I grit my teeth as it rises up to a height of a good fifteen feet, and it lunges at me, swinging a massive fist.

"Alright!" I dive out of the way as the fist passes narrowly over my head. "I need someone else to help me! Uh . . . Krakey!"

My pocket dimension flickers and opens, and half a dozen tentacles shoot out and wrap around the golem-troll-thing. It snarls, then simply begins shifting its rocks, drawing the tentacles inside of itself. When it has them firmly stuck, the monster throws itself backward, pulling the kraken from within the dimension. A powerful scream echoes through my mind, and I grit my teeth and lunge forward.

"No! You're not going to get away with that so—"

SNAP!

One of the tentacles snaps, followed by another. The scream in my head grows unbearably loud, and I fall to my knees, holding my head in my hands. The golem swings a fist around and cuts the last of the tentacles, and my kraken, wounded, slinks back inside the pocket dimension. I can hear it screaming and thrashing about, and I grit my teeth.

"You're going to regret that."

I charge forward, leaping up into the air. My Dagger of Damage seems to fall into my hand, and I unleash a blistering series of attacks against the golem.

[Damage Dealt: 16]

[Damage Dealt: 32]

[Damage Dealt: 64]

[Damage Dealt: 128]

[Damage Dealt: 256]

[Damage Dealt: 512]

[Damage Dealt: 1,024]

[Damage Dealt: 2,048]

The golem snarls and flails about, damaged, but not downed yet. I snarl and strike several more times, increasing the damage more and more, then draw back and race forward.

Wham!

A fist flies out of nowhere, hitting me directly in the gut. I realize that I was *probably* a bit blinded by rage, but there's nothing to do about it as I'm flung into the air, up toward the ceiling. My health drops down to 30 percent, and I grit my teeth and throw the dagger with all my might. It hits the monster in the head, and the whole thing explodes in a massive blast of gravel and stone. Bits and pieces of the thing rain down all across the battlefield, and I land on the ground with a *thud*. Slowly, I rise back to my feet, then regard the area with concern. Nothing moves, and I give a nod.

[FireStorm: Hey, Jason, check out the well!]

It's a good enough suggestion, and I stagger toward the well as best I can. As I arrive, I find myself staring down into the sparkling depths, down a long tunnel that seems to extend to the center of the Earth. Lights flash from within, and I feel myself being drawn down inside. Suddenly, I blink in surprise, finding myself only a fraction of an inch above the water.

[LunarEclipse: It's trying to draw you down inside!]

[ViperQueen: Be careful! It's probably going to kill you or something!]

"I don't think it is." I slowly push myself back up, then reach out and dip my hand into the waters. As I lift it upward, water pours down in a small waterfall, seemingly generating in my palm to burble down like a fountain. I smile, then tip my hand over. The water falls back into the pool with a splash, and that's the end of it.

[Error: Rat King Venom is preventing you from healing.]

"Of course it is." I sigh, then slowly turn toward the open doors. Suddenly, though, the screaming of the kraken echoes through my head once more, and I fall to the ground. "Ahhh! Krakey, come out!"

I'm afraid I cannot. Without water I will die within seconds. My organs cannot sustain my weight without buoyancy.

"Then . . . are you okay?" I ask quietly.

Master . . . I'm afraid . . . I . . . This may be our last conversation.

[Warning: Tamed Kraken's health is low.]

[Warning: Tamed Kraken's health is dangerously low.]

I pause, hardly able to breathe.

[Notice: Tamed Kraken has died.]

I grit my teeth and slowly rise to my feet. A great many angry thoughts flit through my mind, but I simply ball my hands into fists and tuck all my weapons back into my inventory. It was so senseless. He hadn't performed some sort of heroic act to save me. He hadn't been killed in some epic boss battle. He had just . . . died. What sort of life was that?

[RazorEdge: What are you going to do now, Jason?]

[Originalgoth: He's going to go cry his eyes out! And he's going to deserve all the pain he's in.]

[GrendleH8tr: Kid, stuff happens. You know it just as well as I do. Keep yourself together, and you'll make it through.]

I take a deep breath, then check my health. Thirty percent still. The fall from the ceiling didn't damage me at all, which is some small victory at least. Slowly, I turn toward the open doors and stalk forward.

That king is hiding somewhere in here, and he has the antidote I need. More than that, though, he killed one of my pets. For that, he's going to pay. I don't care if he does surrender early. I'm going to find him, and I'm going to kill him.

And then . . . Well, I'll just have to see where life takes me from there.

CHAPTER THREE

The doors stay open as I stride through and get my bearings. As I look around, though, my eyes pop open in surprise.

[ChaosRider: WHOA! Jason isn't going to get through this, I don't think!]

[LunarEclipse: Aw, you have no faith! He'll get through this just fine! I hope.]

[ShadowDancer: This is going to be a battle for the ages, that's for sure!]

[ViperQueen: Please tell me that someone is recording this!]

[IceQueen: Per the terms and conditions you agreed to when you made this account, recording any of this stream is illegal.]

[GoldenShield: Wait . . . What?]

I chuckle idly at the chat but have to turn my attention to the scene in front of me. The room is enormous, spreading out hundreds of feet in all directions. It still looks like a cave, at least mostly, though it's a cave that's been made habitable. There are enormous pillars holding the ceiling aloft, mostly spread around in somewhat random intervals, while around the pillars and spread across the floor is what looks like a village.

Yeah. It's a full village. There are several large gouges in the walls that look like quarries, while the houses and buildings and things are actually made out of the stone. Little strands of smoke drift up here and there to mark chimneys, while I see people striding about, not really taking notice of my presence.

Of course, all the people that I can see are dark elves. Somehow, I doubt they're going to roll out the red carpet and welcome me inside for a hearty meal unless it's to serve me up as the main course. I take a deep breath, then slowly start to look around and gauge my options.

"Burnie, are you available yet?"

Sorry, Master! These new powers I have . . . They're immensely strong, but the cooldown time—pardon the pun—is rather intense. I'm still out of the running for the time being.

"Then I'll just have to ask someone else." I cross my arms. "Bjorn? You're up!"

A portal appears, and, with the softest padding sound, my great Frost Wolf comes striding out from my pocket dimension. He shakes his fur for a moment, looking about, then turns and meets my eyes. His nose gives several small sniffs of the air.

I smell . . . a hundred of them.

"We can take that many." I nod confidently. Of course, doing it all on only 30 percent health . . . No, 29 percent—the poison continues to eat away at my health—is going to be tricky, but I'm sure I can manage. "How should we play this? Stealth?"

Worth a try.

I nod, and I crouch down and start slipping toward the village. My footsteps are so soft I can barely hear them. Hopefully, the dark elves won't be able to hear them either. We reach the edge of the buildings and slip along the backside of one of them, then enter an alley and slowly slide up toward the street. There are several barrels there, and I crouch down so that I can just peek over the tops of them. A handful of dark elves walk back and forth, weapons at the ready. One or two rat-people scurry along as well, though they seem to be living in fear of the elves as servants, or worse—slaves. I draw out my Diamond and Photonic Daggers, then prepare to spring into action. If I'm fast enough, I can probably dart across the street, taking out one or two, and get back under cover before I'm noticed. Then, I can move through the town, slowly, stealthily, taking everything—

"Hey! What's this here?"

I turn around to see a dark elf warrior standing at the end of the alley, a fierce look upon his face. He draws a long, dark sword, and Bjorn bares his teeth.

"I don't suppose you'd have a leader I could go talk to?" I slowly rise back to my feet. "Someone I could reason with, face to face, and—"

"Your face will only come into his presence when I have carved it from the rest of your body!" the elf snarls, then charges.

"Fair enough." I shrug, and Bjorn springs forward. His mighty paws slam into the elf's shoulders and smash him into the ground, and he bounds away. I follow along behind, stabbing the elf in the chest quickly, and we both jump behind the row of buildings.

Of course, by this point, we've been detected. The jig is up, which means our only hope is to fight our way through.

"Alright, Bjorn! Lay down a layer of ice! Let's take them!"

I can hear footsteps pounding on the ground, and a great many dark elf war cries fill the air. Bjorn and I run back down the alley and into the street, and I find myself facing several dozen of the warriors all charging my way at once. The hair stands up on the back of Bjorn's neck, and he howls.

With that, the air chills, and a great wave of frost grows across the ground in front of us. Almost all the warriors freeze under the blast, growing icicles from their weapons, elbows, and feet. A few on the edges skirt around the attack, and they throw themselves at me with immense ferocity.

"Give . . . it . . . up." I transform my Photonic Dagger into a sword and engage in battle with the monsters as they attack with their dark swords. Steel rings against steel, and I find myself fighting three at once. Bjorn snarls and tears into several of them, knocking them asunder and biting fiercely at their exposed body parts. The elf on my left slips ever so slightly, and I land a long cut along his side. That makes him flinch and stumble backward, and I use the opportunity to press my attack against the middle elf.

Strength seems to flow through my body as I let off three quick attacks, breaking through his defense. He falls back, but it's not enough, and I stab him in the gut. With that, he's down, and I turn to the elf on my right. He sets his jaw and lets out a low snarl, then leaps forward. I block the attack, knocking him to the side, and kick him in the knee. *That* makes him stumble backward, and a white blur knocks him down as Bjorn finishes up the job. That only leaves the first elf

I wounded, who, as I watch, smears a little bit of red sap on his wound, grits his teeth, and charges headlong at me.

Power surges through the elf, likely from the sap. His wound begins to glow, and fire trickles from his eyes. I gulp and block his blow, but it knocks me backward painfully. I take a few steps back to get my bearings, but by then he's already upon me. Our blades flash through the air, faster and faster, ringing out loudly. I hear a snarl from behind me as Bjorn readies himself, and I nod.

"Three." I count out loud, not really caring if the elf hears me. "Two. One. Now!"

I drop to the ground just as the elf lunges forward, and Bjorn lets out a powerful howl, freezing him in place. He falls toward me, and I roll out of the way as he lands and shatters into pieces. I nod in approval as I climb back to my feet, and an idea flickers through my head.

"Quick. This way." I turn and run toward the barrels, which have somehow survived intact. "Bjorn, freeze that main group again!"

Bjorn lets out a howl, and I snatch up several of the barrels. Without even bothering to run back to the middle of the street, I spin and launch the barrels at the crowd with all my might.

Smash!

All of them explode into splinters upon the outstretched weapons of the first row of elves, not doing a lick of harm. I scowl, then shrug. "Oh well. Guess we'll just have to get a bit more creative, then. Makes me wish I had a war hammer or something."

[FireStorm: You do have a hammer!]

[ShadowDancer: Yeah! From your fight against the hob-goblin! You never actually dropped it. It just sort of stayed in your inventory!]

"Really?" I blink in surprise, then open my inventory and do a bit of quick scanning. Sure enough, it only takes me a moment to locate the weapon. I pull it out and give it a twirl. It's a large war hammer—not really my style, but useful enough when necessary. I take a deep breath, then march up and swing it with all my might.

Crash!

The blast sends a shock wave through the entire crowd, shattering the frozen warriors into bits. I chuckle and let the hammer drop back down to the ground, then tuck it into my inventory again. You never know when it might come in handy! With that, I slowly walk forward, Bjorn following along behind. I can hear more dark elves laughing and chittering on the far side of things, and that makes me nervous.

As we round a corner, we find what must be the rest of the town. They're just outside the city limits, standing before a large set of stone stairs that slope up to a set of double doors set in the stone wall. Doors that almost certainly belong to the palace of a king. I nod and take my stance, then flinch as the venom knocks my health down to 28 percent.

"Alright, Bjorn." I scan the crowd. For the moment, they aren't attacking; they're just watching me. I can see a collection of mostly warriors, though there are some elves in long robes and pointy hats back near the rear, which look like mages of some sort. *Those* could be a problem. Additionally, I can hear growls and snarls coming from the sides. There's an ambush of some sort waiting, with the main body of the army intent on distracting me. In any case, even without the ambush, this is going to be a fight. My health is steadily decreasing, and there are a *lot* of these guys. Still, what's a guy to do? I have one option and that's to go through them. Turning around will only mean death. "You know what to do. Let's get through this."

Bjorn gives a nod, and the two of us charge forward. The army moves in turn, and Bjorn howls. A blast of ice streaks up the center of the army, freezing well over half of them, but there are still a *lot* that come down to meet me. Additionally, I see a number of dark blurs coming up from the sides, and I risk a single glance.

Wargs. Large dark-haired wargs. Each one is a bit larger than Bjorn, with long black hair and eyes that glow green. The mages all raise their staffs, which begin glowing the same color. They're controlling the animals somehow, I'm sure of it. I nod and run forward all the faster, hoping that I can use them to my advantage.

As the first of the wargs tries to jump on me, I drop to the ground and slide forward. The monster passes over me with a whoosh, slamming into several dark elf soldiers. Meanwhile, Bjorn simply leaps into the midst of the warriors, tossing them aside like rag dolls. I can see him working his way up toward the mages and move to do the same thing, but a great blast of fire falls from the heights of the cave.

No . . . Not fire. Molten rock.

The mages are shooting blasts of magic up into the ceiling, causing gouts of the stone to melt and come tumbling down. I'm forced to stop, and a torrent of molten rock lands in front of me, incinerating a great many of the frozen soldiers. These guys aren't pulling any punches, that's for sure. A warg runs up from behind me, and I turn and dodge, causing it to slip and fall into the pool of molten rock. That's one more down, but a *lot* more left to go.

With no other choice, I simply lurch into the attack. Elves and wargs and lava swirl all around me, but I simply battle with all my heart. My daggers flash, and light gleams from my weapons in contrast to the darkness around me. Monsters fall before me in droves, but I know I'm taking damage as well. I don't even have time to spare a look at my health bar; I simply fight with all my might.

Suddenly, something hits me from behind, and I'm knocked to the ground. This time I *do* risk a glance and find my health at 13 percent. Hot drool lands on the back of my neck. There's a warg ready to eat me, right here, and that means that I have seconds to live.

[FireStorm: Quick, Jason! Perform your signature power move!]

[ShadowDancer: Every move is his signature power move.]

[DarkCynic: Exactly! Get out of there, Jason!]

[ChaosRider: Burnie, help!!!!!!!!!!]

[Burnie: Still recharging. Sorry, guys. Almost good to go again.]

[GrendleH8tr: You know what you've got to do, kid.]

I nod in agreement and take a deep breath. "Tame monster!"

Power flares in my palms and blasts upward, surging and crackling across the beast behind me.

[Dark Warg is resisting your efforts to tame it.]

"I know, I know." I grit my teeth and try to rise, but the warg is still holding me down. Frankly, it doesn't matter whether I tame it or not if I can only use the time it's frozen to escape. Blood pounds in my ears, and I flip out from underneath it.

[Dark Warg is resisting your efforts to tame it.]

I slowly rise back to my feet. Molten rock is still pouring down from the ceiling above. Dark elf warriors lay scattered all around me, dead from blade wounds, teeth wounds, and fire. I can see Bjorn on the other side of the lava waterfall—lavafall?—but his ice powers don't seem to be having any real effect. Meanwhile, the warg is slowly stalking toward me, teeth bared, ready to strike.

[Dark Warg is resisting your efforts to tame it.]

[Dark Warg is resisting . . .]

The warg crouches, and I brace myself. Fire all around. Thirteen percent health left. Time to make my stand.

CHAPTER FOUR

Dark Warg has been tamed!]

With a flicker, the warg blinks in surprise, then crouches down and nods at me.

Apologies, Master. I'm afraid that I was about to eat you for lunch.

"I'll forgive you if you can get me out of this place." I turn and nod at the molten rock. In response, the warg steps up and snarls low in its throat. The lavafall parts like a curtain, then stops flowing altogether. A single mage, standing behind a protective magical shield, blinks in surprise, then turns to run. My new warg snarls and lets out a powerful howl, and the ground underneath the mage's feet simply crumbles. Fire dances about beneath him, and he's suddenly sucked down into a lava pool. It closes and solidifies a moment later, and that's the end of that battle.

[ViperQueen: WOW!!! I love it!!!]

[ShadowDancer: Give it a name! Give it a name!]

[LunarEclipse: Yeah! I'm thinking Burnie! 'Cause it burned that mage!]

[Burnie: Sorry, dude, but that name's taken.]

The warg steps past me and walks up to Bjorn. They sniff each other for a moment, and the dark-haired beast turns to look at me.

My name is Astrid.

"Well, Astrid, good to meet you!" I smile and hold out my hand, and she pads over to rub her head against my palm. "How are you feeling?"

Liberated. That mage was always in my head, ordering me about. I'll do whatever you need me to do. I'm simply glad to be free of all of that.

"Well, I'm glad to have you." I scratch behind her ears, then slowly walk up toward the doors. "Is the king in?"

I believe so, yes.

A smile spreads across my face as Bjorn and Astrid stride up behind me. As we approach the doors, they rumble and open, revealing a grand throne room. High upon the throne, the king is seated rather arrogantly, smiling down upon us. He has a scepter in his hand that I don't like the look of, one that looks rather like those the mages had been holding. Slowly, he rises and gestures for us to enter.

"Ah! You have a new pet! I do hope she serves you well."

"What's that to you?" I ask sharply.

"Simple. If you leave this dungeon, I'd like you to keep clearing out the competition." The king shrugs. "I'm sure you learned a lot from Krak during his time with you. We dungeon bosses don't always get along, and I've been stuck in this low-level pop-up dungeon for millennia, it seems like.

Technically, it's only been eight hundred years, I suppose, but you know how that goes." He sighs dramatically, then pulls out the vial of stardust. Dark energy swirls around it, and it rises up to float over the middle of the throne room.

"What are you pulling?" I demand.

"Simple. If I yield, that vial will float gently down to the floor," the king answers. "If, on the other hand, I *die*, the dark energy will open a portal that will suck the stardust into inter-dimensional space, and you'll never be able to heal again for the rest of your life, which, of course, will be rather short. I do hope I've made my point clear."

"Very." I nod. "Shall we?"

"Indeed."

The king raises his staff, and a great light flares from within. Dark energy seems to flow from his hands up to the head of the staff, and he swings it down grandly. Darkness erupts across the throne room, and I dodge-roll narrowly out of the way. Bjorn and Astrid both leap to the sides and charge up to meet him, but he simply laughs.

"No, no, my dear pups! My battle is with Jason, not with you!"

There's a rumble, and more dark energy shoots up out of the floor. It takes on the form of skeletons—a lot of them, all bearing dark elf weaponry. The wolves don't hesitate as they tear into them, Bjorn on my right and Astrid on my left, and the king slowly marches down the stairs that lead up to his throne.

I charge forward, blade flashing in my hand. Quickly, I switch out the Diamond Dagger for the Dagger of Damage and ready myself for the attack. The king laughs as we come together, and I get the feeling that he's actually rather enjoy-ing this.

"So, you know Krak?" I lunge forward with the blade. I'm able to cut his arm a couple times, then step back as he tries to whack me over the head. I'm able to parry it, just barely, and he spins and lets loose another blast of energy. I'm able to dodge it, but even proximity to the blast drains my health a bit. I lunge back toward him, blade flashing brilliantly, but I can't tell how many times I'm hitting him or how many times he's blocking.

"I know *of* him. Almost the whole dungeon world does now." The king shrugs. "I'd never heard of him before he managed to trick you, but once that happened . . . Well, I made sure I had Wi-Fi installed in the dungeon so I could keep an eye on you."

"You had *Wi-Fi* installed in here?" I dodge another blast, slip around behind the king, and stab him in the back. The damage is slowly rising—it's up to sixty-four now—but bosses are often *tanks*. "How'd you manage that?"

"Opened the portal inside a tech store, kidnapped the staff, and threatened torture until they agreed." The king shrugs and spins. This time he manages to catch me in the ribs and knocks me across the floor like a tumbleweed. My health drops down to 5 percent. "I even paid them well! Loads of treasure."

"Dragon treasure?" I guess as I climb back to my feet.

"What else?" He shrugs. "I heard that the business burned down just a few hours later, but I suppose you can't predict such things."

"Uh-huh."

The two of us come back together in a flurry of blows and strikes. I hit the boss a few more times, raising the damage up to 512. By now I can see a bit of worry in the king's eyes. He might be great at math, or he might be as bad as me, but the potential danger of the weapon is obvious. The attack power grows *rapidly*, which will make it hard for him to determine when to call off the fight. I decide to press that to my advantage.

Suddenly, cracks spread across the floor under the king's feet, and a gout of flame explodes upward. He's sent reeling backward, only to be hit by Astrid an instant later. I spring forward quickly, stabbing the king once more for 1,024 damage. He yelps in pain, though I still don't know how much it's actually hurting him; mid-level bosses like these are hard to read for sure. Astrid grips him tightly in her teeth and shakes him like a rag doll, then throws him up onto his throne. He slams into the stone with bone-crushing force, then falls to the floor and slowly rolls down the stairs. Bjorn leaps upon him as well, and I hear a chuckle escape his lips.

"Bjorn, look—"

A blast of dark energy erupts from his body, and Bjorn is sent rolling across the floor. A bit further back from the blast, Astrid and I weather it a bit better, though I still feel the impact in my chest. My health is down to 3 percent now, which is . . . concerning, to say the least. I can see red flecks around the edge of my vision, warning me of my imminent demise. I take a deep breath and plant my feet, looking up at the stardust high above.

"You're . . . you're not going to get it." The king laughs as he pulls himself to his feet.

"Really? Because it almost seems like you *want* me to take it." I grit my teeth. "You don't want to die."

"I'd rather just defeat you." The king shrugs. From the side, Bjorn springs forward, but the king simply points his staff at him. Dark magic forms ropes around the wolf and slams him to the ground, then slings him back toward the door. Bjorn is flung out into the village, and the doors slam shut. Astrid howls, but as fire belches up from the depths of the Earth, the king simply makes a shield under his feet that absorbs the blast. She springs forward after a moment, but he waves his hands and dark ropes sling her up to the ceiling, holding her fast to the stone high above.

"Is that . . . so?" I slowly stagger forward. My body is aching; my arms and legs don't seem to be working quite right. "The great dark elf king, the one who took down Jason Lee? That's a title that's pleasing to you?"

"Indeed, it is." The king slowly strides forward, a smile on his face. "And I do think I'm about to get it."

"And what will that get you?" I ask, probing for information. "A promotion? A better dungeon?"

"With luck, the ear of the queen." The dark elf king flashes a smile at me. "But I wouldn't expect you to understand that sort of thing. Goodbye, Jason Lee!"

Dark magic flares from his staff, and a great gout of it blasts across the room toward me. Before it can hit, though, my pocket dimension opens, and Burnie shoots out with a blur.

FOOOOOOOOOOOOOOOOOOOOOOOOOOOOOOOOOOOOM!

A great blast of blue flame hits the magic dead-on, turns it around, and sends it all straight back to the king. An instant later, he's hit by the combined torrent of black magic and blue flames, and he's slammed back into the stairs of his throne with enough force to drop an elephant. I grit my teeth, run forward, and leap into the air, wielding my dagger with precision.

As I come down, the king flails up with his scepter, but I'm faster with my knife.

[Damage Dealt: 2,048]

[Damage Dealt: 4,096]

[Damage Dealt: 8,192]

"The next one will deal over sixteen thousand damage," I snarl down at him. "Can you handle that?"

The king chuckles. "Try me."

I stab him once more, and the dark elf roars in pain. His skin seems to sag, and his eyes seem dark and hollow. "The next one is thirty-two thousand. I think. More or less. Care to give it a whirl?"

"I . . ." The king slowly tries to raise himself up. "I think you ought to look at your own health."

I don't dare look away from the king, but I've already seen it. It's sitting at a mere 1 percent. I desperately need that stardust. "Thirty-two thousand damage. If I die, this dagger falls onto you."

The king inhales sharply. Suddenly, before he can answer, Burnie does.

Master! I have the medicine!

I shove the king down onto the ground and stand up, backing away as Burnie drops the stardust vial into my hand. Slowly, carefully, I pop the lid off and take a small pinch out. As I drop it into my mouth, a great torrent of life flows through me.

[Health restored to 100%]

[50% bonus to Stamina for 1 hour.]

[50% bonus to Health for 1 hour.]

[50% bonus to Damage Resistance for 1 hour.]

[. . .]

The list actually goes on for quite some time as it buffs just about every single one of my stats. I nod and slip the vial into my inventory, and the king slowly starts to rise to his feet.

"You . . . won." His voice is weak. "Will you honor your side of the deal and leave me alive?"

"I made no such deal with you." I start to walk toward him, then pause. "That said, you're pathetic to be whining so much. I will leave you alive, but only because I don't particularly fear you."

[ChaosRider: OOH, that's a burn!]

[LunarEclipse: Yeah, go Jason!]

[DarkCynic: Mercy often cuts sharper than vengeance.]

[Originalgoth: If you won't kill him, then I will.]

I blink in surprise at that last one. Originalgoth has been a pain in my side ever since the start of the apocalypse, but she's never said anything like *that*. Suddenly, though, a portal opens just behind the king, and a great deal of fear shoots through me.

It's not just a portal. It's a *terribly* dark portal, one that almost seems to suck me inside simply by virtue of how utterly *black* it is. Lightning rings the edges of the thing, a brilliant red lightning that crackles angrily. The king takes a step back in fear, then turns to run. He makes it exactly three steps before a spear shoots out of the portal and strikes him in the back, passes clean through him, and sticks into the stone floor. He's left hanging there, skewered like a kebab, and the portal closes behind him.

"I . . ." Blood flecks his lips, and he waves at me. Astrid falls back to the floor as his magic fades, and behind me, Bjorn manages to slip in through the open door. The three of us approach him, but I'm not concerned about an ambush. I know when people are faking things—usually—and this doesn't look to me like an act. As I approach him, he looks up and meets my eyes, and he draws a deep, shaky breath.

"What is it?" I ask.

"Beware the queen," he whispers. "She's in control of everything . . . every . . ." He pauses, and then nods once more. "What Krak did was unexpected. Unusual. Thousands of worlds have fallen, and never once has such a thing been accomplished. It's given many people ideas. Strange . . . ideas." His head lolls down, only to rise up an instant later. "Beware, Jason. You seem like a good man. A man I might have appreciated at one point in my life. There's a darkness coming, a darkness unlike anything you've yet seen. Stay strong and stay firm, or it will consume both the Earth and you."

I give a small nod, uncertain what he's talking about. "Can you tell me anything else?"

He opens his mouth, but before he can say a word, another portal opens behind him. Another spear, this one bigger than the first, flashes out and strikes him through the chest. He's dead before he realizes what's happening, and an angry shriek echoes through the cave.

"We've got to go. Now!" I turn and run back toward the exit as fast as I can go. Red lightning explodes through the cave, blasting apart stone and pillars. Bjorn, Astrid, and I run through the village as homes crumble around us. A particularly large chunk of the ceiling crashes down in front of us, showering the town with rubble and dust, but Burnie lets out a blast of laser-like flame, carving us a path back to the safety of the real world.

Desperately, we flee onward. The cave slowly starts to rumble less as we near the entrance, but I still can't turn my mind away from what just happened.

A darkness was coming.

Krak had given people ideas.

It was all so strange and told me that my fight against the dungeons of the world was far, *far* from done. All I could do, though, was to keep up the fight, kill everything in my path, and hope that someday, maybe, I could come to the end.

For now, though, I need a bit of rest, a bit of breakfast . . . And I need to make a phone call to Mr. Wang.

CHAPTER FIVE

By the time I walk out of the dungeon, everything around me is quiet. I can hear off-key singing coming from a bar down the street, and a cat yowls loudly as it gets into a fight with a Dire Raccoon, but otherwise, all is calm. I quickly slip inside the apartment building and take the elevator to the top, where I collapse on my bed with a sigh. My chat goes silent as my eyes flicker closed, and I'm sucked into the wondrous void of slumber.

"Jason!"

The voice blares through my head long before I'm ready to wake up, and I jump to my feet to find Mr. Wang standing in the door of my bedroom, a smile upon his face. He waves to me, and I rather groggily rub my eyes before following him out into the kitchen.

"You know, when I agreed to let you buy a penthouse for me, I didn't *really* mean to imply that I was giving you permission to just walk inside anytime you wanted."

"Jason." Mr. Wang claps me on the shoulder with a broad smile across his face. "It doesn't really matter *where* you live. I'll still have the key, so you might as well live somewhere nice. Plus, I have a feeling that your neighbors would complain if I was always landing the helicopter on the street. Now come, sit down, and have a bowl of cereal!"

"I'd rather have bacon." I sit down at the table and stare down at a rather tasteless-looking bowl of edible cardboard.

"Ah, but this will keep up your strength!" Mr. Wang grins. "The breakfast of champions!"

I fix him with a stare, and he holds up his hands. "Alright, alright! I'll see if I can buy the nearest bacon factory for you."

"I don't need a factory! Just . . ." I sigh as Mr. Wang turns away. Thankfully, one of the servants seems to have heard me and quickly runs to start frying some bacon on the stove. Turns out the place already has plenty. In any event, as I'm being served bacon, along with a healthy portion of eggs and sausage, Mr. Wang walks back over, sits down, and helps himself to a good portion of it all as well.

"Is there a reason why I'm up early?" I finally ask.

"Yes, indeed," Mr. Wang answers around a mouthful of egg. "I've managed to secure a new contract for you this morning, and we need to get out to it just as quickly as possible."

"Somehow, that doesn't surprise me." I have to laugh a bit at Mr. Wang's ability to always have some sort of a business deal on the table at all times. "And what am I clearing out today?"

"It's a company called Oppenheimer Power," Mr. Wang answers. "They operate out of the Bronx, I think."

"There's a nuclear power plant in the Bronx?" I lift an eyebrow.

"Oh, it's not nuclear." Mr. Wang waves his hand dismissively, then frowns. "Is it? If I'm being completely honest, I haven't exactly done a lot of research on them. They offered a great deal of money, so I took them up on it. You're to be there in one hour."

"I'll be there." I give a small nod and take a deep breath. After a moment, though, I frown and nod at him. "I do have a few questions before we take off, though."

"But of course. How can I help?" Mr. Wang folds his hands on the table in front of himself, but I can see him glancing at his watch.

"I'd like to know if you saw the livestream last night. At least the highlights."

Mr. Wang nods slowly. "I did, yes, as soon as I woke up this morning. I've actually already hired a team of experts to look into the matter."

"What *experts?*" I ask. "Unless you know something more than I do, dungeons weren't exactly a staple of Earth's culture until a *very* short time ago."

"I know many more things than you. However, you're quite right in that regard." Mr. Wang shrugs. "As to who they are, who cares? As long as they're an expert on something, no one cares what their field of expertise happens to be. They're experts!"

"Yeah, but I need to know what *queen* is running everything." I lean forward. "This isn't the first time I've heard a queen mentioned, and it makes me nervous. She struck down that dungeon boss in the blink of an eye. She probably could have done the same thing with me, but for some reason chose not to."

[RazorEdge: It's probably because she respects your epicness!]

[GoldenShield: Dude, she's been insulting him on the chat ever since this apocalypse started.]

[IceQueen: Can it really be called an apocalypse if everything is still going on more or less like usual?]

[Originalgoth: Just you wait. You have no idea what's coming for you.]

[LunarEclipse: I do! I bet you're a giant slug! Anyone want to put money on it?]

I roll my eyes at the chat, then nod to Mr. Wang. "Her username is Originalgoth, but I assume you already know that. See if you can get ahold of some tech people to trace it or something. I'd love to pay her a visit."

"You just admitted that she likely could have killed you," Mr. Wang says, pointing a fork at me.

"But she didn't. People don't endlessly insult other people unless they're scared of something, or are trying to feel more powerful than they really are." I cross my arms and try to think, then shrug. "Anyway, I'd appreciate whatever you can come up with."

"I'll see what I can do, for sure." Mr. Wang nods. "In the meantime, we should get going."

"We should." I gulp down the last of my breakfast, then rise. "On an unrelated note, do you happen to know how Ali's doing?"

"Wonderfully, actually. There's a rather massive apartment complex that she managed to purchase with the funds. I've hired a team of workers to head inside and fix the place up. It'll be habitable in no time!" Mr. Wang grins broadly.

"She's very grateful for all that you did. I was told to assure you of that."

I give a nod to him, then slowly rise. Quite frankly, I'd really like to stick around the apartment for a good bit longer, but Mr. Wang is waving me on. Slowly, we walk out onto the rooftop, where his helicopter is waiting. The two of us climb inside, and with that, we're off.

"Oh! One more thing I thought you should know." Mr. Wang speaks through the headset that allows us to converse over the roar of the engines. "The past few days have been exceptional business, but I'm afraid that we may start to see our profits plunge slightly. Not horribly, mind you, but we'll drop from the hundreds of millions into the tens of millions."

"Somehow, I think I'll be fine," I answer with a laugh. "What's happening?"

"Two things. Or three, maybe, depending on how you look at it," Mr. Wang says. "First, the rise of competition. Other warriors are starting to hire themselves out as well, and they're making a pretty good penny at it too. Demand is high, and a lot of warriors are getting tired just running around on the streets clearing out pop-up dungeons."

"Are there still people taking care of those?" I ask, feeling a bit of horror shoot through me. If *everyone* starts doing what I'm doing, then monsters will overrun the normal parts of the city.

"Of course, of course! Lots of people have little to no inter-est in profit. Don't understand it myself, but they're joining the police force or different guilds and things." Mr. Wang shrugs. "But anyway, a lot of the companies are starting to go with these other dungeon-clearing conglomerates. It just means that there are fewer people driving up our bids. And, on that note, the second thing is the fact that I've been hiring. I now have ten warriors in my employment. You'll still be a one-man show most of the time, but here and there I might have you do a team-up. People love a good team-up, and it'll get the dungeons done quicker. I'm hoping that it will lead to more profit overall, but it might mean slightly less in your own coffers. I thought you'd be okay with that."

I roll my eyes. "I already have more money than I could possibly spend, and this apocalypse is a long way from being done."

"Then I was right!" Mr. Wang nods firmly, then leans forward and looks out the window. "Now, that brings us to the third thing. There's been a slight rise in dungeon snipers."

"Snipers?" I raise an eyebrow. "Did someone finally manage to get a firearm drop from one of these monsters? I'd pay for that."

"No, no!" Mr. Wang laughs. "No, it means that there are warriors just wandering around, looking for warriors-for-hire like us. When they see us heading for a dungeon, they step in and offer to clear it for less money. It's caused a handful of issues, at least over the previous twelve hours. I don't know if anyone will dare cross *you*, but they're rather nasty and will often kill for a profit. Kill humans, I mean."

"That's good to know." I nod slowly, mulling it over. I really, *really* don't like the sound of that, but I suppose there's nothing I can do but dive into things and see how it all pans out. "Do you have someone working with me on this job?"

"As a matter of fact, I do! He's not really an employee of mine, but he . . ." Mr. Wang shrugs. "You'll just have to meet him for it to make sense, so I won't ruin the surprise. Ah! Here we are!"

I look down through the window to see us circling a large hotel. Guests up on the roof, relaxing around a pool, stand and point, and a vendor selling some sort of fruity drink pulls the screens shut over his booth. We come down to land on a helipad, and both of us jump out. Mr. Wang shakes my hand, then climbs back into the helicopter.

"Alright, Jason! Get down there and do what you do best! Kill monsters! Bring home the bacon! Make us proud!"

With that, the blades roar to life once more, and I slowly step back. Soon the helicopter is flying off, and I turn to look at the people who are staring at me as if I had three heads instead of one. Slowly, I nod to them, then start walking toward what looks like an elevator shaft at the far end.

I'm almost there when it dings loudly, and the doors slide open to reveal an elegantly dressed butler. Well, not a butler, but that sort of person for a hotel. Of course, right beside him is—

"John!" I grin from ear to ear. John, tall and broad and still wearing a great many animal hides, lunges forward and wraps me in a bear hug. I thump him on the back, and he does the same to me. Of course, his *hurts*, and I gasp a bit as we pull apart.

"I didn't know you were back in town!" I say as soon as we're able to talk.

"Just got in last night! Mr. Wang was going to fly me over to your apartment, but then he checked the livestream and saw you diving into the portal, so we decided to do this instead." John turns and gestures at the elevator. "After you."

I can't deny the fact that I'm *quite* excited. We slip into the elevator, and the butler selects the button for the basement. "So, what brought you back?"

"A helicopter. Run by Mr. Wang," John answers. "He snagged me yesterday afternoon. Promised me loads of money in exchange for coming back to help you on some dungeons. I told him I didn't need the money, and I'd just do it for free, and that seemed to perk him up quite a bit. Then . . . here I am."

"Here you are." I nod. "You went to see your sister, right? How's she?"

"She's good! Can't complain, in any case. Her house is still upright, there are some good warriors in the neighborhood, and her house is in an area that has a much lower portal density than some areas." John nods. "I was planning on staying there for another few days, then coming back and helping clear out more stuff, but now I think I just need to throw myself into the midst of it." He shudders. "All this talk of a dungeon queen has me a little creeped out."

"Me too," I admit, then shrug. "But if that's who's at the top, then I know who to set my sights on."

"You know their title. You don't know *who* it is," John counters.

"Fair enough, fair enough." I nod, then sigh. "I don't know. It's just all weird, you know?"

"Yeah." John nods. "I don't know if it'll help, but my plan after we clear this dungeon is to head out onto the streets. I figure they could use some help keeping them clean, and I'd like to check out these rumors of strange events. Monsters being monsters, I'd rather they not start behaving in an unpredictable manner."

"True." I nod. A moment later the bell dings, and the elevator opens. We've dropped all the way to the bottom floor, and the two of us step out.

Almost instantly I can see that things have changed. Instead of stepping out into a hotel, we step off onto a metal catwalk that overlooks a vast pit. Inside the pit is a classic nuclear reactor, with a great many pylons standing around it hooked up to dozens of enormous cables. The whole things hums loudly, and I slowly cross my arms behind my back. Suddenly, I catch sight of someone on a lower catwalk: a man who looks like the owner of the building. It's hard to say exactly what makes me think that it's the owner; he just has that *owner* bearing: important, but terribly nervous, and rather well-dressed. Standing next to him is a man who's nearly a head taller and dressed as a cowboy. My hands slowly tighten into fists, and John gives a nod.

"Someone beat us to it."

"Snipers." I remember what Mr. Wang was telling me. The cowboy turns and looks up at me, and I get an odd feeling in the pit of my stomach. It's the same feeling I once had when Harold started looking at me weirdly. This man is trouble . . . And I have no intention of letting him steal my dungeon out from underneath me.

CHAPTER SIX

ShadowDancer: Quick, Jason! Do something!]
[ViperQueen: Fight him!]
[ChaosRider: Knock him out!]
[DarkCynic: Challenge him to a game of chess!]
[FireStorm: Or mahjong!]
[Originalgoth: Just kill him, if you want my opinion.]

I grit my teeth, then nod to John. "Throw me."

John looks at me in surprise. "Throw you?"

"You're strong enough to do it. I'm strong enough to survive it," I confirm. "Throw me."

John shrugs, then flexes his hands. The long claws on the end of each finger retract slightly, and he grabs hold of me and lifts me into the air. Now, if you'll recall, each warrior of this apocalypse sort of has their own "thing." Mine is the ability to tame monsters. Harold could turn himself into a fireball, and Ali can do cool stuff with animals. John's ability is the fact that he's *super* strong. Combined with his claws, he can climb up sheer walls with the tiniest handholds, he hardly ever fights with anything more than a dagger—admittedly, neither do I—and, of course, he can throw things *really* far.

Quickly, he grabs me into a fireman's carry, hefts me above his head in something resembling a Superman pose, and then launches me down onto the catwalks below. I fly straight as an arrow, or maybe a torpedo, and land just a few feet from the two men. I quickly transition into a roll, coming up from the motion just in front of the two of them. John starts jumping down from catwalk to catwalk behind me, but I don't look back. Instead, I fix my gaze upon the cowboy.

"I heard that *we* had a contract for this dungeon." I address the hotel owner but don't look away from the newcomer. He's tall, a smidge taller even than me, and wears a ten-gallon hat that looks rather beat up. He's wearing boots and chaps, just about everything you'd expect from a cowboy, and has a whip hanging at his side. Now *that* makes me nervous. Whips are strange things, and you can do a lot with them if you really know how.

"Yes, of course." The owner wrings his hands. "I'm afraid that I—"

"My name is Jason." I turn to him and hold out my hand. "Jason Lee. I presume my reputation precedes me at least somewhat."

"Indeed." The owner flinches backward slightly. "I . . . Well . . . My name is Mr. Harrison, and I'm the owner of Oppenheimer Power. It's a pleasure to have you here. All of you."

"If I might venture a question . . ." I turn pointedly to the cowboy. "What exactly is this feller doing here?"

The cowboy finally speaks up and holds out his hand. "I got here first. Name's Columbus. Columbus Jacobs."

"That sounds made-up." I shake his hand firmly, trying to gauge his reaction to things. Just what sort of person is he? There are a lot of different sorts of warriors, and he just reminds me of Harold in a lot of ways.

"Everything about us is made-up these days." Columbus shrugs. "We both have an audience watching our every move via cameras mounted in our heads. You can't tell me that you behave *exactly* as you did before that happened."

"I certainly hadn't killed as many monsters."

"Nor as many people," John adds as he walks up behind me. "We can always raise the count, though."

"Boys." Mr. Harrison holds up his hands. "Please don't misunderstand me. No one is getting cut out of the contract. The fact of the matter is that you're all going in there. I've made a deal for Jason and John's services through Mr. Wang, and I've made a deal with Columbus a bit more privately. You'll all three be heading into the dungeon, and you'll all three be coming out."

"I wouldn't count on that fact," John growls.

"Then allow me to make it clear." Mr. Harrison raises an eyebrow. "If you don't all three emerge, none of you get any payment. You will focus on getting the dungeon clear, and you will not waste time infighting. Is that clear?"

"Clear as the sky on the plains." Columbus nods with a rather sly sort of a smile.

I don't say anything and neither does John. After a moment, Mr. Harrison nods and turns and gestures at the room around us.

"Now, I'm sure you're wondering why exactly we have a power plant underneath a luxury hotel. The answer, I'm afraid, is quite simple." He lets his arms drop back to his side. "The power plant was here first. It was built about fifty years ago, during a time when nuclear power was illegal and highly regulated. The purpose was to give electricity to the poor neighborhoods of the area, neighborhoods that were regularly getting shut down due to a lack of payment or simple scare tactics from the larger companies."

"Does this have a purpose?" Columbus asks.

"Indeed. Be patient." Mr. Harrison nods. "The power plant worked wonderfully for a time, receiving deliveries and things in a nearby warehouse, but eventually, the police started to catch on. Realizing that they needed to do something more, the owners built the hotel over top of it. Nowadays, water used to cool the power plant is also used to heat the assorted hot tubs, showers, and other such things in the hotel above. The power itself, of course, is quite useful in operating the business, while the majority of it is still sent out into the neighborhoods for the poor of New York."

"I still don't see the point." Columbus crosses his arms. "Does any of this have a bearing on what's inside the portal or how to kill it?"

"Not directly. I simply want you all to know what the stakes are, in addition to your precious money." Mr. Harrison shrugs. "If this power plant goes down, it will take down power to every low-income residence in a fifty-block radius. Additionally, the hotel itself, where every last penny of profit is turned around to benefit these poor neighborhoods, will shut down. It is *imperative* that you close this dungeon before it does any harm."

"Then point us in the right direction." John steps forward and cracks his knuckles. "Where are we looking?"

In response, Mr. Harrison turns and points down the catwalk to where it runs up to a wall in the concrete cone of the nuclear plant itself. A small door sits there, which has a single reinforced window. Through that window, I can just see the crackling of a portal. My hands ball into fists, and Columbus tips his hat.

"Well, then. If it's alright with you ladies, I'm heading over there to take a look around."

"Not without me, you aren't." John stalks after him, but I hold back for a brief moment. Mr. Harrison fidgets for an instant, and I nod to him.

"Has anything come out of the portal yet?"

"No." Mr. Harrison shakes his head. "Nothing at all."

"And you're sure there's nothing else happening here?" I ask pointedly. "No unlawful nuclear research? Development of an atomic bomb or something?"

"If there *was*, I certainly wouldn't be telling it to you with a live audience." Mr. Harrison counters. After a moment, he sighs. "Forgive me. In answer: no, there's no unsolicited nuclear research happening here. Just a nuclear power plant that doesn't want monsters to come out and cause an explosion that launches half the city into orbit."

[FireStorm: Actually, that's not how an explosion like this would work!]

[ShadowDancer: Yeah! The hotel above you would get blasted into rubble, but everything else would mostly still be okay!]

[IceQueen: The radiation, though . . . You wouldn't be able to drink water in the city for like . . . a zillion years.]

I nod after a moment. I can't sense if Mr. Harrison is lying, but it does seem like he's hiding something. In any case, he's paying me, and Mr. Wang is going to be upset with me if I don't get inside and clear the place out. I turn and walk after the other two warriors, and we soon come up to the entrance of the portal. John and Columbus are eyeballing each other warily, but I walk past them and step through the crackling energy.

If by some chance you've forgotten, traveling across the interdimensional border between Earth and the dungeons is *beyond* unpleasant. I've been stabbed, beaten, kicked, burned, frozen, crushed, and poisoned, and trust me, I'd just about rather go through all of that a dozen times over than to cross one of those boundaries. It feels like your entire body turns to liquid, and then you get sucked through some sort of interdimensional straw, only to get spat out the other side like some sort of spitball. You take on the right form when you come out the other side, mind you, but it feels like the parts of you that used to be in your toes are now in your brain, and the parts now forming your toes came from your gut.

And, of course, there are loads of things attacking you that prevent you from actually taking the time to re-orient yourself.

The moment my feet hit the ground, I lash out with my daggers—the diamond and photonic ones, respectively. The blades chop a massive spider in two, and I blink spider guts out of my eyes as my vision slowly returns to normal.

Now, all entry chambers are more or less the same, and this one is no exception. It's maybe a hundred feet in each dimension, with a large tunnel leading down into the darkness. In this dungeon, though, everything is covered with thick cobwebs.

Massive cobwebs.

Cobwebs with equally massive spiders crawling down them toward me.

"Alright." I take my stance as several dozen of them all begin to converge on me. I can see their fangs dripping with venom, their legs crackling with electricity.

Wait. Crackling with *what?*

Several of them all discharge massive blasts of electricity at me at the same time. Lightning arcs from web to web, flickering and flashing across the walls and floor. I spring up into the air, landing on a nearby stone that *just* peeks out of the webbing. John and Columbus both take that exact moment to step through, and they're blasted with lightning as they set foot on this side of the portal. Columbus falls almost instantly, though John grits his teeth and manages to bear it.

"Don't worry! I've got you!" I fling one of my daggers at the spider emitting the electricity. It's struck firmly in the side, and with a squeak, it falls over and dies. The electricity ceases briefly; however, I can see all the spiders massing for another attack. "Let's go!"

I fling myself forward as the spiders rise to the occasion. Thankfully, they aren't hard to chop through, and spider body parts fly through the air as I hack them into little bits and pieces. Suddenly, though, I feel legs clamp down onto my back, and a great blast of electricity arcs through my body.

"Ahhh!" I fall to the ground, momentarily paralyzed. The spider crawls forward, but a sharp *ping* strikes it dead as John throws a pebble clean through its body. It collapses in a heap, and I shrug it off as the spiders all surge around us.

"Yeehaw!" Columbus spins his whip wildly, almost hitting

us as many times as he hits the spiders. His whip is deadly—I have to give him that much—and he strikes down a dozen of the things in as many seconds as monsters come from every side. He's got a smile across his face, and I get that nervous sort of feeling in the pit of my stomach again.

"Come on." John takes a deep breath. "We need to get through these things, and now."

I see what he means. Columbus is starting to laugh, apparently enjoying killing the things so easily. Don't get me wrong, I enjoy the thrill of the hunt as well, but he's just *relishing* it. I watch him for a moment, glance around the room, and spring into action.

A group of the spiders is rallying over on the side of the area, stacking themselves up into a pile. They hiss as I charge forward, and all of them spit blobs of webbing at me. I dodge most, but a few hit me on my arms and legs. Lightning arcs briefly from the points of impact, and I stumble and fall head-long across the floor. The spiders spring on me, and I take a deep breath.

"Stop! Drop! Roll!"

With that, I roll to the side. Most of the spiders jump free, but a few of them are squished underneath. As I climb back to my feet, three of them jump at me, and I lash out reflexively. The first one is cut clean in half, but the second and third get past without a scratch as Columbus's whip lashes around my wrist and holds it tight.

"Give me back my whip!" Columbus orders.

"You give me—" I have to stop talking to him as the spiders reach me and start clambering up my legs. I shake one free and kick it, but the second one scampers up onto my chest.

"I said . . . give . . . it . . . back!" Columbus snaps. The whip comes free, and he lashes it across the spider, splattering me with spider guts. Of course, this *also* lashes me across the chest, and *that* stings. I grimace and put my hand to the wound but make no further movements. Columbus just snickers and turns back to whipping the spiders. I watch for a moment, then open up my pocket dimension and let Burnie fly out. John snatches up a massive stone and smashes three spiders at once, then blinks in surprise as my Phoenix flies past his head.

"Isn't it a little early for that?"

"Nah." I give the bird a nod, and Burnie opens his beak. A great searing blast of fire streaks around the room, burning up the last of the spiders in the blink of an eye. As the ash settles, he ducks back into the pocket dimension, and Columbus slowly lets his whip fall to his side.

"And there we go!" He slaps his thigh, then starts walking toward the exit. "Now we just need to move onto the next room. Let's get moving, partners!"

I frown, then give John a knowing glance. He nods back. We have to watch this guy and watch him like a *hawk.* Crackling noises emerge from deeper within the passage, and the three of us slowly enter. It's going to be a long way to the bottom. And I have to do it all with someone who just *might* be a homicidal maniac.

CHAPTER SEVEN

The tunnel grows dark around us—oppressively so, but that's hardly unusual. I take a tighter grip on my daggers, knowing that at any moment a great many things could jump out to ambush us. Ahead, I catch a small flicker of light, and the crackling noises grow louder.

"Do you get the idea that this place is being affected by the power plant?" John glances at me a bit nervously.

"Either that, or the dungeon chose the power plant as a place to open because of the unique adaptations of its residents," Columbus points out. "From what I'm starting to hear, these dungeon bosses have a whole lot of free will."

I can't argue with that. First, a dragon possessed a ring and followed me from dungeon to dungeon trying to possess me. Then, Krak managed to trick me into thinking that I'd tamed him and managed to take over a rift. Now, word on the street is that things are getting even wilder. I don't really have a clue what that means or how you can get much crazier than that, but I suppose I don't know everything.

[DarkCynic: Do you think Jason's going to keep running into electric stuff through the rest of this dungeon?]

[ShadowDancer: Uhh . . . Yeah. Don't you?]

[DarkCynic: I dunno. Seems like he might find something unexpected, you know?]

"I'd rather *not* find something unexpected," I murmur. John and Columbus both look at me, and I shrug. "Chat."

"Yeah, I just let my fans watch what I do. I don't talk to them," John snorts.

"And how many fans do you have?" I ask. "I bet you're under a thousand."

John blinks, then scowls. "Nine hundred and five. I thought that was pretty good."

"I'm at one million, nine hundred eighty-five thousand, seven hundred forty-five . . . forty-six . . . forty-seven." I shrug. "Always going up."

"Are there that many people actually watching?" John raises an eyebrow. "Don't people like . . . I don't know . . . have to work or something?"

"Teenagers don't," I point out. "And in the realm of things, watching a livestream apocalypse is *probably* more likely to get them permission to stay at the computer all day. After all, it's basically like watching news, as opposed to watching livestreams of a game."

At that, John laughs. "Oh, you're sweet. Thinking kids actually ask permission for things these days."

I just shake my head. I'm not from New York, and even after fighting monsters here for what already seems like a life-time, I really just don't always fit in. Oh well. At present, I don't fit in because I'm a better warrior than a lot of them, so I can't really complain about that.

In any event, the crackling ahead of us grows brighter, and we come up to the entrance of a long and broad cavern. There aren't any webs here, which is nice, but there *are* a great many scorpions.

Scorpions whose tail barbs are flickering with electricity.

"Hmm." I pause for a moment. "They're all distracted for the moment, but as soon as we appear, there are a *lot* of lightning bolts that are going to be coming our way. Does anyone have a shield?"

"Nope." Columbus shakes his head. "I just dodge or kill whatever's coming at me before it gets to me."

John looks pointedly at me, and I hold up my daggers. "What are you looking at *me* for? I'm a close-range melee fighter! A shield would only get in the way! Come on, you're like a tank. You ought to have one!"

"I'm a berserker! Well, barbarian. Some sort of similar thing to you." John shrugs. "I just figure my body is the shield, you know?"

Columbus and I glance at each other, and for the first and last time, we wind up thinking the same thing. A few moments later, John is shoved into the room—willingly, of course; we'd never have been able to budge him if he didn't want to move— and all the scorpions turn toward him. Lightning flares along their tails, and a dozen lightning bolts flash toward him at once. He braces himself and grits his teeth, and with a brilliant eruption of light, electricity courses over him.

He groans as the lightning dies away. "Alright! You asked for it!"

With that, he leaps forward, smashing a fist into the closest scorpion. It crumples up like a little ball, and he scoops it up, spins, and throws it into a second scorpion so hard that *it's* killed as well. I race into view an instant later, pounding toward the rest of the monsters, blades flashing in my hands.

One of the scorpions looms before me, and I dive to the side as it fires a blast of lightning at me. Quickly, I slash my knife through its tail, cut off the barb, and snatch it out of the air. I spin like a top and throw it into the body of another nearby scorpion, causing a blast of electricity to arc across it. Legs twitch and sizzle, and it drops like a rock. The scorpion I injured lunges forward and snatches at my leg with its pincers, and a moment later, it slams me to the ground.

Oomph!

All the air leaves my lungs as I hit the cold, hard stone, and it jumps on me a moment later. Legs scramble to find purchase, and it lifts its mouth and readies its large mandibles. I head-butt it as hard as I can, making it stager a bit, and kick upward with everything I have. The scorpion is knocked up into the air, and I spin and punch it into a nearby wall. A resounding *boom* shakes the area, and with that, I jump back to my feet.

All around me, chaos rages, but I don't take the time to absorb it. Instead, I run forward, preparing my blade. Several notifications pop across my vision, and I ignore them.

[You have leveled up!]

[Congratulations! You are now Level 27!]

Twenty-seven? That doesn't make sense. I was a level twenty-five, wasn't I? I don't have time to sort things out right now, so I dismiss the prompt and fling myself into battle once more. Scorpions approach rapidly, and I hack them apart just as fast as my hands will allow me to. Suddenly, all falls quiet, and I pause as I realize that all the scorpions are dead.

"And that's how we do it around here." Columbus snaps his whip loudly, the *crack* echoing through the chamber. "Anyone else? No? I didn't think so! Run, you little cowards, run!"

I think he's planning on saying more, but he's cut off as a crack opens in the back of the cavern and an *immense* scorpion, the size of a bus, comes walking through. It snaps its pincers once, then lets off a blast of lightning that hits John in the chest.

Zzzzzzzzzzzzzzzzzzzzzzzzzzzat-booooooom!

He's lifted off his feet and blasted back into the wall behind, where he vanishes in a cloud of dust. *That's* not good. I snarl and run at the thing, hoping that its tail has a bit of a cooldown period.

It does but, as I find out, only one that lasts for about three seconds. A second blast of lightning erupts from the tail and, catching me completely off-guard, hits me in the chest. Light explodes through my vision, and I lose just about all sense of . . . well . . . anything.

[ShadowDancer: OUCH! That has to hurt!]

[ViperQueen: JASON! Are you okay?]

[GoldenShield: His health is still registering at a decent level, so I think he's fine. Just stunned!]

[FireStorm: Fine . . . for now.]

I find myself lying flat on my back, staring up at the ceiling as my vision returns. I didn't even feel myself falling to the ground. John jumps over me, and I try to stand up, but find myself unable to move. It's almost like when you wake up with your arms over your head and they're completely numb, except this is my entire body. Which, of course, means that in just a few seconds . . .

"AHHHHHHH!" I can't help a scream as my limbs start to move again and the worst case of pins and needles hits me an instant later. I rise halfway to my feet, only for my body to tense up under the extraordinary pain. I grit my teeth as the giant scorpion charges at me, knowing that I have a matter of seconds. "I . . . will . . . not . . . fall!"

With that, I spring forward. My intent was to jump over the thing, but with my legs still mostly numb, I just succeed in throwing myself straight into its head. Still, as it wasn't expecting that move in the slightest, I knock the thing off-guard. I grip my daggers tightly—my hands clenched when I was hit, ensuring they stayed in my grasp—and I stab the monster in the eyes. They sink through the gaps in the armored chitin, and I rip with all my might.

The scorpion screams in pain and fires another blast of electricity at me, but I dodge out of the way in time. Columbus steps into motion, whip whirling over his head. He cracks the thing up and down the length of its back, even as John snatches up several rocks and pelts the scorpion fiercely. Suddenly, Columbus lashes the whip around its tail and pulls, yanking the barb end of the tail downward.

[ChaosRider: Now's your chance, Jason! Get it!]

[RazorEdge: YEAH!!!! Show that thing who's the real boss!]

[ViperQueen: Technically, that's not a boss. Not even a mini-boss, really. Just a big monster.]

I ignore the chat and spring upward, preparing to cut off the barb to use it against the creature.

I really should have known better.

As my feet hit the back of the scorpion, Columbus's whip comes loose, and the barb flashes back upward. It hits the ceiling and lets a massive electric blast loose, shattering a great deal of the stone. Rocks and debris come tumbling down, hitting me rather hard, and the tail flashes back down to hit me. Exposed, I parry the sharp tail head once, then twice, and then scream in pain as it shoots past my defenses and buries the stinger deep in the flesh of my shoulder.

[IceQueen: OH NO!!!!!]

[GoldenShield: Jason, get out of there! If that thing hurt you so badly from fifteen feet, it'll kill you this close!]

[FireStorm: Can you really call it *close* if it's in his body?]

I grit my teeth as lightning flares around the base of the stinger. I have mere moments before it's discharged into my body, and that's *not* going to end well no matter what I do. I try to fling myself backward, but the barb on the tip holds me tight. Quickly, hoping that it'll work, I transform my Photonic Dagger into a sword, then jab it downward into a crack in the scorpion's back.

BZZZZZZZZZZZZZZZZZZZZZZZT!

Lightning explodes down from the scorpion's tail and through my body. Thankfully, due to the little bit of high school science that managed to stick in my brain, I remember that electricity likes to take the shortest path through things. Sure, it might have a great deal of fun zapping my body into oblivion, but it would have a great deal *more* fun escaping through the scorpion's grounded feet and into the stone around it. Thus, as electricity arcs through my body, I wind up in an immense amount of pain but find the vast majority of the lightning flashing down my arm, through the sword, and back into the scorpion itself.

Whatever the scorpion was expecting, *that* clearly wasn't it.

It lets out a piercing scream—side note: scorpions, at least the giant variety, apparently have vocal cords that allow them to scream—and collapses, yanking the stinger out of my shoulder. I stagger backward and fall to the floor, but this time I'm able to jump back to my feet almost immediately. The scorpion is injured but not yet out of the fight.

"Why'd you do that?" John roars at Columbus as the scorpion slowly gathers itself.

"Do what? The whip slips sometimes!" Columbus shrugs. "Just tough luck, I'd say. Now, should we kill this thing, or what?"

"We should." I take a deep breath, then run forward. I almost draw out the Dagger of Damage, but I don't know if I'll be able to get in that many hits. No, this time I need pure, simple violence, and I think I know just how to do it. "Astrid! I could use you!"

My pocket dimension opens, and Astrid bounds out. She takes one look at the scorpion and snarls, and cracks explode through the stone underneath it. Fire and steam belch upward, cooking the scorpion from beneath, and it scuttles forward. Before it can do anything, though, I stab it in the face with my sword of light, driving the weapon between its mandible and deep into its gullet. I can hear things cracking and breaking under the impact, and the scorpion draws up short. A moment later, as it's driven to a halt, John steps up, folds his hands together, and brings a crushing blow down onto the back of the creature. Bone and chitin shatter under the impact, and it's smashed down into the ground. Lightning crackles around the stinger, and I nod to Columbus.

"Now!"

The cowboy lashes the tail with his whip and yanks downward.

The tail barb points straight downward and discharges into the scorpion's back, and with that, the scorpion drops dead. I let out a gasp of relief and step backward, drawing out my sword as I do so. Astrid dips her head and retreats into my pocket dimension, and Columbus glances at me and shakes his head.

"Just how many of those things do you have in there?"

"Quite a few." I shrug.

"They seem a bit overpowered to me," Columbus snorts.

I can only shrug once more as I start walking toward the crevice at the back of the room. "Well, in all fairness, this dungeon does seem a bit lower-leveled than what I normally take on. Almost makes it easy."

"Coming from the guy who wound up on the floor in a twitching heap." Columbus laughs.

"I wasn't twitching!" I protest.

"Yeah, you sort of were." John shrugs. "Not that it's important, really, but . . . yeah."

I roll my eyes, and the three of us start forward once more. As we do, though, I keep my eyes on Columbus. I think John was a bit premature when he yelled at Columbus for the whip coming loose, but only because I *do* suspect that it was intentional and letting *him* know that we think it's intentional is only going to make matters worse.

Either he knew that I would be able to get out of the attack, or he truly doesn't care about the money being offered to him, whatever it happens to be. Something's odd about him, that's for sure, and I have to figure out what it is before he manages to get the drop on me.

CHAPTER EIGHT

This next crevice isn't a long one, and it's one where I have the distinct feeling that we're being watched. It's hard to say exactly what makes me think that, but I can tell you that the hairs on the back of my neck are standing up quite fiercely, and I can practically feel something breathing on me from the darkness.

Thankfully, it's not long before I come to realize just why that is.

Because we *are* being watched.

As we come to the end of the crevice, we find another cave, this one larger than any of the rest, with three small tents sitting around a small campfire. I can see a large pot burbling and bubbling over the fire and three hags tending it. They turn and look at us the moment we step through, and one of them beckons with a crooked finger. I should say that each of these things is probably only about half my height, and all of them are entirely cloaked in tattered rags. One of them wears black rags, one green, and one red. I don't really know the significance, and, frankly, I don't really *want* to.

"Come!" Her voice is just as *hag-y* as you might expect. "Come and join us for dinner!"

"Are we the main course?" John crosses his arms, then draws out his bone daggers. "I'd hate to kill a little old lady, but something tells me that you aren't the kind that offers cookies."

The three hags all cackle and turn to face us. Their faces are horribly twisted and wretched, covered in warts and boils and fungi. They're vile looking creatures, and they all raise their hands and start walking toward us.

"Would you like to know your future?"

"We can tell it to you!"

"Yes, for no price at all!"

"Other than being allowed to watch events play out!"

I take a deep breath, then shake my head. "Afraid we'll pass, ladies. John?"

John, who had been quietly slipping his right foot underneath a small boulder, kicks out with all his might. I hope I've been clear that he can generate a *lot* of might. The rock hits the hag wearing black quite firmly and blasts her across the cavern, where she hits the wall with a resounding *boom*. Dust fills the air, but a moment later, she simply walks out as if she was going for a leisurely stroll on a Sunday afternoon.

"Alright, then. I guess that tells us a bit more about what they are." I nod to John. "You take the black one, and I'll get the red one? Columbus, you've got the green—"

"Yeehaw!"

Columbus runs forward, cracking his whip. The red hag

simply stretches out her hand and catches the flashing end of the whip, then yanks him forward. Now, by this point I know that they're powerful, but even I have to admit that I'm surprised when she rather effortlessly throws him across the room, where he smashes into a stalactite and slumps to the ground.

"Poor boy!" She cackles. "He'll go well with my soup!"

"Alright, then." I nod. "You get black, I'll get red, and we split green?"

"How about we just dive in and—WHOA!"

The three hags suddenly cast aside their rags, revealing that the cloth was covering immense bat-like wings. Harpies, not hags, then. As a quick side note, they *are* still wearing clothing: more rags that match the color of their upper layer of rags, but without covering their wings. Anyway, they all come flying toward us, and the two of us rush into action.

The red one comes first, swooping down to attack John. He jumps up into the air and punches her, hard, slamming her into the wall. The green one, though, catches hold of his arm and flies high into the air, shooting upward as fast as if she'd been fired from a gun. I grit my teeth, but a moment later, the black one is upon me, and I'm fighting for my life.

She grabs me around my throat and flies up into the air after the green one, cackling the whole way.

"Aren't you a pretty boy? Yes, you are! And you'll go nicely in my stew!"

I can't answer, as she's pinching my vocal cords. That said, I don't really want to. Instead, I simply draw out my daggers and stab her, driving the weapons into her gut. It doesn't seem to affect her at all, so I stick them back into my inventory and yank out my Dagger of Damage.

"You think *that* will kill me?" She laughs. "Let us see if your tricks can best me!"

I shrug, then stab her a dozen times in rapid succession. The damage dealt quickly rises up into the thousands, and she yelps. Obviously in pain, she throws me down, and I find myself tumbling toward the pot of stew below.

[RazorEdge: Ahhhhh! Jason, you're about to get cooked!]

[ShadowDancer: I hope that's just for decoration!]

[Originalgoth: I wonder how he'll taste? Maybe I should come down for a bite.]

I grit my teeth and desperately try to think of a way out of the predicament. Thankfully, my pets are way ahead of me. Unbeknownst to me, Bjorn has already snuck out of my pocket dimension, and he howls loudly, freezing the fire and the pot solid. I hit the stew an instant later, and let me tell you, it *hurts*, but I survive the impact well enough and bounce to the floor. John follows within a second and smashes the whole thing to bits.

"No!"

"Our precious stew!"

"How will we kill them now?"

"The normal way! The question is how to eat them!" The black harpy flashes down and lands in front of me. "I think we can figure that out later, though. Get them!"

Lightning pulses through her hand, and she throws a massive blast of electricity at me. I dodge it, but only just, and Bjorn howls. She freezes momentarily, and I leap forward and punch her. I might not be able to hit quite as hard as John, but I can still pack a pretty good punch. Ice explodes from her skin as she's flung backward onto the ground, and I leap upon her, stabbing her rapidly with the Dagger of Damage. She hits me in the jaw before I can do much, knocking me up into the air only to flash upward and snag me by the foot.

I'm carried high into the air once more, hanging upside down from the harpy as she sails to the top of the cave. Suddenly, I see the other two harpies circling below, and the black one drops me. I plummet down . . . down . . . and the other two flash up to meet me.

Wham!

Smack!

Both of them land solid punches and scratches along my face and body as I fall, and I hit the ground with quite a lot of force. My health drops down to the yellow, and I groan and slowly climb back to my feet.

"I need some Pumped!." I open my inventory and yank out a bottle, drinking it as quickly as I can. My health starts to rise as soon as I've finished, and with that, I twirl the bottle and throw it up at the harpies. The red one catches it and throws it back down, then dives at me, drawing several large knives as she does so. I grit my teeth, then run forward and jump up to meet her. Daggers meet daggers, steel against flint. Neither of us manage to hit the other one, but I'm knocked flat to the ground as she casually throws me down. The green one uses a similar move on John, but he grabs her arm, slings her over his head, and brings her crashing down to the ground. Stone cracks under the impact, and she discharges a blast of lightning into his body before escaping to the skies once more.

Suddenly, I notice that the three of them have started flying in a tight circle just above the spot where the fire used to be. Chanted words drift down, though I don't recognize the language they're spoken in. The fire bursts back to life, filling the air with green flames, and both of us brace ourselves.

"What do you think's coming next?" John murmurs.

I don't have a clue, but an instant later I get the answer. The flames roar higher, and a spindly, flaming figure steps out of the fire. It seems entirely made of the flame and looks rather like a stick figure that a child might draw. It looks around for a moment, then raises its hands. Fire erupts from its body and courses across the ground, melting stone into lava. Bjorn howls, and the creature's fire dies out, exposing it as being made entirely of ash. I leap forward before it can start to burn again and slash my dagger through the thing.

That does it, and the monster crumbles into nothingness. Before I can move, though, another of the flame monsters steps out of the fire, and then another. Bjorn howls again, and I manage to strike them down, but I know Bjorn has a limit. It won't take much for the harpies to exhaust him, and that's a problem.

We need to end this, and we need to do it quickly.

"Bjorn, target the harpies themselves!" I order. "John, I need you to throw me again!"

This time there's no hesitation or argument. John jumps forward, grabs me, and throws me up into the air. As I fly upward, the air grows cool. Above, all three harpies suddenly freeze in mid-flight and come tumbling down, and I draw out my Dagger of Damage.

"Alright . . . Die!"

I stab upward as hard as I can, hitting the black one with extraordinary force. The accumulated damage I've already built up along with the frozen state of harpy and the manner of the strike all combine to cause the thing to explode into slivers. I'm flipped end over end by the impact, but the harpy is dead, so I don't rightly care. A moment later, John catches me when I fall back to the ground, and I spin to look at the remaining monsters.

"Astrid! I need you!" She's at my side instantly and gives a small yelp. "Swallow those monsters into the ground."

Astrid snarls loudly, and the green one suddenly thaws as cracks explode through the ground underneath her body. Steam and fire belch upward, and the stone just sort of collapses. An instant later, she's sucked down into the depths of the Earth, and I give a small cheer. Bjorn helps by freezing the lava over top of it. Two down. One to—

WHAM!

The red harpy seems to have recovered while I was preoccupied and is not happy that her sisters have died. She starts to fly up into the air, then spins and throws me into a wall. I hit hard enough to send out a shockwave, then slowly fall back down to the ground. Before I hit, though, the harpy snatches me up, swings me around, and throws me into a different wall.

"*Bleh!* You know . . . your table manners . . . aren't the best." I drop to the ground as she swings around and flashes back down for the kill. "If you invite someone to dinner . . . at least . . . serve them an appetizer first."

The harpy doesn't seem to appreciate my clever(ish) joke. Okay, so it wasn't really funny, but I *am* recovering from being smashed into two walls. Now, far more in line with my expectations, she *also* doesn't seem to appreciate the massive boulder that John throws into her body. She smashes into the same wall that I just hit, stone crumbling all around her, and I step forward and lunge with my Dagger of Damage.

"And now, you die!"

I plunge the weapon deep into her heart, twist, and with all my might, rip it back out.

[Damage Dealt: 1]

The harpy laughs, then lifts her hands. Electricity explodes across my body, and I stagger backward into the wall. I can't move, I can't breathe, I can't . . .

No. No, I have to be able to move. My hand tightly grips my Dagger of Damage, which is trying desperately to fall from my hands. As the harpy approaches, John bounces a rock in the palm of his hand but can't get a good shot. Tossing it aside, he runs toward me, but I can see that it won't be enough.

And so, with every last ounce of strength in my body, I lunge forward and plunge the dagger into the harpy's shoulder. Electricity flows from her hands into my body, down my arm, and back into her body. She grits her teeth against the attack and pours the lightning ever harder.

As she does so, I can see my health bar start to drain: 85 percent, 80 percent, 75 percent. That said, I can see something that she's apparently missing, blinded as she is by rage. The lightning entering her body is counting as an attack as well, draining *her* health. As near as I can tell, it's registering an attack about every half-second.

And the Dagger of Damage compounds fast.

She continues to snarl, and I watch the numbers tick upward. Suddenly, she lets out a scream and is blasted backward, away from me, like she was fired from a cannon. John reacts just fast enough and punches her in the back of the head. She's slammed into the ground with immense, impossible force, sending out a rolling shock wave. Astrid gives a single bark, and the ground collapses around the red harpy, sucking her down to the depths of magma and torment below. Bjorn seals the gap once more, and the group of us all stare at each other.

[You have leveled up!]

[Congratulations! You are now Level 28!]

I dismiss the prompt. I'm too busy right now to worry about leveling. I give John a simple nod before crouching down and scratching my beloved pups behind the ears.

"Alright, you two. Get back inside and stay alert and ready. I might need you again before we get to the end of this dungeon."

They both lick me, and with that, they retreat through the portal to the pocket dimension. I slowly rise to my feet, and John and I start walking toward Columbus. A great many thoughts swirl through my head about how to deal with him, but before any of them can come to fruition, he stirs and slowly sits up.

"Huh? What'd I . . . What'd I miss?"

"A fight where we really could have used your help," I mutter.

"Maybe. Your help almost got Jason killed in the last room," John retorts.

I don't say anything more, but Columbus's face sets. There's certainly no love lost between us, and the deeper we get into this dungeon, the deeper the divide between us will likely grow.

CHAPTER NINE

In any event, the three of us soon pick ourselves up. It takes us a short time to find the exit, which has been carefully concealed by the harpies. My best guess is that they don't want people running away from them before they can properly take them down, but that's entirely conjecture. After about ten minutes of searching, we find a small pile of rubble that looks slightly different from the rest and dig it aside to find a small tunnel just beyond. I get down on my hands and knees and start crawling inside, and Columbus reaches down and taps my shoulder.

"And what makes *you* get to go first?" he sneers at me.

I shrug. "The fact that I don't trust you."

"I got knocked out in that last fight!" he protests. "I don't understand why that's such a crime."

I just stare at him. I don't have any real evidence against him, but something just seems off. Anyway, I crawl into the hole, and he comes next, with John bringing up the rear.

Quietly, carefully, we steal along through the darkness, seeking the far end.

As it happens, the other end winds up seeking *us*. The ground, quite suddenly, gives way beneath my hands, and I find myself tumbling down a long, steep slope. Columbus screams above me as he falls as well, and I hear claws scraping on stone. Likely, John is able to control his descent, but I have no such ability.

Thankfully, I keep myself oriented forward, with no tumbling or turning. A few brief seconds pass while I shoot down the long funnel, and then, with a great rush of air, I shoot out into a dark cavern. A few bits of light stream down from cracks in the ceiling above, but that's it. I slam into the rocky ground, tumble several times, and manage to get to my feet. As I stand up and look around, Columbus falls at my feet, then leaps up and slaps his cowboy hat back over his dark hair. For a moment, we just stand there, and a deep laugh floats down through the air.

"You have fallen into my lair." The voice sounds amused, and I grit my teeth and ball my hands into fists. "You will pay for that mistake."

"Might I point something out?" I hold up my hands and take a step forward. My intention is to stall; I know I have no chance of talking him down from anything, *but* at present, I can hardly see a thing through the gloom, and I'd like to get my bearings before something comes out of the darkness to kill us. "Anyone who enters this dungeon will fall into your lair, due to the design of the dungeon. You can hardly consider that a *mistake*."

"It was a mistake to enter the dungeon!" The voice continues to laugh.

"If no one ever came into the dungeon, you'd die of boredom." I shrug. "Still not really something you can call a mistake."

The laughter slowly dies away. "Well, I can certainly call *you* annoying. I can also pound you into the dust without any scruples of conscience! What have you to say about that?"

"Bring it on."

There's a pause, then a rumble. I draw out the Photonic Dagger, and its pale illumination shines throughout the area. The battle arena isn't large, maybe fifty feet on each side and a hundred feet tall. It feels more like a pit than anything else—a battle pit—but as per usual, I don't really see any way out, and there's nothing inside it to kill us.

At least . . . for the moment.

Shadows begin to flicker across the cracks, and Columbus and I look up. Something's moving above us. Suddenly, things begin to fall through, tumbling down to clatter on the stone far below. One of them, a particularly round one, lands on the ground right in front of me and bounces up to my feet.

A skull.

All around me, the bones tumble down faster, forming great piles that rise to a height of almost five feet. I see finger bones, shins, hips, ribs, and a great many skulls. When they finally stop, I find myself utterly surrounded and start to get a bad feeling in the pit of my stomach. Over on the side of the room where the shaft exits, I see John slowly poke his head out, and I give a brief shake of my head. He nods, then starts climbing up the wall toward the ceiling. Columbus and I slowly ready our weapons, preparing for what comes next.

"So, you're a necromancer, then?" I ask softly. "Are you the boss of this dungeon, or just his servant?"

"We're all servants." The voice cackles, back to its darkly joyful self. "These people served me in life, with the promise of a reward after their death. Little did they know exactly what that would be, eh?"

Green fire suddenly pours down from the ceiling and washes across the bones. With a rattle, they begin to draw themselves together, bones snapping into bones, taking on the general form of people once again. The skull next to my feet bounces across the ground like a soccer ball, reunites with its jaw, and then flies over to snap onto a spine writhing around on the ground like a snake. Soon, it's connected itself with the rest of its bones, and the whole thing raises itself up.

Then, with a great flare of magic, the bones all take on flesh.

Well, *flesh* is a bit of an exaggeration, but they certainly take on form. Fire blazes up and down the length of the bones, forming robes of sorts, the type with pointy hoods that sort of look like they're meant to mock the habits that monks wear. As the bones all finish their shifting and re-sorting, I find myself facing an army of . . . I don't know, a hundred skeletons? More than I might have liked. All of them draw out spectral swords at the same moment, and I gulp.

"So, you *are* a necromancer." I raise my voice. "Lame."

"Lame?" the voice shrieks. Apparently, I've struck a nerve. "No! Totally cool! Epic!"

"Are you kidding me?" I hold my hands up and wink at Columbus. "You just have other things do all your fighting for you! That's lame with a capital *L*."

"I . . . AHHHH!"

His shriek explodes through the room, and the skeletons all lunge forward at once, lashing at me with their weapons.

Columbus cracks his whip wildly, swinging it in a broad arc, and the whole things flares with light. Several of the skeletons in the lead are struck and collapse, but more are coming, and they look ready to kill.

"Alright, then. I guess we'll do this the hard way!" I run forward, blades shining in my hands, and lunge at the one closest to me. It brings its sword crashing down, and I raise my Diamond Dagger to block it.

Only . . . the sword, being entirely spectral, passes through my blade and slashes across my arm. *That* hurts, and I yelp and jump back in pain. Skeletons laugh and press forward, and Columbus cracks his whip again and again. I'm starting to see fear in his eyes, and I take a deep breath.

"Bjorn? I could use your expertise right about now."

With a flicker, Bjorn emerges from my pocket dimension and snarls softly. The skeletons scream and lunge forward, and Bjorn gives a mighty howl. All around, the air chills, and almost three-quarters of the skeletons suddenly cease to burn. They collapse to the ground as soon as their magic fire is gone, leaving them as little more than a few scattered piles of bones.

"*Now* who's having something else fight for him?" the necromancer screams. "If I'm lame, you're lame too!"

I shrug, then run forward. Now that the skeletons are a little more spread out, I find my task a lot easier. The closest one stabs at me, but I dodge to the side and let the blade flash past me. I spin my own dagger into position and drive it into its spine underneath the skull, breaking bone and fracturing the magical ligaments. With that, the head is blasted clean off, and the whole pile of bones drops to the ground. Quickly, I run toward the next one, light flashing in my hands.

"And . . . you're next!" I leap forward at the next one. He slashes at me as well, but I duck underneath this one and slam into his torso full force. Magical fire roars around me but doesn't hurt as I smash him back into the wall and shatter the skeleton into dust and broken bones. As the last of the ribs fall to the ground, I turn to the last of the undead monsters, take a deep breath, and nod at Bjorn.

"Let's do this!"

The two of us lunge forward as Columbus cracks his whip, smashing apart several more of the creatures. With Bjorn at my side, we tear straight through the last of them, leaving bones scattered here and there across the ground. I take a deep breath and ball my hands into fists, then laugh.

"Is that all you've got? Your little army didn't fare so well against us, now, did it?"

"That was just a practice run." The necromancer's voice suddenly sounds a great deal less annoyed and is instead *far* more confident. "I was measuring you. Testing you. Putting up with your little insults. Now . . . Now, I know enough to defeat you."

Fire once more falls down from the cracks in the ceiling and pours across the bones. Of course, at this point, the bones are all around us, and I flinch as they roll past me. Suddenly, bones are rolling across the floor, being pulled together into a single, central point. Bone piles on top of bone, and . . . well . . .

[DarkCynic: AHHHH! That's *disgusting!*]
[ViperQueen: Positively revolting!]
[Originalgoth: I think it looks kind of cute.]
[ChaosRider: No one cares, scary lady!]

[FireStorm: Just . . . Ugh.]

Let's just say that what forms from that mass of bones is quite hideous, an abomination of the worst kind. A conglomeration of a hundred human bodies, its shape is at least tacitly insectile, with half a dozen legs or more, but generally speaking, it just looks like a blob with a whole bunch of sharp pointy things across it. Red fire blazes within, and the whole structure lurches forward.

Bjorn howls once more, piercing to the core of the monster, but nothing happens. All of us dodge out of the way as it lumbers through, striking at us with immense arms made from dozens of skeletons. One of the legs sweeps around and hits me firmly in the torso, blasting me across the room and into a wall. I groan as I slump to the ground, then push myself back up. By then, though, the monster is upon me, and I grimace.

The thing attacks quickly, launching a blistering series of piercing strikes. I parry as many of them as I can, but the thing has a dozen little arms that are all striking at me, which makes it impossible to avoid every hit. I can see Columbus deploying his whip with vigor, but it doesn't seem to be working. Near as I can tell, the monster did indeed analyze our attack patterns and is now responding in kind. I have to find a way out of this, and quickly, or it's going to kill me.

Thankfully, John takes this moment to join the party.

He falls from the ceiling, slamming into the back of the monster with a power-punch that smashes the whole thing into the ground. That frees me up, and I leap into action, clambering up onto the back of the construct. I yank out my Dagger of Damage and attack as quickly as I can.

[Damage Dealt: 1]

[Damage Dealt: 1]

[Damage Dealt: 1]

[Damage Dealt: 1]

"What?" I growl. "Why won't this go higher?"

"Each individual skeleton probably has its own hit box," John answers. "There will be a collective health bar, but when you're dealing with the number of times things are attacked . . ."

He lets the sentence trail off. A moment later, one of the legs reaches up and grabs him, and he's thrown into a nearby wall. I dive out of the way before the same thing can happen to me, then frown.

"John! Can you open up a hole in the shell of this thing?"

"We'll see!" John punches a large stalagmite, hefts it over his head, and throws it as hard as he can. It smashes into the shell of the monster, piercing into the heart of the beast. Bones go flying through the air, slicing me in several places. I don't hesitate, though, as a small crack opens up through its shell, and I dive inside.

The interior of the monster isn't solid but hollow, with the bones all wrapped around a central flame that animates the whole thing. As I fall inside, I fall into the flame, and the fire starts to rage against me.

The necromancer laughs. "You've stepped into my flame of control! Stay in there very long, and you'll become one of my lieges whether you want it or not!"

"Then it's a good thing I don't intend to stay here very long." I wince as the flame starts to lick into my skin. It's a spectral, magical sort of fire, so it doesn't burn me—at least not physically. "There was something I learned once, when fighting an undead monkey."

"What's that?" The necromancer laughs at me. He's not taking me seriously at all, but that'll change in a moment.

"The fact that for undead things, poison will heal them but healing items will kill them." I open my inventory and scroll to my Pumped! stash. Quickly, I pull out a bottle, twist off the top, and start to pour it out. "How's this feel?"

The fire immediately withdraws from me, which is nice. Even nicer is the fact that as the soda pours across the bones, the whole structure rattles and quakes, as if the very health is draining from its body. Which, strictly speaking, it is.

"That's a parlor trick!" The necromancer laughs once more as the bottle empties, though he sounds a good deal less confident now. "You could dump out a hundred of those soda bottles and it wouldn't kill this thing."

"No." I shrug. "But pouring it out means that you didn't see me get *this* out of my inventory." I lift my hand to display the vial of stardust, which has been uncorked. "Sweet dreams."

With that, I tip out the tiniest little shake of powder. The glittering dust is instantly caught up in the flames of control and swirls through the bones.

And, with a resounding *boom*, the structure explodes.

[ChaosRider: Yeah! That's our Jason! Always showing them who's boss!]

[LunarEclipse: What a clever trick! I never would have thought of that!]

[IceQueen: I might have thought of it if I'd been in that same situation. Or I would have just called Burnie. He could have done it!]

I clap the lid back onto the vial and tuck it into my inventory as I'm launched through the air. I then come down quite hard on a great pile of bones and groan as I slide down to the ground once more. The pain vanishes as a bit of the dust settles onto me, and I slowly climb back to my feet and shake my head.

"Done and done." I take a deep breath. "A bit more violent than I anticipated, but nothing I mind."

"I didn't take you for the type to care all that much about violence." John walks toward the side of the pit and starts climbing upward.

"I don't," I answer. "Now, what exactly are you doing?"

"I'm getting us out of here," he calls down. "And then we're going to track that guy down and put an end to his little reign of terror."

CHAPTER TEN

When John gets to the top of the ceiling, he starts punching the stone. At this point, I'm fairly certain that the way we're *supposed* to climb up to the ceiling is by hooking the bones together to make a ladder, but I don't really like the idea of doing that with human remains, and besides, John's way looks a lot more fun. After a couple of punches, he simply digs in his claws and rips out a chunk, revealing the sky above. With that, he scrambles up, then drops a rope down below. Columbus and I both start climbing up, and John hauls us along.

When we reach the top, he pulls us up onto what seems to be a rather desolate place. We're actually up in the open, seemingly on the surface of a world, in a setting that looks something like the wild west. The sun beats down upon us, and in the distance, large red walls rise up to mark the bound-ary of a small and barren valley. None of that is really of any concern to me, though. No, ahead of me, I find that we're standing just outside a particularly large cemetery. There are three tombstones marked with our names standing right above open graves. I raise my eyebrow, and John chuckles.

"That's sort of cliche."

"Yeah, but you do have to admit that it's kind of cool." I start walking forward, balling my hands into fists. "Now, where's that necromancer? He has to have a bit of a headache after what I did to him, but—"

Dark smoke erupts from the central grave—mine—and takes on the form of a wraith just above the pit. A dark hood veils any features on its face, and smoke billows from its sleeves. Still, as it raises its arms, I have the distinct feeling that a lack of hands isn't really going to be altogether too detrimental.

"You laugh at me." His voice is louder than before, but it's obviously the same person from the cave. "You mock me! Now you will die and rise up again as my slave!"

"Yeah, gonna pass on that." I cross my arms.

"I am not offering you a choice!" the necromancer snarls. "Now die!"

Lightning erupts from the wraith and sweeps across the ground, blasting cracks in the dry dirt. I dive out of the way, and as usual, John simply takes the brunt of it. Columbus ducks behind a large tombstone and draws out his whip, then spins back into view and cracks it loudly. The weapon lashes across the wraith and cracks inside his body. That seems to actually hurt the thing, and he's knocked backward across the graveyard. I don't hesitate but instead run forward just as fast as I can, angling for the thing. I draw out my Dagger of Damage as well as my Photonic Dagger and leap at the mage as fast as I can.

"Nettles!"

The word comes from the necromancer, and suddenly, fiery thorns spring up all around me. They wrap around my legs and feet, and I'm dragged to a stop almost instantly. Quickly, I slash across them with my daggers, cutting them loose, but the distraction is enough for the wraith to rise up into the air once again, recovering his balance.

"And now, warriors, you will die!"

Thunder claps and a great cloud begins to form over the head of the monster. Lightning pulses down from the clouds and into his body, and a glow starts to come from within the necromancer's chest. With a mighty *pzzzzzzzzzzzzzzzzzzzeeeeeeeeew* the lightning is discharged across the graveyard, arcing from stone to stone to stone. I'm struck firmly in the chest and knocked backward, while John leaps over the arcing electricity and charges the monster.

He reaches out and grabs a tombstone, ripping it out of the ground with one mighty heave, and throws the impromptu weapon at the necromancer. The thing simply raises a hand, and the tombstone changes course and flashes off across the desert, sending up a cloud of dust as it hits with a *boom*.

"You will not defeat me with such paltry toys."

John doesn't seem to care and jumps at the wraith. He sails through the air, balling his hands into fists, preparing to deal a fatal—or near-fatal, certainly—blow against the thing. Instead, though, the necromancer simply puffs into smoke and reforms as John sails through the space where his body had just been. Ropes lash around John's body, and with a mighty heave, John is smashed into the ground, sending up an immense cloud of dust.

"Looks like it's up to us!" Columbus shouts to me.

"Nah." I shake my head. "Up to me, maybe."

"What do you have against me?" Columbus shouts out. "Alright, so I showed up to do the dungeon as well. What does that—"

Crack!

The necromancer fires a bolt of lightning into the ground in front of one of the tombstones, and with a roar, one of the harpies erupts upward into the air. Clods of dirt fall down from her body, and Columbus fires away with his whip. The weapon cracks across her wretched, withered body, and she's blasted back into the ground. But still she gets up again, and I run forward.

"Would you *stay* down this time?" I snarl and jump at her, kicking her in the chin. She's launched backward, smashing into another tombstone, and I slash my dagger across her neck. The head comes clean off, and the entire body crumbles back into dust. With that, I spare a single glance back at Columbus. He returns the look as another blast of electricity hits another grave.

This time an immense blast of fire shoots up from the ground, and a rotten, burned hand shoots up from the soil to grab the edge of the grave. I feel my world freeze as Harold slowly pulls himself up. His eyes are yellow, and he sneers at me through cracked lips.

"You killed me," he snarls softly. "You killed me, and now I'm going to—"

Crack!

Columbus's whip lashes around the zombie's neck. Harold turns and sends out a blast of flame that rolls down the length of the whip, but Columbus is too fast, and he pulls with all his might. The whip cuts through the rotten neck, severing it cleanly, and the body falls to the ground with a *thud*. The necromancer laughs, then begins to drift toward me.

"You think you can defeat me, but as you see, I have far more than mere minions," the necromancer gloats. "I *can* fight with my own two hands."

"And where are they?" I snap up at him. "I sure don't see th—"

My voice is choked off as a pair of hands materialize around my throat and begin to squeeze.

[ChaosRider: Oh, Jason, you really walked right into that one.]

[IceQueen: Yeah, that was a good one. Don't get me wrong, I hope you escape, but you fell for that trap hook, line, and sinker.]

[Originalgoth: Bwahahahaha!!!!]

I grit my teeth as my lungs strain to draw air. It's a losing battle, and I reach up and grab hold of the hands to pull them away from my neck. Unfortunately, his magic hands are a bit stronger than my non-magic hands, and I see darkness flickering around the edges of my vision. John is starting to stir on the other side of the graveyard, but he's not going to be up quickly enough.

Lacking any other option, I throw myself forward, smashing my neck into a nearby tombstone. Stone cracks and crumbles around the point of impact, and I gasp in relief as the hands loosen for a split second. However, they clamp back down a moment later. I've bought myself mere seconds, no more, and that's a problem. Quickly, I stand back up, draw out my Diamond Dagger, and stab at my own throat.

Now, please don't get me wrong. I know exactly what the

necromancer would do in such a situation, and he almost immediately does it: he lets go. As such, with my blade poised at my throat, unable to stop, I'll stab myself in a rather vulnerable location. At least . . . that's what I *would* have done had Columbus not been there with his whip.

I let go of the blade, and Columbus's chosen weapon lashes down around the hilt and yanks it away at the last second. Now in possession of my dagger, Columbus whips it around his head and uses the whip to hurl the blade straight through the wraith. The movement is so fast I can hardly follow it, and the necromancer isn't fast enough to follow it either. The blade, my lovely Diamond Dagger, streaks out into the desert, while the wraith is knocked from the sky to land in the corner of the graveyard. John finishes rising to his feet, sees the fallen thing, snatches up a tombstone, and lunges forward to smash the wraith flat.

Once more, the wraith is just a hint faster than John and explodes again into darkness. This time, though, the cloud of smoke flows upward and flashes into John's head, pouring itself in through his nose and ears, and John spins around, snarling at us.

"I'll kill you both, or you'll kill this body!" John starts to stalk forward. His eyes dart wildly between the two of us, and they look terrified. "Either way, I win!"

John lunges forward, and I narrowly dodge out of the way. Before I can do anything, though, he spins like a top and hits me in the chest, blasting me across the graveyard so hard that I break half a dozen tombstones as I'm thrown through them. I land in my grave under a small pile of rubble from all the stones I just busted and lie there for a moment, thinking.

This isn't a good sign, not at all. With John possessed by some sort of necromancer, the odds of us getting out alive are dropping. We have to get the necromancer out of John's body in order to save him, but getting the thing out will involve killing him, right? Killing him or knocking him out, neither of which are going to be easy to do, and besides, that's *John!* I don't want to hurt him! I'd like to have a beer with him, sure, but not *kill* . . .

A beer.

A soda.

Healing.

The thought enters my head just as several undead undertakers arrive and start to throw dirt on top of me. I leap upward, drawing my Photonic Dagger again and allowing it to transform into a sword. Light blazes in the noontime sun, and I cut through the skeletal diggers as fast as I can. Bones drop across the ground, and I run toward John with every ounce of energy I have. I give Columbus a nod, and John spins to face me.

"No, I don't think so," the necromancer says through John, and he lifts a hand. Dark ropes explode out of the ground, and I'm slammed to the dust. Quickly, dozens more ropes flash up out of the cracks in the soil, and I find myself fighting a losing battle.

At least for a moment.

I grit my teeth and heave upward, snapping the bonds, and climb to my feet. The stardust drops out of my inventory and lands in my hand, and I shake the tiniest bit out onto my palm. The necromancer laughs as I start to heal, and I step forward toward him.

"You're not going to—"

Before he can say anything more, I wipe some of the dust onto the blade of my Dagger of Damage, then lunge forward and slam it into John's chest, driving it in up to the hilt.

[Damage Dealt: 1]

The dust flows through him almost instantly, healing the wound and the single point of damage. With a shriek, the necromancer erupts from John's body, escaping in a cloud of smoke. John reacts instantly, snatching the cloud of smoke with his hands and yanking it down.

I'm not exactly sure how he does it, but he manages to keep hold of the slippery little monster and brings it crashing back down to the ground. The wraith takes on human form, and I plunge my dagger down into it—my dagger that still has a bit of the dust on it. Light explodes through the body, and with that . . . it explodes.

Or, rather, it dissolves. The wraith loses form, and a great deal of smoke erupts through the graveyard. When it fades away, all that's left is a small wraith-shaped burn on the ground. John and I stand back up, and Columbus tips his hat to us.

"Much obliged."

"I have to thank you too." I give him a nod. "You're the one who got the thing with that dagger. I wish you had managed to keep the dagger, but . . ."

Columbus shrugs. "Well, you know how that goes. Not always the easiest to hang onto things with this whip."

"If you're still practicing, maybe you should try a different weapon," John mutters.

"Well, I'd love a couple six-guns, but I only have what I

was given when I got my powers." Columbus shrugs. "Now, if you don't mind, we need to figure out how to get on with this place."

The ground rumbles, and a cloud of dust shoots up from the graves. I walk over and find that the three graves have transformed into long chutes that lead down into the ground.

"I think I found our path." I give a nod into the darkness, then draw out my Photonic Dagger. "Let's go see where these things go."

CHAPTER ELEVEN

I go first, jumping down into the pit. At first, I think it's just a short drop, but as the walls whir around me and I plunge into the inky blackness, I realize that the hole goes a *long* way down.

[ChaosRider: Where's Jason going???]

[FireStorm: Do you think he'll be able to come out of it alive?]

[LunarEclipse: Anyone want to place bets on what he'll face when he gets there?]

[GoldenShield: Something electric!]

[ViperQueen: The harpies and the necromancer weren't electric.]

[DarkCynic: Dude, controlling undead bodies is totally all about controlling electricity.]

[ViperQueen: WHOA.]

I briefly read the chat but keep myself primed for whatever I'll find down at the bottom. The air begins to growl around me, and I hear voices drifting through my head.

"You think you're the best."

"You're nothing."

"You'll fall to my power."

"You'll give yourself to my control!"

I shake my head and try to force the voices back out. "No, I won't!"

Air whirls around me, and I'm slammed into the wall. Sharp stones and something that feels like tree roots batter against me, and pain flares through my body.

"You will!"

"Never!" I grit my teeth against the pain. "I'll never yield. Not now, not—"

With a loud *snap*, the wall seems to open up, and I'm tossed out into a darkened cavern. It's *pitch* black, and as I roll to a stop, I sit up and hold out my Photonic Dagger. Its faint beams don't seem to penetrate more than a few feet, and I take long slow, even breaths. I don't see John or Columbus anywhere, which means that they've likely wound up in different places. I don't know what that means, but I suspect that it's not great for me.

"You *will* bow to me." A single point of light appears ahead of me, something like a spotlight on the bare ground, illuminating a figure clothed in dark robes. Honestly, he looks like the most cliche dark lord I could imagine, but I also suspect that he can pack a punch.

"You're the real necromancer," I say, wagering a guess. "What we just fought on the surface was an illusion."

"Something like that." The figure slowly walks forward, lightning crackling from his fingertips. "I'll admit, you're a fun one, Jason Lee."

"What do you want from me?" I ask pointedly. "You want

me as one of your lieges? I'll be as weak as any other random skeleton you could dredge up. If that was all you wanted, you'd just pop over to a random cemetery anywhere on the planet, suck up a bunch of bodies, and go on with life."

"I do want you as my liege, yes, but . . ." The necromancer shrugs. "It would take too long to explain to you why I *cannot* do what you've just stated, along with why I wouldn't want to do that anyway. You're a powerful one, Jason Lee, and I have many uses for you. Starting, of course, with taking down the boss of this dungeon."

A smile slowly spreads across my face. "So, we're going off-script here?"

"If that's how you care to look at it, then please do." The necromancer spreads his hands wide. Now he actually *does* have hands, long and bony ones that look sort of like spiders. "Now, allow me to tell you what will happen here. You'll bow to me. You'll help me defeat the boss of this dungeon. You'll rule by my side as we embark on a journey to become the most powerful dungeon lords in the known world. Is this clear?"

"Sort of." I shrug. "You have to realize that I've fought monsters more powerful than you."

"Indeed." The necromancer shrugs. "That's why I need you. I know my strengths and my weaknesses, and I know you have what I need in order to begin my rule."

That makes something spark in the back of my mind. "You need the stardust."

The necromancer doesn't say anything, but it makes sense. The stardust is extremely powerful and, as deadly as it is to the necromancer . . . well . . . the exit of the dungeon opens into a nuclear reactor; playing it safe likely isn't something in his, or the boss's, toolbox.

"You have to know I'm not going to give it to you." I shrug. "I'm also not joining you on your little quest."

"Then your friends will die."

Two more spotlights appear, illuminating John and Columbus. They're both being held by massive grim reaper skeleton things. They flail against their captors' grasps, then vanish as the light goes out once more.

"Yield, or your friends die!"

"If I yield, it only means that they're already dead." I answer. My Photonic Dagger transforms into a sword, and I point it into the darkness. "Burnie! I could use your help shedding some light on this situation!"

[RazorEdge: YEAH, JASON! Now we're going to see you kick some butt!]

[FireStorm: This will be epic! And it's not even the boss fight!]

[IceQueen: Hang on, everyone! Here we go!]

Burnie flashes out of my pocket dimension with a great rush of flame and lets loose a massive *FOOOOOOOOOOOOOM!* Fire explodes across the cavern, a great wash of blue flame, setting a great many things alight. Mushrooms, a few piles of debris, the cloak of the necromancer, and both of the grim reapers all burst into flame. Suddenly, I can see a great deal better. John breaks free of the reaper holding him and punches it in the face, scattering bones everywhere, while Columbus turns around, draws a machete, and hacks off its head. Bones collapse in a heap, and the two of them run over to join me.

"No!" the necromancer screams, then turns to walk away. "I've had enough of this."

"So have I."

With a hiss, a great explosion erupts at the end of the cavern, letting more light stream in. From beyond, I see a great many blue crystals glowing brilliantly. Into the cavern comes a giant spider, twenty or thirty feet long at least, with venom dripping readily from its fangs. The necromancer snarls up at the thing.

"I have this under control!"

"If that was the case, I wouldn't be here!" the spider practically screams down at the necromancer. "You're fired!"

"No! I will be the boss!"

The necromancer raises his hands and blasts the spider with lightning. The spider is launched backward into the cavern, and the necromancer rises up into the air to start floating toward the monster.

Which is when Burnie flies back into things.

He hits the necromancer from the side, blasting him with flame and knocking him from the sky. He falls to the ground with a scream, hitting the ground hard enough to send out a shockwave. I spring forward and race toward him as fast as I can, with John right behind me. Columbus hangs back, and I see him pulling some items out of his inventory, though I don't have time to really watch him right at the moment.

As we approach the necromancer, Bjorn and Astrid join us as well, and the whole group of us charges forward. The necromancer rises up and spins to the spider, hitting him with another blast of lightning, then spins to us. Boulders come racing across the ground, leaping and spinning and crashing about.

I leap over the first one. Astrid howls, the first one I think I've heard her make, and the rest of the boulders shatter into rubble. Burnie then flashes down, hitting the necromancer with another gout of flame. This time, though, the necromancer is ready, and catches it all with one smooth motion of his hand. He balls it all up into a fist, then spins and casts it down again at us. I brace for impact, but Burnie swoops into the path, catches it all on his feathers, and with a wonderful spin of his body, flings it all straight back. That one can't be caught so easily, and the necromancer is knocked through the air, spinning.

"Astrid!" John calls. "Give me something to throw!"

Astrid growls, and cracks spread through the ground. With a loud *whump*, a small boulder is blasted up into the air just in front of John. He snatches it, spins, and throws it with the force of a cannonball at the necromander, who is *just* able to divert it, and the projectile is redirected to slam into the spider with immense force.

Ssssssssssssssplat!

A great wad of string flashes from the spider's abdomen and hits the necromancer, and with a practiced twist of the abdomen, the spider slams him down to the ground. I leap forward, blades flashing, and drive both of my weapons, the Photonic Dagger and the Shadow Dagger, into the monster's back. He flings me up into the air as if shrugging off a fly, and with another *splat*, a wad of string hits *me* and flings me back to the ground, where I stick rather firmly in a large cocoon of web.

"Bleh! I hate spiderwebs." I flex my muscles and manage to get the tip of my dagger to pop out through the coating. Slowly and carefully, I draw it upward, slicing my way out, and climb back to my feet. Bjorn howls and freezes the necromancer, bringing him crashing down to the ground, then leaps to the side as the spider fires a blob of web at him. Meanwhile, John snatches up a boulder and throws it at the necromancer, smashing into him and sending his frozen body bouncing wildly across the ground.

The spider, sensing his chance, scampers forward. I charge across the ground to meet him, preparing my attack patterns. Suddenly, though, the necromancer lets out a scream and staggers back to his feet.

"I'll not have any of this!"

A great pulse of green lightning erupts from his hands and flickers across the ceiling, blasting stone from the edifice, sending a great torrent of rubble raining down across the spider. The monster steps backward, and with a loud *clunk*, a final boulder falls into place, temporarily sealing the thing away from us. With that, the necromancer drifts up into the air, and aims the blast of lightning at the center of the arena.

"You don't have a choice!" I throw my Shadow Dagger at the necromancer with all my might. A small flicker of lightning flashes out from the monster and hits the weapon, knocking it away. The blade clatters to the ground, and I grip my sword of light a bit tighter as I run closer. Suddenly, though, a low rumble shakes the ground, and I lose my balance, falling to the stone.

With a great *crack*, something explodes upward from the middle of the cavern. A stone giant begins to emerge, pulling himself upward just the same way that a corpse might pull itself from a grave. I feel a flash of horror shoot through me. Horror and . . . well, if I'm being honest, a bit of excitement.

I've never fought one of these before. I'm not sure I can take it, but if I can, it'll be epic. I turn toward the thing, only to hear Bjorn's voice in my head.

It's a trick, Master! I can't tell exactly how, but something's wrong with that thing. Also, where's Columbus?

I glance around the room and find that he's indeed vanished. I grit my teeth as I catch sight of a rope on the far side of the room, near where we came in. It goes up through a crevice in the ceiling. I have no idea how he managed to get the rope up there, but he's absconded, and I turn back toward the necromancer.

If the giant is a trap, that means that I need to get to the necromancer, and quickly. I race across the ground just as quickly as I can, but the giant continues to pull himself upward, and his head hits the ceiling. *That* causes an immense quake as cracks explode across the entire upper half of the cave.

Suddenly, it makes sense. The trap of the giant is that the monster is too big for the cave. It'll bring the whole thing crashing down, and the only thing to escape will be the necromancer himself. That means that I need to kill him and kill him now. I open my inventory and reach for the admittedly overpowered stardust but pause as I realize that it's missing.

Let's see . . . I took it out when I attacked the wraith above, but I thought I put it back into my inventory? I can't remember either way, but I suppose I must have dropped it somewhere along the line. Making a mental note to look for it later, I reach the spot where John is standing with my pets, and I nod.

"Alright! Astrid, warm up this dagger." I throw my Dagger of Damage to the ground. "Bjorn, knock that thing out of the sky."

The ground cracks, and steam hisses upward. Within seconds, my dagger has turned red-hot. Bjorn, meanwhile, howls loudly, and the necromancer falls from the sky. John, not to be outdone, steps forward and punches him back up into the sky—once, just for good measure—but doesn't deal any real damage to him. As he lands with a mighty *crash*, I snatch up the burning-hot dagger and plunge it into the heart of the necromancer.

The effect is similar to the electricity on the harpy. At first, even though heated to the point of melting, it only deals one or two points of burn damage per second. A smidge of smoke rises up from the cloak, but that's it. After a moment, though, the burn damage grows more intense. Flames shoot up higher and higher, and the monster tries to rise, but a mighty blow from John drops him back to the ground. Suddenly, with one final *whoosh*, the necromancer is consumed, and the giant collapses with a mighty roar of stone.

I let out a sigh of relief and slowly sheath my dagger.

[You have leveled up!]

[Congratulations! You are now Level 29!]

I give a nod to the notification and close it down, then slowly turn to the pile of stone.

"What now?" John glances over at me.

"Now, we start digging," I answer. "If I had to wager a guess, Columbus took off to try and clear the dungeon before us. Maybe he wants our cut of the money. Maybe—"

Maybe he stole my stardust.

It's an absurd thought. Most likely, I just dropped it while falling through the long chute, but then again . . . I don't know. If he did take it, he's armed with something strange

and mysterious and powerful, and that's not something I like
to think about.

Still, there's nothing I can do about it at the moment. All
I can do is try to get to the boss as quickly as possible. And
then, once I meet up with him, I can ask him nicely.

CHAPTER TWELVE

We waste no time moving on from that cavern. I can hear thunking from deeper in the ground, likely the spider rummaging around. I'd really like to meet him on my own terms, as the thing seems particularly vengeful and won't be in a good mood given that one of his own mini-bosses just tried to stage a coup. Of more concern, though, is the fact that Columbus and the stardust are missing, so I step back while John and Astrid start working to clear a path through the rubble.

"Did anyone happen to see what happened to Columbus?" I ask my chat. I duck as John throws a boulder over my head, then straighten back up. "Or my—"

[ChaosRider: <sent an image. Click to download.>]

[GoldenShield: Whoa! That's really cool! How'd you get that?]

[ChaosRider: I'm recording it, so I just went back and took a screenshot.]

[FireStorm: Wasn't there a discussion earlier about how that's illegal?]

[ChaosRider: Hey, if it helps keep people alive, I don't really care.]

I ignore the banter and download the image. There's a pause, and it appears a moment later. It's a scene of the fight, from my own viewpoint, as I'm running back toward the necromancer. In the corner of my vision, I can just see Columbus firing some sort of grappling hook up into the air. He has something glittering in his hand, and my jaw sets.

"Do we have any idea how he managed to get ahold of the dust?"

[RazorEdge: None. It doesn't look like he has an active stream following him.]

[IceQueen: What??? Really? Why not?]

[ShadowDancer: Probably because some people value their privacy and don't want every waking moment to be watched by everyone on the planet who cares to tune in.]

[IceQueen: But . . . but fame!]

[ShadowDancer: <eyeroll emoji>]

I grit my teeth. I can only imagine that I dropped the dust and he picked it up. I know pickpockets are a thing, but I have pretty high perception, so unless Columbus is a lot sneakier than I gave him credit for . . .

Then again . . . Well, he's not really all that good with the whip. To me, it looks more like a normal weapon that he's struggling to master, not actually something that's his *thing*. Frankly, I haven't seen him display anything that really stands out to me. Maybe that's because there's nothing that *does* stand out, but instead something that blends in. I don't know, and that fact frankly annoys me a great deal, but I swallow it down. I have things to do, and I'd rather not voice my suspicions. If it somehow got back to Columbus, which is quite likely given the nature of the livestream, I'd rather not have it bite me in the rear.

In any case, John grunts as he heaves aside a particularly large boulder, then brushes off his hands and steps to the side.

"Alright, there we go! You first."

I chuckle and nod, then slowly walk forward toward the small gap. My pets all scamper back inside their homes in my pocket dimension, and I slip through the path in the rubble, ducking underneath several low-hanging boulders, and into the crystal-lit chamber that I saw earlier.

[LunarEclipse: Whoa! That's cool!]

[DarkCynic: Kinda hurts to look at, I think.]

[ViperQueen: Yeah, but . . . it's so pretty!]

I have to agree, frankly. The crystals are wonderful, sparkling in the low light of the cave. There are a number of scratch marks on the floor indicating that the spider was here at one point, but I don't see him now. John comes through the gap, and the two of us start walking down the path, which leads around a gentle curve and into the distance.

"So, are you enjoying your return to the dungeon life?" I glance over at my friend, happy to have him at my side.

"Well enough." John shrugs, then scratches his head. "I have to admit, I do like punching things. And throwing things. And smashing things. And your pets are *super* cute." He pauses for a moment. "Any idea what happened to Columbus?"

I explain to him what the people in the chat saw. He frowns and scratches his head some more.

"That sounds an awful lot like Harold."

"I was thinking the same thing," I agree. "It doesn't make a lot of sense to me unless he happens to know something we don't. My best guess is that he's trying to solo the dungeon before we can, but if that's the case, he has to have seen a way out that we didn't. The original path through the dungeon, not the way that the necromancer took us."

"I just hope we don't—" John freezes, then motions to be silent. He darts forward behind a boulder that just sticks out into the curve of the passage, and I do the same. Slowly, we peer around the stone, where we're able to look into the boss chamber.

As far as boss chambers go, it's pretty stereotypical: huge, with plenty of room to move around, and a few odd outcroppings of stone to hide behind. A massive spiderweb clings to the ceiling and walls, where the enormous spider is currently hanging from a thick thread.

Of course, standing in the middle of the floor, looking up at the spider, is Columbus.

I can hear his voice as well as the voice of the spider, though I can't make out any of the words. Quietly, I murmur for my chat to hear.

"Someone record this and then analyze the audio later. I need to know what's being said, but I don't need to know it right this second."

[ChaosRider: We're on it, Jason!]

[ShadowDancer: My cousin is an audio guy! He'll be able to have this audio cleaned up straightaway!]

[ViperQueen: Shhhh! I'm trying to listen!]

I smile and lean forward, as if moving my head an extra

two inches will help the audio get picked up better. Suddenly, I see a flash of silver in Columbus's hand, and my blood goes cold.

The stardust.

He's offering the stardust up to the spider.

Rage fills me, and I climb to my feet. John seems to be of the same opinion and rips up the boulder we're hiding behind. Columbus turns and looks at us just in time to get hit with it, which blasts him across the chamber and into the wall. There's a loud *crack* as he hits, and the two of us stride inside.

"Well, well. I was wondering when you two would show up." The spider slowly turns to face us. "What exactly may I do for you?"

"Die," I snap. "Die like any other dungeon boss."

"Is that so?" The spider seems amused. "Are neither of you even the least bit curious why I opened the dungeon portal in a nuclear reactor?"

"Curiosity is a vice distracting us from our purpose," I answer curtly.

"Perhaps." The spider slowly lowers himself down until he lands on the ground. Columbus saunters out of the dust, a smirk on his face. "Still, it would prove most useful to *me* if you would ask a few more questions."

"Stow it," I snap. "Columbus! What are you thinking?"

"I'm thinking that the two of you aren't going to make it out of here." Columbus shrugs and starts walking toward the exit. "And I'm afraid that I have business to attend to."

He doffs his hat as he reaches a small tunnel that leads away from the boss fight, and I grit my teeth. Suddenly, the great spider begins to glow, and I get the odd feeling that I'm about to find out exactly what the whole mystery of the power plant happens to be.

The spider launches a web a moment later, glowing with nuclear fire. John and I both dive out of the way, and it scorches the ground between us, melting a great deal of the stone into lava. John snarls, then digs his claws into the ground, rips up a small boulder, and throws it with all his might. It slams into the spider's face and knocks him asunder slightly, but not enough. Meanwhile, I charge at the thing, my feet pounding across the ground.

PZZZZZZZZZZZZZZZZZZTEEEEEEEEEW!

The spider lets loose a great blast of nuclear energy. I drop to the ground and slide underneath it, but only barely. Suddenly, I see my pocket dimension open, and my three most faithful warriors come racing out. Bjorn tilts his head back and howls fiercely, and the air grows cool.

Well, it grows cool everywhere *except* around the spider.

A few traces of frost seem to flit around the spider's legs, but they don't adhere. Instead, the spider merely glows a bit brighter, driving back the freezing air. He's entirely unaffected and spits a blob of nuclear fire directly at Bjorn. The glowing blast of flame nearly hits him, and he dodges narrowly back into the pocket dimension. Meanwhile, Astrid and Burnie both let loose attacks, Burnie from the air and Astrid by opening up a geyser from underneath.

As you might expect, both attacks are at least somewhat useful but don't do nearly as much damage as I might have liked. The spider weathers them without even flinching, and I wave at the two of them.

"Get back to safety! I'll be fine!"

They need no encouragement and dive back into my pocket dimension. I frown as I continue to run forward, looking for any weakness, any gap. The spider fires another blob of webbing at me, and again I only narrowly dodge it. With that, I reach the spider, draw my Dagger of Damage, and leap up at the thing with all my might.

[Damage Dealt: 1]

[Damage Dealt: 2]

[Damage Dealt: 4]

[Damage Dealt: 8]

I unleash a long string of attacks across his belly, hardly even pricking the thing enough for him to notice. It seems foolish, I know, but I have a strong suspicion that the scaling of the dagger is the only thing that's going to allow me to get any sort of leverage over this monster. I'm able to raise the damage up to 128 before being forced to dodge out from underneath him, and with that, John enters the fight.

He throws a massive boulder into the spider's head, then runs underneath him, just like I had done. Instead of stabbing him, though, he snatches at the legs of the creature and yanks them out from underneath him, ripping two of them clean off. *That* makes the spider angry, and he whacks John with one of his back legs quite forcefully. John is thrown across the room, where the spider hits him with a blob of fiery webbing an instant later. He screams in pain as he starts trying to cut his way loose, and I look around frantically.

Just *how* is this spider powering up like this? There has to be a way it's happening. Simply opening the portal inside the reactor isn't going to do anything, just like the way that putting a microphone in a crowd of people isn't going to pick up any noise unless you connect it to a speaker or computer or something.

Suddenly, as I step back away from the spider, I see it: there's a strand of webbing that comes in through a small crack in the ceiling, a strand of thread that's glowing brilliantly. It connects to a small node that, frankly, looks something like a Wi-Fi broadcasting device. That's how the spider is getting the power, I'm sure of it. In order to defeat the thing, I'll need to get up there. The only question is how to get up there. I can think of a dozen different possibilities; perhaps three of them are actually plausible and really only one of them makes much sense.

"John!" I race over to where he's slowly ripping himself out of the burning web. Thankfully, his constitution seems to have prevented most of the damage, but he's still burned pretty badly. "I need you to throw me again, up at that glowing thing!"

"Again? Why not have Burnie turn into a set of stairs or something?" he grumbles. Apparently getting zapped by the nuclear thread has made him a bit grouchy.

"Because this will be faster. Just do it!"

The spider fires another blast of thread at us. John snarls and stomps on the ground hard enough to make a chunk of the floor erupt upward, blocking it. With that, he rather angrily grabs me, winces in pain, and launches me upward.

I fly as straight as an arrow, with the force of a rocket. When I hit the ceiling, it's with a good deal more force than I might have liked, and all the air leaves my body on impact.

[ShadowDancer: Ouch! That's got to hurt!]

[LunarEclipse: Yeah! Jason, are you okay?]

[ChaosRider: John! You shouldn't be mean like that!]

Before I fall, I reach out and grab the glowing thread. John, despite his anger, actually had pretty good aim. Pain shoots through my hand, but I ignore it and draw out my dagger. The thread is thick, almost as thick as my arm, and I stab the blade into it with all my might.

Foooooom!

A great deal of fire and light pours out of the scratch in the thread, pouring over me like a burning waterfall. I scream in pain, then reach up and, with the last of my strength, cut through the thread. Now energy *really* pours down over me, and I lose my grip and fall.

Down . . . Down . . . Down I go. The light is blinding, and with a loud *smack*, I hit the back of the spider. I stab him as many times as I can, but before I can really do much, John grabs me.

"We've got to go—now!"

My vision hasn't yet returned when he throws me with all his might. I sail off into the darkness, only to hit something with extraordinary force. With that, I slump down to the ground, health flickering in a single digit percentage, and do everything in my power not to succumb to the void.

CHAPTER THIRTEEN

Come on, Jason. Don't die on me now." John's voice echoes through my ears, and I hear the sharp *crack* of a bottle top being twisted off. Suddenly, I feel the sweet flavor of Pumped! flowing into my mouth, and I gulp it down as quickly as I can. My health rises back to a respectable, though still quite low, percentage, and I cough and sit up.

We're in the tunnel just outside the spider's room. I groan and climb to my feet, then shake my head.

"That Pumped! is disgusting." I choke down the last of it left in my mouth, knowing that I need to heal. "What flavor is that, and where did you get it?"

"Uh . . ." John looks down at the bottle. "Looks like it's marshmallow."

"Marshmallow." I cross my arms. "You gave me marshmallow Pumped!?"

"You were dying!"

"My health was still at like four percent!" I scowl at him.

"That's low!"

"Not low enough that I needed to drink that stuff." I scowl at him, then chuckle. "That said, thanks. And I killed the spider."

"Did *you* kill the spider or did I?" John lifts an eyebrow.

"Me. I cut the cable," I answer, then shake the last vestiges of pain from my body and start walking down the tunnel toward the exit.

"Yeah, but I threw you," John says. "If you threw a spear into the heart of a dragon, who would be the one who killed the monster? The one who threw the spear or the spear itself?"

"I'm not a spear!" I cross my arms.

"Alright," John presses, though he has a wide grin across his face, "let's say that you throw . . . a robot."

"A robot doesn't have a soul!" I snort. "I do."

"I imagine that at least one or two people would debate that fact," John retorts.

"Well . . ." I can't come up with a good response, so I just smile at him. "Much appreciated, in any case." Suddenly, I remember to check my levels. I'm still at level twenty-nine, but I would wager a guess that I'm not far from level thirty. In any case, I'm satisfied with it. I have four level-ups to go through, but I don't really want to do that here.

John and I continue to walk back through the tunnels. We find a number of dead monsters, most of them killed by what look like whip marks. I can't really tell what direction Columbus was going when he killed them, though. Soon, we make it back to the bone pit; there, we find a rope dangling down from the ceiling as well as the entrance, which was concealed by a boulder. The necromancer had directed us upward instead of allowing us to proceed to the boss. Interesting. Suddenly, though, my chat comes to life.

[DarkCynic: Hey, Jason! We worked out what Columbus was saying to the spider!]

[ShadowDancer: Yeah! Take a listen to this!]

[ShadowDancer: <sent an audio file. Click to download.>]

I pause and motion for John to do the same thing. Quickly, I download the file, and we stand there to listen to what comes next. Columbus's voice springs to life in my ears, crackling and harsh, but recognizable.

"I've got it right here."

"I'm impressed you managed to get it from him," the spider says.

"He's powerful, but he's a fool."

"Then you're a fool. He's no one to mess with. He's almost here; I can sense him."

"Then take it!" Columbus sounds desperate on the recording. "Take it now before he—"

WHAM!

The recording ends, and I frown in thought. So . . . the spider had asked Columbus to get the stardust, but then . . .

"I'm confused," John murmurs.

"As am I." I nod. "We'll just have to get out of here and track him down."

"Do you think that will even be possible?" John frowns. "He's got a pretty good head start on us."

I give a simple nod. "Yeah. Yeah, I think it'll be more than possible. Come on, though! We need to hurry."

The two of us pick up speed and soon come back to the

entrance. We step out into the nuclear reactor, where we find Mr. Harrison standing, a bit of a bewildered look on his face.

"I . . . You two are alive?"

"Where did Columbus go?" I snap. "Tell me now."

"He just left, not two minutes ago," Mr. Harrison answers. "We . . . What happened in there? The power was suddenly drained into the dungeon, almost everything we produce, and then it went away, and then he came out and said that you'd both been killed by the boss!"

"Did you give him the money?" I snap.

"I gave him his cut of it. Your share is still fine." Mr. Harrison nods. "It'll be transferred to Mr. Wang right away."

"Good." I nod and start to run forward. John follows closely behind. "Then I'll leave it to the two of you to work out the details!"

"And where are you going?" Mr. Harrison calls after us.

"Doesn't matter! We're no longer working for you!" John calls over his shoulder in return. Before I can say a word, John grabs me and throws me up into the air. He's a bit short of the mark, and I snatch hold of the railing of the catwalk to haul myself up to the entrance of the room. John climbs up, leaping from rail to rail with the grace of a cat. We both reach the elevator and push the button to go up, but as we do, the elevator falls dead.

"That's only a delaying tactic." John scowls. He reaches up and punches out the panel that allows him to climb up onto the roof of the car. We start to move quickly upward as he simply takes over for the motor.

"Yeah, but all he needs to do is slow us down long enough

to get away," I answer, bracing myself to run the moment the doors are open. "Come on . . . Come on . . ."

"Ding!" John calls out as we move up to the correct floor. "Ground level. Home to our—"

I know it's a joke, but I don't stay to hear the punch line. I lunge forward, push the doors open with my bare hands, and run out into the lobby of the hotel. There, I see guests looking about wildly. More than a few stare at me and John as we both run out the front doors and onto the streets of New York once more.

Traffic blares loudly as taxies and elephant-mounts vie for road space. A woman sprays a goblin with a vial of pepper spray to prevent him from stealing her purse. Two muggers push an old man into an alley, only to be jumped in turn by a couple of trash trolls. Yes, all is normal in New York . . . And I don't have the faintest idea where Columbus might have gone. He could have run down the street; he could have ducked into any old store; he could have—

"Burnie!" I call out. "I need you to be my eyes in the sky, and I need Lightfax!"

With a flash, the portal to my pocket dimension opens. Burnie flies out and shoots up into the sky, Lightfax steps out, and an old lady whacks me with her handbag for blocking the sidewalk. I climb up onto my noble horse as quickly as I can, then glance at John.

"Do you think she can hold me?" John asks. "I'm awful heavy."

I grimace. "I don't know, honestly. I—"

Chopper blades echo through the air, and my phone rings. I frown, then answer it quickly. All around, a crowd is starting to look at me, but I ignore them.

"Hey, Jason!" Mr. Wang cries out. "I'll get John! You head toward Central Park! That's where Columbus is heading. You've got to admit, this is *great!* The publicity, the money, the—"

I hang up the phone. The *danger.* If Columbus sells the stardust to a monster, it could make them invincible, and that's not something that anyone wants to deal with. I tap my heels into Lightfax's sides, and we shoot off like a gun. John, behind me, jumps up into the air and starts climbing the side of the building even as the helicopter slowly drops downward.

Lightfax pounds down the sidewalk as fast as she can, though it's difficult with the amount of pedestrian traffic. I swerve out into the street to allow us to go faster, weaving between the taxis, and that works a *little* better, though the amount of horn honking that it creates almost makes it not worth it. In any event, but the time I reach Central Park, I can see Columbus ahead of me. He bolts through the gates and runs toward a shelter, and I spur Lightfax on all the faster.

Suddenly, Columbus turns and flicks his wrist. A lasso shoots through the air from his palm and slaps down around my torso, pinning my arms to my body. I'm not exactly sure how it works, but I'm pulled from Lightfax's back almost instantly and come tumbling to the ground. I hit the dust hard and roll several times. Lightfax charges Columbus and rears up to strike at him, and he draws a pistol.

Now, I've seen guns deployed against monsters. They're utterly useless, and there's simply no other way to describe them. That said, I don't really know what they might do to a tamed beast like Lightfax, so I give a wave of my hand. She's sucked back into the pocket dimension instantly, and the gun discharges with a sharp *crack*. With that, Columbus spins toward me, and I flex my muscles as hard as I can. Ropes snap, and I climb to my feet and stalk toward him.

"Give it back to me," I demand. "Right now. You know what I'm talking about."

"I—I . . ." Columbus stammers. "Jason! What a surprise! I—"

He raises his gun and fires three times. The bullets hit me in the torso, but they feel more like gentle punches instead of gunshot wounds. Apparently, *I'm* a bit more immune to them as well. That's nice to know. In any case, he draws back in fear as I approach, and I ball my hands into fists.

"Give it back to me," I snap. "You know what I'm talking about."

"The stardust?" Columbus questions, trying to look innocent.

"Yes." I nod as I reach him. I grab his shirt with my left hand and lift him up into the air, then ball my right hand into a fist. "You know how strong I am, and someone who's a whole lot stronger is about to arrive. We heard you talking to the spider. We know you were hired to steal it. We know—"

"You don't know anything," Columbus snaps. I lift an eyebrow, and he sighs. "Look, I—"

Snip.

The noise is quiet, but it's there. I spin to the side, throwing Columbus out of the way. A dart flies through the space he was just occupying and slams into the dust. There's a brief flickering, and a great blast of electricity arcs upward. To my great surprise, an electric sprite takes shape in the air, a flickering ball of electricity that looks *quite* angry at my presence.

Columbus gasps, then breaks and runs. I ball my hands into fists and prepare for battle, then turn to look in the direction that the shot came from. Something flickers on top of a rooftop nearby, and I hear the same noise.

This time I'm not fast enough, and the dart hits me in the shoulder.

I've felt a lot of pain since the start of this apocalypse. Some of it's been worse, and some of it's been not as bad. *That* pain I would rank near the top. Electricity explodes from the dart the moment it hits me, arcing through my body like a child running through a playground. I fall to the ground and grit my teeth, desperately trying to stay focused. A moment later, an electric sprite shoots out of my chest and joins the first one, and I'm left weakened.

The two sprites seem to confer for a moment, and then they charge me. Well . . . they explode across the distance like lightning bolts, hit me in the chest before I can process what's happening, and knock me flat on my back. Once more, it hurts a *lot*, but that's all I can do. My arms and legs won't move, my—

"I am *not* going down like this!" I managed to blurt out. Electricity is coursing through my body. Thankfully, I know something else that can hold a lot of electricity. With every last ounce of effort I have left, I haul myself to my feet, turn, and throw myself into the nearby lake.

Well, I *fall* into the lake, but the effect is the same. The electric sprites are sucked from my body as they encounter a much larger body to disperse themselves through. I'm relieved of the pain, at least somewhat, and splash back onto shore as the water flickers with electricity. Suddenly, with a great explosion of water, the sprites shoot back up into the air, hover there for a moment, and flash back at me.

Now, at this point, I don't really have anything that'll let me fight against non-corporeal creatures like these. My last fight against a sprite, an ice one, was *hard*. Right now, I honestly don't know what to do, but I know I have to do something. I draw out my Photonic Dagger and transform it into a sword, hoping that I'll be able to use it to some effect. I swing it sort of like a baseball bat as the two enemies attack, and, to my delight, they're both absorbed by the weapon, just like a lightning rod. Lightning rings the weapon like a wreath, and, just as quickly as I can, I plunge the blade into the dirt. There's a soft *hiss* as the electricity is discharged into the bulk of the Earth, and I sigh as I pull the weapon free.

Thunk!

John comes down with a crash just next to me, and Burnie flies down to land on my shoulder. He looks around, then frowns.

"Did I miss the party?"

"Afraid so." I wince as a bit of smoke rises up from some of my armor, and I look around for Columbus. "Burnie, did you happen to see where the cowboy went?"

I'm sorry, Master. I didn't.

"Then we'll just have to figure it out later," I answer.

"We're not going to keep going after him?" John demands.

"Not right now." I shake my head. "Someone just tried to kill him. Wherever he is, he'll be hiding *deep* down. If we track him, we'll only be giving information to whoever is trying to knock him off."

"Then, what are we going to do?"

I frown, then look up at the sky. Mr. Wang's helicopter hovers overhead, and I give it a wave. "We're going to head back to the apartment and figure things out from there. Once we're all settled, we'll track him back down, and we'll make sure we put an end to this for good."

CHAPTER FOURTEEN

Mr. Wang's helicopter shoots through the air back to my apartment, but I can't focus enough to enjoy the view. Soon, we come down for a landing on the helipad, and John and I jump out and walk into my living room. A few moments later, an arrow flies through one of my open windows and sticks into a chair, and with a flash of teleporter light, Ali is brought in. John jumps with a start, and I laugh.

"John, meet Ali," I say, introducing the two of them. "And Ali, thank you for coming. I know you're busy with your construction project, but I appreciate you taking the time."

Ali smiles and nods. "But of course! How can I help you?"

"We're in a bit of a—"

Fzzzzzzt!

A hologram comes to life over the coffee table in my living room, adding Mr. Wang to the discussion. He gives a bow at the waist, and the three of us slowly look up at him.

"Apologies for not being there in person! I'm afraid I'm

being asked to a conference in China with a number of governmental agencies whose identities I cannot reveal." Mr. Wang gives a wink to us. "That said, as I feel that I'm an integral part of this discussion, I must include myself."

"We're happy to have you." I give him a nod as I slowly sit down and cross my arms. Ali's already seated, and John drops onto my couch. Mr. Wang looks at all of us, and his hologram slowly takes a seat as well. He doesn't seem like he really wants to be here for a terribly long time, but that's the way it goes. "Now, we have some things we need to discuss."

"And what would that be, Jason Lee?" Mr. Wang folds his hands into his lap.

"There are three of them." I hold up a finger, adding another with each point. "First, we need to figure out what exactly this stardust stuff is. Second, we need to figure out what Columbus did, or is doing, with it. Somehow, I doubt he still has it on him. Third, we need to figure out what's going on with these dungeons around here."

"The first one I can help with." Ali holds up a hand. "I've been doing some research on it since it first started getting mentioned. As a bit of a healer, I've managed to get my hands on some books that have come out of the dungeons. Game guides, so to speak. One of them was an item manual." She opens up her inventory and pulls out a massive book, which she drops onto the coffee table and opens up. "Stardust is the product created by refining Fallen Stars. Each Fallen Star will produce one ounce. A single grain will heal one percent of health and temporarily increase all stats and abilities by point-five percent. For every grain consumed, this effect compounds."

"So, it's a healing item, just like I'd used it." I nod slowly.

"Yes and no." Ali gives her head a small shake, then keeps reading. "Additionally, stardust may have other properties when combined with magical items. It can augment the power of any magical property and, upon consumption, can be used to target specific skills instead of overall health and stats. The relative value of this product is unthinkable."

"Target specific skills," I murmur softly. "Augment magical properties. For a dungeon boss with an ambition to rise in rank, this could be the key."

"Especially because that sort of thing could be abused pretty easily." John nods. "If you have a skill that increases the effectiveness of enchantments, for example, and then an enchantment that increases the effectiveness of skills, you could potentially loop them together to break the system."

"You could probably do that *anyway*," Ali argues.

"I'm just giving an example!" John shrugs. "That seems like the sort of thing that would be able to circumvent the rules that the system ordinarily sets up."

"To that, I entirely agree." Mr. Wang nods. "How rare is stardust, Ali?"

"As near as I can tell, virtually none of it has ever been produced in the history of the dungeons," Ali answers. "Fallen Stars are a rare phenomenon that only appear in Astral Dungeons, but those can't even start appearing until warriors hit level fifty. Right now, no one is even close, except for maybe Jason."

"I've still got a long way to go." I grimace. "Too far, if you ask me, but you know how that goes."

"Right. Even if they did exist in our world, the chance of a Fallen Star appearing in any given Astral Dungeon is something like point zero one percent, and even once it *does* appear, very few are ever processed, as they're quite powerful in their own right." Ali shrugs. "I'd say that vial is the single most valuable *thing* on planet Earth right now, given that we've estimated it to hold almost five ounces of dust."

I frown and lean back in my seat. "Then *why* did that boss offer the dust to me? He dangled it right there!"

"You heard him," Mr. Wang jumps in. "He'd poisoned you. He wanted you at his side, remember, helping him rise in rank. Maybe he thought you would recognize the significance of what he was offering, especially once you'd turned and joined his war of terror."

"Maybe." I nod with a frown. "It still seems odd, but it does give us a bit of a leg up. Now, moving on slightly, how many people know about the stardust? I mean, everyone will know *now*, but . . ."

"Prior to this moment, word was spreading pretty fast, at least as near as I can tell." Ali shrugs. "If you're trying to figure out who was trying to kill Columbus, it could have been any-one—another dungeon boss, a human, who knows? People will kill each other over gemstones and things that are *way* less important than that vial."

"Most likely, Columbus tried to snipe the dungeon, just like we assumed." John shrugs. "Once he was inside, the spider's minions got to him and asked him to betray us. He was already planning on doing it anyway, so he agreed."

"Maybe," I muse. "It still doesn't make a lot of sense. He seemed like he had come to the dungeon intentionally. It wasn't an accident. I think there's more going on right now. Have we managed to track the assassin yet?"

"My people are working on it right now," Mr. Wang assures me. "We're working on accessing some of the security footage of the buildings nearby to see if we can identify the perpetrator, but that could take some time. What we *have* managed to do, somewhat more successfully, is actually quite similar to what Ali did. Some of my staff have been acquiring books brought out of the dungeons, and we found what we think was the weapon used in the attempt on his life. Or at least part of the weapon." Mr. Wang reaches out of the frame, then pulls his hand back. He has a small crystal in his hand now, no longer than an inch, shaped rather like the diamond that might be floating over someone's head in a video game to mark a quest. "This will generate an ice wraith if activated. Activation can be with a verbal command or by impact."

"Impact," I murmur. "That sounds about right. You think someone used that as a bullet?"

"The little bit of footage we *have* managed to get our hands on suggests that someone got ahold of electric wraith crystals, then managed to jury-rig a gun of some sort," Mr. Wang answers. "We're running tests and simulations now to see just exactly how fast the item could be fired without activating it inside the barrel of the gun, since we know that the punch of being fired didn't set it off. Perhaps some sort of magnetic acceleration, or compressed air. The short answer is that we just don't know what we're dealing with, but we're working on it. In any event, these items are quite easy to get your hands on if you know what you're looking for."

"Good to know." I cross my arms in thought. "Well, in that case, finding Columbus needs to be our top priority. Like I said, my guess is that he hid the stardust after the assassination attempt, but that also means that he knows where it is. Every half-baked dungeon boss in the tri-state area will be trying to get their hands on him, and when they do, they'll get the information out of him."

"You think he'll cave that easily?" John raises an eyebrow.

"He was terrified of me when I caught up to him, and his escape was, frankly, childish," I answer. "He'll cave, yeah, and I doubt it'll even take that much."

"I'll put every spare resource I have on it," Mr. Wang promises. "In the meantime, Jason, I do have another job for you."

"Another job?" I climb to my feet. "Surely padding your pockets isn't more important than finding this stuff!"

"There are few things that I find to be more important than padding my pockets," Mr. Wang answers with a small smile. "That said, in this case, I actually do agree with you. Finding the dust is of the utmost importance, and that's why I don't want you on the case. You or John, actually. Both of you subscribed to the livestream, and that means that your every move is being watched. If you're on the case, our enemies will be watching you like hawks. You'll do all the work, and they'll swoop in at the last moment to score the prize."

"What about Ali?" I gesture to her. "She has the livestream too!"

"Actually, I took it down." She shrugs. "Not voluntarily, but I started to dig up some . . . we'll call them *governmental oversights* in my campaign to provide affordable housing to all my warriors. The moment everyone started seeing the same things, the government turned off my feed. I don't mind it being gone, mind you, and I'll be throwing myself into tracking all of this down."

"Alright, then." I nod slowly, then turn back to the group. "In that case, I've only got one question left. The odd behavior of the bosses. What does anyone know? Specific incidents? Odd scenarios? Anything out of the ordinary, I need to know about it."

There's a brief moment of silence, and Ali shrugs. "I can ask my warriors if they've noticed anything, but outside of all the crazy stuff you've been experiencing, I've not heard of it."

Mr. Wang reaches out and taps on a computer just beyond the range of the hologram. "I've got a few reports here. One from Hong Kong where a dungeon boss, an octopus, left the dungeon and raided a military base nearby. It's uncertain what he was looking for—he was killed within a few moments of entering—but it's of some concern to the people there. Another involves a dungeon in London that opened up quietly in a clothing store and sent out its warriors to steal clothes from the racks overnight. They then closed the portal and re-opened it elsewhere, where a group of orcs tried to slip into society dressed as ordinary humans. It didn't work, but it made for some *epic* memes."

"But no reports of dungeon bosses trying to increase their ranking among the other dungeon bosses?" I press.

"Jason?" Ali bats her eyes at me, and not in the flirtatious way. "No one other than you bothers to talk to the dungeon bosses or the dungeon minions. They just kill them."

"Well . . ." I scowl. "They have good information."

"Be that as it may, the rest of us can't tame them," Ali points out. "The whole ruse that Krak pulled on you? Yeah, for most people, that would have just been impossible since most people don't routinely go around trying to tame dungeon bosses. Or dungeon *anythings*."

"Well . . ." I shrug. "It's a fun hobby."

"And I sense that this meeting is at an end." Mr. Wang, never one to waste a moment, stands up. "Jason, I'll let you know the moment I know something. In the meantime, I have a new assignment for you. Head to the helicopter and you'll have the details."

I nod, and the hologram flickers and vanishes. Ali sighs and stands, then unslings her bow.

"I guess that's my cue to go." She fits an arrow to the bow. "Keep up the good work, John. I don't know where we'd be without you, and that's just a fact."

With that, she fires the arrow out through my window, then slings the bow onto her back and waits for a long moment. Suddenly, there's a loud yell from below followed by a resounding *boom*, and she blinks in surprise.

"Oh! I used the wrong arrow type. My bad." She draws out another arrow and fires again, and after a long moment, she vanishes in a burst of teleporter light. I chuckle, and John and I walk back out onto the helipad. The pilot is just changing out with another pilot, so we pause for a moment on the edge of the roof.

"Are you coming with me?" I glance at my friend. "I could use your help in there, especially if there are any more snipers. And to be clear, I mean that in all senses of the word now."

John laughs at that. "Nah. I'll come back when you're ready to tie everything together, but for the time being, I'd like to get back onto the streets. I'll see you around."

"Catch you later." I throw him a salute, and with that, he

jumps off the building, digging his claws into the stone to slow his descent. The sound is just awful, but I have to laugh as he skates down the side of the building just like he was born into it. After a moment, the helicopter blades start to whir to life, and I run back and climb in.

With that, we lift off, and I'm taken away to my next adventure. Whatever, and wherever, that might be.

CHAPTER FIFTEEN

The helicopter roars through the sky, and this time I allow myself a bit of free time to look down at the landscape below. Buildings, trees, people, cars, monsters—it all blurs together. We pass over a river, where boats chug back and forth even as serpent tails curl beneath, and I have to smile.

New York. There really is no other place in the world like it.

"What's that?" Something catches my eye, and I point across the bay. It looks like some new construction is going up, and it's going up *fast*. Monsters of some sort—they look almost like dinosaurs with longer arms—are slapping steel beams in place far faster than I would have imagined was possible. Well, it certainly *is* far faster than would be possible with standard cranes. Workers crawl over the structure like ants, presumably stitching the whole thing together just as quickly as they can.

"I think that's the new Pumped! factory!" the pilot calls back. "Yeah, I was hearing about it on the news just this morning! They've been analyzing the chemical formula of the stuff that's been brought out of the dungeons, and someone's managed to recreate it using ordinary food. Since it's so popular, they're just going to make a whole factory! Cool, huh?"

Frankly, I don't know what to think of it. I can see a number of issues. A scenario comes to my mind where I'm in the middle of a fight, snag a Pumped! off a counter, and wind up chugging a bunch of sugary syrup instead of actually getting a health boost. In any case, the helicopter soon starts to descend, and I'm drawn back to the reality of my job. I stand up even before we land, and as we come to a stop, I slide open the door and hop out. My feet have hardly hit the ground before the helicopter roars and flies off, and I turn and put my hands behind my back.

I have to admit, the place isn't what I expected. Instead of looking at a big, rich corporation, I find myself looking at D20 Games, a board game cafe. I blink in surprise and slowly turn to look up at the retreating helicopter, but before I can do anything, the door swings open. A man walks out, dressed in a sweater, khaki pants, and a beanie. He has a five-o'clock shadow and is holding a cup of coffee in his hand.

"Hey! You must be Jason Lee, world-famous dungeon warrior!"

"That's me." I hold out my hand. The man blinks, then grins.

"Oh! Yeah." He shifts the cup of coffee to his other hand, shakes mine, and then nods at the store. "Shall we?"

"Let's do it." I nod and follow him as we walk inside. A bell jingles, and I find myself standing in a wide-open game room. There are dozens of tables, many of which already have people playing board games. I see the classics, chess and checkers, alongside card games like Wonder: The Get-Together, worker placements, roll n' writes, and, of course, everyone's favorite gateway game: Settlers of Catan. Off to one side is a coffee bar, and around the room are shelves upon shelves of board games. It's a lovely atmosphere, and everyone inside cheers as I enter.

"I . . . I have to admit that I'm a bit confused." I scratch my head.

"You won't be! Come here." The owner of the store points to a door at the back of the room. "Now, this used to be our immersive escape room, but then the dungeon opened up, and with OSHA rules being what they are . . ." He waves his hands around in the air as if he's annoyed, then grabs the handle and pulls it open. Inside, I see an area that looks like a rather messy hotel room, the perfect setting for an escape room, along with a flickering portal. Of course, I also see a handful of other warriors standing in front of the portal as well. One of them is a woman dressed in long red robes; one of them is a man wearing a monk's robe, complete with the hood pulled *far* over his face; and a third is dressed like a pirate, complete with a peg leg.

"Yeah, I'm still confused." I cross my arms. "What . . . I . . ."

"You're wondering how we managed to hire you." The owner holds out his hands. "Of course, of course. You're used to working for multi-zillion dollar corporations, but those aren't the only ones in town. As soon as this popped up, we started up a Kickstarter campaign, sent out an email to all our subscribers, and offered ten percent off any product in our store to those who forwarded it. That email went viral, and we raised a hundred million dollars in thirty minutes flat!"

"And who are these guys?" I gesture with my thumb at the other warriors.

"Stretch goals!"

"Ahh." I take a deep breath. "I'm surprised Mr. Wang agreed to work for so little," I can't help remarking.

"He thought it would be a good PR stunt, and I happen to agree." The man seems over the moon. "Now, for the specifics of the job, we'd like—"

"Specifics?" I frown. "I go in there and kill things."

"Yeah . . . I mean, feel free to do that. We have a *lot* of people counting on a good livestream, so I do think that's a good idea, but we're going to need a smidge more than that." The man slowly folds his hands. "So, the whole point of the Kickstarter is that instead of just clearing the dungeon out, we're going to turn it into an immersive experience."

"A what?" I honestly can't believe what I'm hearing right now.

"An immersive experience!" The man smiles and holds out his hands as if framing a sunset or a skyline or something. "Picture this! People come into my game store, my lovely store, for the only dungeon in the world that you can walk through as a normal civilian! All the monsters are in cages, so you can observe what they look like firsthand. The boss is dead, or maybe just caged, and you can walk around inside the actual boss room, and it's just going to be epic!"

I have a hard time keeping a straight face. "There is *absolutely* no way this will work."

"Give me one good reason why not." The owner turns to me. "I paid good money for you."

"Yeah, without telling me what it was for!" I protest. "Look, the individual monsters are going to be hard enough! I don't have the faintest idea how I'll cage any of them, but the boss . . . If you kill the boss, the dungeon will close as soon as it's empty, and if you don't kill the boss, the boss *will* kill your customers. I guarantee it."

"Then . . . How about this?" the man offers. "You go in there and do your best. Give us a good show and capture as many monsters as you possibly can. When you get to the end, kill the boss. After that, I'll just make sure there's always someone inside! It'll work great!"

"Just so that it's on the record, I want *everyone* to know that I think this is a terrible idea." I hold up a finger. "Does everyone on my chat have that fact down?"

[IceQueen: Got it, Jason!]

[ChaosRider: Are you kidding me? I paid $1,000 for the full VIP experience! If I don't get to explore my own dungeon, I'm holding you personally responsible.]

[LunarEclipse: I paid $100 for a discounted rate once the dungeon opens. I'd still like to cash in on it, so I *would* appreciate it if you could make it work.]

"Alright." I rub my jaw. "Then I guess I'll try."

My chat explodes with cheers, and the owner grins. "Great! I'll start getting things set up on my end! You just . . . I don't know, have a brief chat with your team, then get inside and get to work. Got it?"

With that, he turns and runs out of the room. I rub my jaw again, then turn to the other three people standing there.

"Does anyone happen to know what his name is?" I ask, gesturing over my shoulder with my thumb.

"I think it was James," the woman in red answers. "Or Felix. Something along that line."

"Interesting." I shrug. "And your names?"

"My name is Ella." The woman draws a Samurai sword. "But I go by Electra!"

"That name is taken," the pirate says.

"Then just Ella." The woman shrugs. "I kill things. I don't require that they have my name right ahead of time."

"Well, I'm Tom." The pirate draws a cutlass. "But I go by Blackbeard! See!" He sticks out his chin. I can *maybe* see a single hair there, but to each his own, I suppose.

The monk stays silent and just shifts his hands inside his cloak a bit. Tom turns to him and elbows the monk, making the man rock sideways.

"Hey! What's your name?"

The monk doesn't say anything, but I have a pretty good idea what's going on.

[ChaosRider: Hey, is that Columbus?]

[ViperQueen: Yeah, that's totally him.]

[ShadowDancer: Let me get my cousin to run a body-analysis scan. He'll be able to tell if the monk's build is the same as Columbus.]

[RazorEdge: But . . . if that's Columbus, are these other clowns the people trying to kill him?]

I don't have an answer for that final question, but it bothers me as well. I sit back and try to think, and the monk slowly starts shuffling toward the portal.

"Hey! I think Jason should have the opportunity to go first!" Tom says, holding the monk back.

Frankly, I'm not convinced that that's a good idea, for a wide variety of reasons. If Columbus is here to kill me, hitting me from behind after I enter the portal is a good way to do it.

Secondly, if he's here to hide, and one of the others is here to kill him, that gives them several seconds without my presence for them to act. Of course, if it's *not* actually Columbus, then all of this conjecture is utterly useless.

"Quick question." I turn to the three warriors. "Do *any* of you have experience actually fighting?"

"I cleaned out a dungeon that opened in my sister's basement." Tom shrugs.

"Really?" I cross my arms. "A whole dungeon? What level are you?"

Tom winces, and he slowly takes a step back. "Three. And . . . Well, I guess it was just a cockroach, but still! It was a big cockroach, and it spat poison at me."

"And you?" I turn to Ella. "What have you done?"

"I've fought my way through three dungeons and two rifts." She crosses her arms in defiance. "Level fifteen."

"That true?" I ask my chat.

[DarkCynic: Not even close! It looks like she's a Level 5, has about twenty subs, mostly relatives who never log on, and has only been in two dungeons.]

[IceQueen: She's got spunk, though.]

[ChaosRider: She doesn't seem evil, if that's what you're asking.]

I raise an eyebrow, and Ella seems to shrink back. I turn to the monk next, and he simply lowers his head. After a moment, I cross my arms.

"In that case, I'll be going inside with just him."

The monk nods, then shuffles across the floor and slips into the portal. I nod to the other two, then walk into the portal after him. Ella and Tom both protest, but I hold up a finger as I step into the interdimensional straw, and they fall silent. They know they can't stand against me, and that saves me at least some hassle. The door flies open as someone barges in, but by that time, I'm getting sucked inside.

As per usual, the crackling, whooshing, interdimensional trip is entirely unpleasant, painful, revolting, and in all other senses of the word undesirable. When I come shooting out the other side, I find myself standing in a large cavern that feels like it's located *far* beneath the planet's crust. Cracks in the ground emit steam in sharp, hissing blasts, and the whole thing is lit by glowing lava crystal things stuck in the walls. Yellow eyes peer at me from the darkness, and I slowly draw out my Photonic Dagger and the Dagger of Damage. You have no idea how much I miss my Diamond Dagger, but I suppose some things just aren't meant to be.

"Level up!" I smack my forehead as I step into the dungeon. "I totally forgot to level up! I might have gotten some better weapons!"

[ShadowDancer: Yeah, that was sort of a stupid move.]

[ViperQueen: I'd have remembered to level up if I were in your shoes.]

[FireStorm: Yeah, but you spent so much time gabbing with your friends that you forgot the most important thing!]

"And did any of *you* remember to remind me?" I raise an eyebrow. The chat falls silent at that, and I glance over at the monk. Slowly, he reaches up and pulls back his hood, revealing, of course, Columbus. He starts taking off his monk's clothing as I watch, revealing his cowboy outfit.

"Uh . . . Thanks." He bows his head.

"Don't thank me yet." I shrug. "Thank me once we manage

to get through this dungeon. Caging up everything we . . ." I pause, trying not to laugh. "I have no idea how we're going to do this!"

"Well . . ." Columbus shrugs. "I have a lasso."

"Then put it to good use!" I point into the darkness as forms start to emerge, and the yellow eyes grow closer. "Here we go!"

A loud snarl echoes through the cavern, and a great, black cat springs forward. I have to describe it as a lava-cat, there's just no other real word for it. The fur is jet-black, the claws are glowing orange, and the eyes are, of course, glowing yellow. It's somewhere in the ballpark of three feet long.

And it looks like it wants to eat me.

The first one springs forward, claws outstretched, raking at my face. I slam my Photonic Dagger into its chest, and, just like the cat I had growing up, it claws at my face and manages to rake several red-hot claws across my cheek. I snarl and smash it into the ground, trying to drive the point of the weapon down into the stone below. As I do so, I stab it several times with the Dagger of Damage, but I only manage to raise the damage up to the level of an ordinary dagger before the lava-cat twists out of the way and springs off into the distance. More of the cats rush forward in a great blur, and Columbus and I settle in for the fight.

Suddenly, though, there's a sharp *hiss*, and a new figure steps through the portal and into the dungeon. It's wearing deep black robes, holding a staff set with a glowing crystal, and it looks rather like the necromancer that I fought in the last dungeon. You know, bony hands, a dark hood, that sort of thing.

"Columbus! You've made your last mistake."

His staff flares with light, and another cat jumps at my head. I'm in *way* beyond what I signed up for . . . And there's nothing I can do but grit my teeth and fight my way through as best I can.

CHAPTER SIXTEEN

ChaosRider: Who's this new guy?]

[IceQueen: I'm checking . . . I can't find a matching feed!]

[ShadowDancer: Order them alphabetically! I'll check A–C, you check D–F, and so on.]

[DarkCynic: Got him! His name is Deathhands. Doesn't look like the type you want to mess with.]

[LunarEclipse: Oh . . . Yeah, Jason, you're going to want to be careful here!]

I blink as I watch the scrolling chat, then turn my attention to the newcomer. Or at least I try to. The cat that suddenly hits me in the head and digs its claws into my shoulders makes it a good bit more difficult, and I flail around as I try to get the thing off.

Whooooooooooosh!

A blast of necrotic energy erupts from Deathhands's staff, hitting Columbus at point-blank range. The cowboy is blasted backward into a nearby wall. He draws a pistol and fires into the dark lord's face, but the weapon remains just as useless as when he shot me.

"Stupid . . . cat!" I stab the creature with my Photonic Dagger several times, then run forward and smash my head into a wall. The cat cushions the blow to my skull, and it drops to the ground rather senseless. I quickly turn the weapon into a sword and cut off its head, then spin back to the newcomer. He fires a blast of damage at me, but I duck under it and charge forward at him.

"Oh no, you don't!" He laughs and lifts a hand. I feel invisible cords wrap around my wrists and feet, and I'm lifted into the air and cast to the side like a puppet. As I come down, I land right in the middle of a small gang of the cats. They jump on me with lightning speed, and I react in the only way that comes to my mind.

I grab their tails, hold on tightly, and spin with all my might. They lose their grip on my skin and are slung around rather like . . . well, like anything you might spin by the tail. I throw them at the newcomer, then charge at him. He blasts them out of the sky with two quick bolts of lightning, killing them both instantly, and holds out his staff. I freeze solid— not from cold but from simple paralysis, and he cackles.

"You're useless, Jason! All you can do is watch as I—*hrrrrrrrk!*"

Now, the word *hrrrrrrrk,* when translated from lizard speech—I picked up a book on it from Ali—means something akin to the English word "hello," though it also has the connotation "I'm keeping an eye on you." Lizardmen aren't, by nature, trusting creatures. That said, in this case, the word *hrrrrrrk* is the sound of Deathhands choking on a lasso that suddenly wraps around his neck. Columbus emerges from the darkness, lasso in his hands, and gives a sharp jerk of his wrist. The man is slammed into the ground so hard that I hear his back pop, and I run forward to snatch up his staff.

"Ah-ha!" I dive forward and grab the weapon, then spin and point the crystal at him. "Don't move!"

The cats behind me don't get the memo, and three of them leap onto my back at the same time. One of them has the nerve to breathe a great deal of fire across my back, ruining my shirt and dropping my health down into the yellow. In the chaos, I lose my grip on the staff, which clatters to the ground. Deathhands telekinetically yanks it back into his palm, and I grit my teeth against the pain and throw myself backward into a wall. This time the cats are too fast, and they all jump off me before I impact the wall, which leaves them without a trace of injury. I, however, wind up with more than a trace of a headache and three cats all ready to jump back onto my *front* now. Deathhands fires a bolt of fire at Columbus, making the cowboy relax his control of the rope, which the assassin burns away before standing back up.

"Alright. I need help." I stab one of the cats in the neck, then twist the blade and rip it through the being, cutting off its head. "Astrid! Bjorn!"

With a flicker, my two wolves leap out of my pocket dimension and into action. Astrid snarls, making the ground tremble, and a great deal of fire explodes up out of the ground, roasting the cats. Bjorn, meanwhile, runs at Deathhands. The two cats left on my chest dig their claws in deeper, and I take a deep breath.

"Alright . . . Brief Acquisition!" I grate out. A blast of energy flashes from my palm and hits one of the cats. It instantly lets go and attacks the other one, and the two of them roll across the floor in a tangle of claws and flame. Astrid keeps up her own attack, focusing her ire against the other felines of the room, and I run toward Deathhands.

By now, Deathhands is backing toward the portal. A constant blast of flame surges from his staff at Bjorn, who's sending a blast of ice out at the assassin. Columbus, meanwhile, stands nearby, watching them while holding his whip idly in his hand. He seems torn between what to do, and I'm reminded that he *did* still try to kill me and leave me for dead. Whether or not I need him, whether or not there are darker forces trying to get to him, he's not exactly the most upstanding of characters, and I can't let my guard down.

Not if I want to live.

I pull out my Photonic Dagger, heft it a little in my hand, and throw it with all my might. It flashes straight through the torrent of competing energies and hits Deathhands in the chest, knocking him backward. Columbus takes the opportunity to use his whip and lashes the end of it around the staff. He yanks it free, and a blast of ice from Bjorn freezes the man solid. I slowly walk up to find Deathhands bending over backward, halfway through a fall, entirely encased in ice.

"Kill him now." Columbus walks up to me, anger written across his face. He's holding the staff in his hands, and the crystal starts to glow. "We can end him."

"Hold on." I lift a hand. "We can't kill someone who can't defend themselves! He's just . . . trapped in there! That wouldn't be humane!"

With a mighty *crash*, Deathhands erupts from the ice. Invisible cords wrap around my neck, and I suddenly find myself unable to breathe. In fact, my entire body seems to grow numb, and I feel myself fall to my knees. Columbus does the same thing, and Deathhands chuckles.

"You should have killed me while you had the chance!"

Bjorn lets out another blast of ice, but a twitch of a finger causes a chunk of stone to erupt from the floor and hit the wolf in the chest, smashing him up into the ceiling. He falls to the ground, not dead but quite pummeled. Astrid lets out a howl and comes running as well, but a stone falls out of the ceiling to smash her into the ground. Deathhands chuckles deeply, his voice echoing throughout the room.

"And now, I, the great Deathhands, will do what no monster, no dungeon boss, has yet been able to do! I will kill Jason Lee, I will take the stardust from Columbus, and I will—"

The noise he makes this time is more of a gurgling sound and isn't something that can easily be written down. As it just so happens, it more or less translates to the word "shoe" in a particular dialect of sea-orc, but that's a side note. In any case, the noise is made because the cat that I temporarily tamed sneaks up behind him, jumps onto his back, and drives his claws deep into Deathhands's throat.

With that, the invisible holds on my own throat go away, and I lunge up and forward as quickly as I can. Without really thinking about it, I grab the staff from his hands, twirl it around my head, and whack the dark lord like a baseball player hitting a ball.

The attack, to my great surprise, works wonders, and Deathhands is blasted across the room and into one of the walls. Several cats jump on him, and I feel him tugging at the staff, trying to call it back to him, but I give him no chance to strike back. Instead, I lift the weapon and smash it into the floor, shattering the crystal on the end. A great torrent of spectral magic explodes through the room, briefly lighting it, and I lunge forward, holding the broken remains of the staff. Deathhands looks up and blinks in surprise, and I drive the weapon straight through his heart like a spear.

There's a long pause, and Deathhands slowly goes still. The remaining cats turn toward me, but a growl from Bjorn freezes most of them and sends the rest running. The room goes quiet, and I bend down to start patting down the assassin.

"What are you doing?" Columbus steps up behind me.

"Searching his body," I answer. "Why don't you go see if you can tie up any of these cats for the cage project thing."

"Are you sure that's a good—"

"I almost died because of you." I stand up and stare Columbus in the eye. "More than once, as a matter of fact. *Most* of the time, I kill whatever happens to put me in that sort of situation. If you want my help, and it sure seems like you do, I want you to go tie up some cats with your magic lasso, and I'll get back to you in a minute."

Columbus gives a single nod of his head, and I crouch down and continue searching through Deathhands's robes. He seems to be a rather average man once I pull the hood back away from his face. Early thirties, most likely. A bit scraggly and unkempt. Looks to me like the type that lives alone, probably works retail, and hangs out with his friends on the weekend. Not a bad guy by any stretch of the imagination.

So why was he trying to kill me?

I get my answer as I find something hard in one of his pockets. Slowly, carefully, I pull out a small wooden token. It's the size of a silver dollar but has a *vastly* different design. On one side is a skull with the letters *MM*. On the other side is a single phrase:

Live the Game.

[ShadowDancer: Whoa! I've heard about those but never seen one in person!]

[RazorEdge: You're still not seeing it in person.]

[ChaosRider: Wait, what are those?]

I have to agree with ChaosRider, but I'd rather hear it from Columbus. I turn away from the corpse to find him just tying up a third cat, which looks to be the last one in the room. His lasso seems to have the ability to heal itself as well as the ability to change material. All the cats are bound with steel cable that their claws can't cut through, though they sure are trying awfully hard as I walk up. Columbus turns to look at me, and I toss the token to him.

"What's this?"

He looks down at the item, then sighs. "The 'MM' stands for 'memento mori.' I'm sure you've heard it before. It can be translated as 'Remember your death,' 'Remember that you must die,' and so on."

"Right. Keep talking." I continue to stare at him.

"Well . . ." He scratches the back of his neck. "There's a bit of a guild forming, you might say. They call it just that— MM. Their slogan is 'Live the Game.' Essentially . . . do whatever you have to do to become more powerful."

"They're people killers," I answer.

"They call themselves player killers, Awakened killers . . .

Call it whatever you want." Columbus shrugs. "The facts are the same."

"And how did *you* get mixed up with them?" I point at him.

"I'd rather not say."

From deeper within the dungeon, something roars. The ground shakes, and Astrid and Bjorn whimper. I can tell that they're both injured, so I open up my pocket dimension.

"Get inside, both of you. I want you back on your feet as soon as possible. This place creeps me out."

They waste no time running inside, and I slowly let out a long breath and close the portal after them. With that, I turn to Columbus, who winces once more.

"Where's the stardust?"

"I don't have it," Columbus answers. "And I'm not revealing where I hid it, either. I know how much that knowledge raises the value of my life."

"True, but you're only valuable as long as there's a chance you'll reveal it." I shrug. "If there's no chance it'll come out, you're just an obstacle." Columbus clamps his jaw shut, and I turn away. "Well, then. I've got a dungeon to clear. Come with me if you want or stay here. I frankly don't care. If you come with me, I'll do my best to protect you from anyone else who comes after you, *but*"—I hold up a finger—"there's a catch. If I'm going to protect you, I need answers. I need to know who needs the stardust, and what for. I need to know who hired you, I need to know how many people are trying to kill you, and I need to know anything else that's going to prove pertinent to this whole ordeal."

"I'm not saying anything," Columbus snarls softly.

"Then I'm sure the next sniper with a gun full of elementals will love to have the same discussion." With that, I start down the corridor. "See you around."

[FireStorm: Hey, Jason!!! Don't forget to level up!!!]

[IceQueen: Yeah! We want to see you get some new weapons!!!]

[RazorEdge: DO IT!!!!!!!!!!!!!!]

A smile flickers across my face, and I come to a stop. The path ahead of me is dark, so I draw out my Photonic Dagger and let its soft illumination shine into the inky blackness. At present, I have only two daggers. The diamond one was lost while fighting the necromancer, and the Shadow Dagger was actually lost in the same fight, though down in the cave below.

"Alright, then." I open up my interface. "Let's do this. I've got four levels to claim. Let's see what I can get!"

The cave flares with light as I start making my selections, and, as seems usual in such situations, the crowd in the chat goes absolutely wild.

CHAPTER SEVENTEEN

[Weapon Acquired: Seeking Dagger]

[Level: C]

[Details: When thrown, Seeking Dagger will seek out an intended target.]

[Weapon Acquired: Dagger of Kings]

[Level: E]

[Details: Has lots of jewels built into the hilt. Increases Charisma when worn in public and serves as a nice wall piece.]

[Weapon Acquired: Dagger of Doom]

[Level: B]

[Details: Deals damage based on the target's weakness. Warning: This may also be your weakness.]

[Skill Acquired!]

[Innocence: For 30 seconds, hostile mobs will take no notice of you. Effect will not work if they are actively attacking you. Effect will be broken if you attack anything.]

I look down at my new weapons with satisfaction. These

are going to make my life *much* easier, at least in some respects. I tuck them away as the chat scrolls rapidly past my vision.

[ChaosRider: WHOA!!! If I had that Seeking Dagger, I'd be unstoppable!]

[DarkCynic: He really should have taken a new creature instead of that third weapon. The Dagger of Kings is just going to get in his way.]

[IceQueen: Okay, but he didn't *know* that! We have to rally behind our favorite dungeon crawler!]

[Originalgoth: He's not *my* favorite.]

[RazorEdge: Are you sure about that? You sure spend a lot of time bashing him. Hate and love are *very* closely linked.]

[Originalgoth: I can smite you too, you know.]

[RazorEdge: MURDER!]

[GoldenShield: Can we get back to talking about Jason, here? These new weapons are going to make him impossible to stop.]

I tune out the chat after a few more moments, slip all my new weapons into my inventory, and turn my attention down the tunnel. I can see light at the end, a red, fiery light. There are a lot of different types of dungeons, but the ones that really embrace the whole "underground" theme, especially the ones that incorporate lava, are my least favorite. I suppose that just makes them more of a challenge, and thus more rewarding to defeat, but . . . still.

"Jason." Columbus walks up next to me and clears his throat. "I . . . I might have something to say to you."

"I thought you might." I nod at him. "Fire away."

"I'll start . . . MM." He sighs, takes off his hat, and wipes his brow. After a moment, he sighs once more and puts it back on. "Formally, they're the MM guild. Terrible folks, if you ask me. The initial core group formed within a few hours of the apocalypse starting, at least the way I've heard it. They started recruiting about a day later, scooping up everyone who wasn't ready to drop their lives and just start dungeon crawling for a live audience at the whim of the government. I got invited to a meeting, and I was sort of hard up for friends at the time, so I agreed."

I nod slowly. "Lost most of your friends when they found out you had superpowers?"

"Something like that." Columbus shrugs. "Anyway, I went to the meeting and found out that they were planning some roundly terrible things. I got out of there just as quick as I could. The very next day . . . I don't know."

He looks down at the ground. I don't say a thing, but I get the feeling I know where he's going with this.

"I was asked to come and help. I went with the intention of stopping them, but . . . then I got cold feet." His voice is quiet. "I saw them trap a party of warriors coming out of a dungeon. I stood there, and I watched. I watched them . . ." He groans and rubs his jaw. "Anyway, after that, they had leverage over me. Since the victims were all livestreaming, the police saw me there. I'm a wanted man. The only reason they haven't come after me yet is because they have bigger fish to fry, but their own warriors will be along in due time, once they get the chance."

"And somehow, that led you to the stardust," I surmise.

Columbus doesn't say anything more. I know there's more to the story, but if he's not ready to talk yet, there's not a whole lot I'm going to be able to coax out of him. I could just try to beat it out of him, of course, but doing that will only mean that he might hide something from me. I need him to trust me.

Thankfully, there are a lot of monster fights coming, so hopefully I'll be able to convince him that I'm worth trusting.

Ahead of us, the light grows brighter and brighter. Soon we come to the end, where the tunnel opens up into a vast chamber. The floor is, of course, lava, hot and boiling and glowing. Cinders pop up in the air with sharp *hisses*, while something dark moves about beneath the waves. Well . . . more than one something, now that I look at it a bit more closely. They look almost like snakes or eels or something, but I can't quite tell for sure.

More importantly, though, I can see the way out of the cave, as well as the path to get to it. Unfortunately, the path leads straight up and consists of a great many stairs strung out between stone platforms, which slowly climb up to a hole in the middle of the ceiling. The stone platforms, as well as the stairs, are built upon immense columns of stone rising out of the lava, though I can see scratch marks and things on a great many of them.

"This is . . . interesting," Columbus muses.

"I know." I look at the first stair, which is only a few feet away from me. "Get ready to run, and *fast*."

"Why's that?" Columbus adjusts the cowboy hat on his head.

"Because I used to play a game as a child that reminds me a *lot* of this," I murmur.

[ChaosRider: Ooh! What's that game? It sounds like fun!]

[LunarEclipse: Dude, are you serious? How boring was your childhood???]

[DarkCynic: Can we focus on the fact that there are lava snakes??? Snakes are bad enough by themselves, but LAVA snakes???]

[GamerBro: Bigger issue. I asked you to find a way to cage up these animals, and I don't know how you're possibly going to do that. Just know that I'm paying you based off your success.]

"No, you're not." I raise an eyebrow. "You already paid Mr. Wang. I'm sure of it."

"What's that?" Columbus looks over at me.

"Nothing. Just talking to the chat." I frown, then take a deep breath. "Ready?"

"Can I say no?"

"Nope." With that, I dart forward, pounding up the stairs as fast as I can. Columbus comes along behind, and almost immediately, I hear a loud roar.

Though . . . it's not the roar of a monster.

It's the roar of a volcano.

Ka-blooooooooooooooooooooooooom!

Fire erupts upward just to my left, shooting high up into the upper reaches of the cave. Molten stone then showers back down behind me. I turn around just in time to see Columbus dive forward. The lava hits the stairs just behind him and melts them into slag, and the whole chunk below us collapses into the fire beneath. He turns rather pale, and I see something even more frightening.

The lava is starting to rise.

"Alright, move!" I race upward even faster, and a moment later I come to the first platform. Another blast of lava shoots through the staircase leading off of it, crumbling a good twenty feet of stone. Now I'm left on the platform with a gap to the stairs that's twenty feet wide and at least that high. I bounce on the balls of my feet, trying to figure out where to go from here.

"I wish I had John here," I murmur. "He could just throw me to the top and then climb up with his claws."

"Well, you have me instead." Columbus reaches the platform as well. "My whip can probably reach that far."

"Yeah, but there's nothing for it to grab onto, and even if there was, I don't exactly trust the track record that your weapon has left for itself," I mutter back. Maybe a bit harsh, but I'm getting a little stressed. "Alright. Burnie, I need you! We're going to try the staircase thing again."

Burnie shoots out of the pocket dimension and starts to circle the stone platform, getting his bearings. I glance over the edge, finding that the lava has now risen to within only a dozen feet or so. I take a deep breath, prepare myself, and run forward.

"*Screeeeeeeeeeeeee!*"

A lava snake explodes up out of the molten rock. Now, this thing is big, though not so big as you might expect a magic snake to be. Picture a python or an anaconda, just one that's made out of living fire, and you're pretty close. Anyway, it comes up out of nowhere, snatches Burnie in its jaws, and vanishes back beneath the surface of the lava in the blink of an eye.

"Burnie!" I flail as I try to avoid jumping off the edge of the platform. As I come to a stop and look down, more of the snakes come shooting up. Several manage to get their upper coils onto the platform, and they start to slither up . . . slowly . . . menacingly.

"Ahhh!" Columbus shouts, draws a machete, and, lunging forward, slashes off the head of one of the closest snakes. The thing cools into pumice, then cracks and crumbles, falling back to the stone below. I take a somewhat blunter approach and simply kick the closest snake in the head. That knocks it free, and maybe kills it—I can't quite tell for sure—and it falls back down. With that, I draw out my daggers as more of the monsters drag themselves up.

One of the snakes quickly coils itself onto the platform and raises itself into a striking position. It opens its jaws, revealing white-hot fangs. I draw out my Photonic Dagger and transform it into a sword—I don't want to get too close to those fangs—and lunge forward, slashing at its throat. The snake is fast, though, and whips back before striking. I manage to dodge out of the way just in time and slash through the back of the neck, killing it, but the thing manages to scrape up my left arm pretty badly in the process. I wince, looking down at the burns, and prepare myself for the next attack. It comes almost instantly as two more of the snakes lunge at me, and I throw myself into a somersault over the top of them to avoid being bitten. I'm unable to score any more strikes, though. On the other side of the platform, Columbus seems to be having the same issues.

"Alright." I step back and draw out my Seeking Dagger. "Time to see what you're made of. Go!"

I throw the weapon with all my might. Now, I've thrown plenty of daggers before, but this time I actually see it curve through the air as the snake lunges at me. The weapon slams into its throat, and the thing collapses and crumbles. With that, the weapon flashes back to my hand, and I smile and throw it again. Another kill . . . but now there are more and more snakes crowding the platform, and the lava is getting *very* close.

"Alright, Columbus." I grit my teeth. "Get ready to get out of here."

"How?" He slashes at one of the snakes with his machete, then takes a step back. "They're all around!"

"I know." I draw my arm back, then spin and throw the Seeking Dagger off into the distance, putting every ounce of strength behind it. "Just . . . wait!"

The dagger flashes across the room, straight as an arrow, only to curve as it reaches the far side. Moving just as fast as before, it flashes back and carves a neat circle around the two of us, striking down each of the lava snakes in one quick blow. The dagger lands in my hand with a satisfying *smack*, and I twirl the weapon once.

"Okay, I do have to admit, that was cool." Columbus dips his head.

"Right?" I take a deep breath and look at the swirling lava. It's getting closer . . . and closer . . . "I'll go first. Be ready with your whip."

With that, I run forward. I see the snakes churning beneath the waves, and I jump with all my might, aiming toward the stairs. Thankfully, I've timed things well, and one of the snakes explodes up from the lava right as I leap. My feet land squarely on its head, and I jump once again with every-thing I have left in me. The stairs come closer . . . closer . . .

Smack!

My hand whacks onto the last remaining stair, and though I hear cracks echoing through the stone, I don't stop. I pull myself up, then turn around and hold out my hand. Columbus lets his whip fly, and the end of the weapon wraps around my hand. With that, I start pulling him upward, and after a few moments of struggling, I've pulled him up to join me. The lava absorbs the platform just below, and I gulp.

"Well, that was—"

"*Screeeeeeeeeeeeeeeeee!*"

More snakes come shooting up, landing on the stairs ahead of us. Those things have some *strength* to be able to jump so high! I charge forward, weapons in hand, and hack through everything that dares to stand before me. Below, the lava continues to rise, and I continue to fight, desperate to reach the top.

We don't get trapped on any more platforms, but we do have the stairs collapse ahead of us several more times. The expanses are shorter, though, and each time we're able to jump across the lava snakes. As we get closer and closer to the top of the room, the lava rises faster and faster until we're pelting along just as fast as we can, with the lava only feet behind us.

I can see the exit ahead of me: a small dark cave entrance. Cinders pop up from the rising lava below, scorching my pants. A lava snake erupts from my right side, but I cut off its head before it rises as high as it was intending. Suddenly, I hear a cry from Columbus and risk a glance over my shoulder.

He's a few stairs behind me and only inches above the lava. His pants have caught on fire from it, but we both know we can't stop to put out the fire. His face twists in pain, and I put on a burst of speed. If we can just make it out, we can—

CRA-FOOOOOOOOOOOOOOOOOM!

A massive snake, this one the size you would expect a

mythical snake to be, rises out of the lava and smashes through the final set of stairs before the cave entrance. Its head is a dozen feet wide, and as it opens its mouth, I see that each fang is as long as my body. They would *not* be pleasant to be bitten by, I'm certain of that. I grit my teeth and brace for impact . . . and Columbus screams again.

I glance back over my shoulder once more, just in time to see the lava turn white-hot. There's a blast of energy and a great figure shoots out of the molten stone like a rocket, flies between us, and lets loose a burst of what seems like pure light. The snake explodes under the blast, and Burnie spreads his wings to slow down as he reaches the safety of the cave. Columbus and I put on one more burst of speed, and we come tumbling out into the cave. With that, we both collapse on the ground, laughing and gasping, just happy to be alive. Burnie swoops down and lands next to us, and I sigh with relief.

We've both made it out, and Burnie is still alive!

Really, what more can I ask for?

CHAPTER EIGHTEEN

Columbus and I take a moment to recover before we really get up. Columbus beats out his flames, then applies a bit of healing ointment to the wound. I glance over at him, wondering if I can help but not wanting to intrude. The flesh is dark and scarred, and while it does heal, it remains as black as coal. He dresses it quickly with a bandage, and I grimace and look away. I don't really need to heal, but the rest is still nice. Burnie takes almost ten minutes before he's cool enough to touch, which he spends preening his feathers to pick out all the cooling stone.

[IceQueen: That was really cool, Burnie! Feel free to keep up all the neat tricks!]

[ShadowDancer: But don't scare us like that again!]

[GamerBro: And get me some snakes!!!]

[Originalgoth: Yes, Jason, get him some snakes. This I'd *love* to see.]

I sigh as the chat scrolls by. Originalgoth's call is picked up by the others, all of whom really, *really* want to see me capture a snake and *somehow* secure it so that others can enjoy it.

"You do realize that there's no way this room is safe, right?" I walk up to the hole in the floor that had once been the entrance to the chamber. It makes my stomach queasy to think about how much lava is underneath my feet. "I mean . . . even if there were no snakes—and these looked to me to be the infinitely generated sort—that lava is *fast!* There's no way you get clearance from any competent authority to open this room up for public access."

[GamerBro: I already have the cats! One of my employees snagged them from the opening chamber, and I'm working on designing a cell that will hold them. Even if I can't open the room up, I want as many weird creatures as I can get!]

"Alright, then." I roll my eyes. "Columbus, come with me."

"What? Why?" Columbus slowly climbs to his feet and follows me over to the lava pool. "Please tell me you're not about to do what I think you're about to do."

"Aw, it'll be fun." I kneel down next to the lava and rub my hands together. "How many other people do you know who have caught lava snakes?"

"None, and for good reason!"

"Then you'll have something to brag about when we make it back to Earth." I shrug. "Columbus, the snake-wrangling cowboy!"

"I would be the laughingstock of the west," Columbus snorts.

"Only if you actually use that name." I chuckle. Some of the lava snakes start to swirl beneath the waves. "Columbus the valiant!"

"Too generic."

"Columbus the . . . hottest gun in the west!" Columbus just stares at me, and I laugh. "Alright, alright. Just get ready to lasso whatever comes out of here."

There's a great *foom* a moment later, and one of the snakes erupts to charge me. It looks sort of confused, probably about why someone would come back, but it's ready to eat me, nevertheless. Anyway, I punch it in the bottom of the chin, slamming it up into the ceiling, and Columbus slings his lasso around its neck. The lasso changes to a silvery bronze that doesn't catch fire, and we quickly work to tie up the snake, touching its body as little as possible. It flops around a little bit, but, stunned by the blast, it doesn't react altogether too strongly. When we finish, I wipe my brow and look down at the knotted serpent. It's a mess, but it's there, and I give a nod.

"There you go, GamerBro. Have fun with it!"

With a crackling sound, the snake suddenly cools into pumice, forming a statue that's about as appealing to look at as . . . Well, to be honest, it actually looks better than a lot of the modern art that I've seen.

[GamerBro: What have you done??? I can't put *that* in my store!]

I start to walk away. "Just, I don't know . . . Call it a metaphor for our minds when we try to do too many tasks or please too many people at once."

[GamerBro: That's . . . brilliant!]

[ViperQueen: WONDERFUL!!! I'll buy it for $100!]

[RazorEdge: I'll buy it for $1,000!]

[GoldenShield: I've got a friend who works for the MOMA! They might want this!]

I can't help laughing. Columbus looks at me, and I can only shrug. It would be too complicated to explain, and if I were to actually *voice* how much I dislike modern art, I would risk alienating anyone in my chat who actually did like the stuff. Of course, do I really *want* anyone in my chat who enjoys looking at banana peels taped to walls? It's a conundrum, to be certain.

In any case, Columbus and I are once more meandering through a small passage, though this one appears to be far shorter than some of the others. Already, there are dozens of crystals decorating the walls, glowing ones of all different colors: reds, yellows, greens, blues—every color of the rainbow. Soon, we come up to the entrance of a much larger cavern, one with a great deal more personality than some.

Crystals hang from the walls, from great stalactites, from protrusions on the floor, from just about everywhere. Additionally, there are a number of small, den-like holes carved in the walls, holes surrounded by scratch marks in the stone. The floor of the chamber is flat, while sloping ramps wind up the sides of the walls to the ceiling. This is proving to be a *very* vertical dungeon, which I'm not the biggest fan of.

"What do you think are in those holes?" I gesture toward them. "I'm guessing goblins."

"This is too high a level for goblins." Columbus shrugs. "Goblins only infest the lowest-level dungeons, not these."

As if in response to his voice, a loud cackling voice echoes through the air. Bright yellow eyes appear in a great many of the holes, and, slowly, several goblins step out into view. They're holding typical goblin weapons: wooden spears, rusty swords, that sort of thing.

"Aw, they're sort of cute." Columbus draws his pistol and takes aim. *BLAM!* As per usual, it has absolutely no effect, save to make the little creatures start walking forward. "Bummer. One of these days . . ." He drops the pistol back into its holster, then draws out his machete. I ready my Seeking Dagger . . . And then, something happens.

All the goblins burst into flame.

The cackling noises grow louder, and they start to dance about, leaping from one foot to the other, giggling wildly at our confusion. I take a tighter hold on my dagger, then throw it with all my might.

Ziiiiiiiiiiiiiiiiiiiiiiiiiing-thwack!

The blade flashes through the air and slams into the chest of the nearest goblin, sinking in up to the hilt. The goblin snarls and staggers, then slowly fixes his gaze upon me. To my great annoyance, he doesn't seem particularly bothered by the attack. Slowly, he pulls out the weapon and drops it to the ground, where it hesitates before flying back to my hand. I grit my teeth, then slip that weapon into my inventory and draw out my Dagger of Doom. Time to give it a whirl.

The goblins come racing forward, ready for war, and I charge forward to meet them, leaving Columbus behind. The first of the goblins leaps forward, swinging a fiery sword at me. I duck past the first stroke, then block the second with the Dagger of Doom. A layer of ice forms across the weapon, and the fire licking across the enemy's blade seems to be tempered somewhat.

[Dagger of Doom has discovered an [Ice] weakness.]

"Good to know." I whistle sharply. "Bjorn! You're up!"

With that, I launch myself into a blistering series of attacks against the goblin. I manage to land several strikes along his arms and torso, crippling him somewhat. Before I can kill him, though, another one comes up from the side, striking at me with a spear. He manages to score a blow across my chest, which *hurts*. I let out a yell and retreat slightly, and Columbus nods to me.

"Throw it and I'll get it back for you!"

I nod, then throw the weapon into the goblin. It hits the beast in the stomach, and he suddenly stops emitting flame. A few moments longer and he freezes solid. Columbus lashes out with his whip, snags the hilt of the dagger and yanks it back out. Of course, his aim is off, and it only clatters to the floor on the other side of the room. I scowl at him, and he shrugs before simply lashing out with his whip even more.

"*Kalalalalalalallalalalalalalalalalaal!*"

That particular cry, I believe, translates to something akin to "I've got you now, sucker!" and is called out by a goblin who, at that moment, jumps down onto my back from above and wraps his arms around my neck. Ordinarily, it wouldn't have bothered me that much, except for the fact that he, of course, is on fire. Flames lick around my face, and I scream in agony as his very touch seems to scald me to the core. More goblins take the opportunity to attack, and I suddenly find myself pressed by spears, swords, claws, and a great many other things. I stagger backward, gritting my teeth . . . And that's when I hear Bjorn snarl.

A blast of cold air washes over me, and every single one of the goblins on me freezes solid. I get pretty chilled as well, but not nearly to the same extent. Of course, that means that I now have a dozen goblins frozen to my body, and I have to throw myself against a nearby rock to smash them off me. Soon, I'm standing there in the midst of goblin bits while Bjorn steps around the room, freezing what looks to be the last of the creatures. Then, from above, I hear more of them laughing and giggling, and Columbus tilts his head back and squints.

"That doesn't sound good to m—"

Booooom!

A crystal—red, I think—flashes down from above and hits the ground, exploding like a grenade. Little bits of stone fragments flash everywhere, and I feel several slam into my cheeks and forehead. More start to rain down, and I groan.

"We've got to get moving. Bjorn, up and at 'em!"

Bjorn tilts his head back and howls. The sound echoes up the chamber, resounding from wall to wall. Frozen goblins suddenly tumble downward, bouncing off the walls and hitting the stones below, as we start to run up the stairs. I snatch a crystal off the wall as we run, a red one, and throw it upward. It hits one of the slopes where I see a goblin, and it explodes violently, making the goblin ragdoll as he's thrown out into the abyss. Columbus nods, and he starts doing the same thing.

The battle rages fiercely as we move upward. Goblins throw crystals down at us, and we throw the weapons back up at them. They're resilient little buggers, way stronger than any of the ones I've fought in the past. I can see half a dozen of them swarming up from below, recovered from their fall, and there are countless more above.

Suddenly, one of them leaps out of a hole next to us and hits me in the face. He wraps himself around my head and starts whacking me on the top of the head with a rock, and I reach up, grab the thing, and rip him off.

At least, I try to.

He hangs on with all his might, digging in his claws, and whacks all the harder. My world starts to spin a bit, and I suddenly feel the ground starting to give way beneath my feet. I grit my teeth and try to throw myself forward, but I only succeed in accidentally tossing myself off the slope altogether. Quite suddenly, I'm whizzing through the air, falling, and the goblin laughs wildly.

And then I land.

The goblin, thankfully, serves as a rather excellent cushion. He's beaned rather badly, but I'm only battered and a bit bruised, not fully broken. I groan and climb to my feet, and with that, all the goblins in the area turn to look at me. Seemingly as one, they burst into flame, snatch up the crystals from all around, and throw them at me in one concerted salvo.

I really can't describe just how much the blast hurts. Dozens of the crystals hit me all at once, and my health falls down to the red. Suddenly, as I fall to my knees, I catch a glimpse of several of the crystals on the wall. There is more than one color, but so far we've only used the red ones. I reach over and snatch at one of the blue ones, then throw it with all my might.

The crystal hits a goblin charging headlong at me, and great ice crystals erupt off him as he freezes solid. I nod and smile, then grab two more and squeeze with all my might. Cracks spread across the surface of the crystal, and with a mighty *boom*, they shatter, sending waves of freezing energy across the floor. That freezes the rest of them solid, in a wide variety of poses, and I let out a sigh of relief.

Suddenly, my Dagger of Doom catches my eye, and I quickly snatch it up and drop it back into my inventory. With that, I turn and head on upward, climbing toward the summit once again. As I do, I snatch open a bottle of Pumped! and start to drink it, watching with satisfaction as my health climbs to a more reasonable level once more.

High overhead, the battle rages, and I quickly jog upward to meet it. I'm eager to defeat the goblins and get on with this dungeon. Somehow, so far, it's all seemed too easy to me. It just feels like there's got to be another foot, another boot . . . And I have a feeling that it's not going to be particularly pleasant when that boot drops.

CHAPTER NINETEEN

The rest of the trip doesn't take long. Columbus and Bjorn haven't made it much further from where I fell, but once I get back there, we're soon able to clear out the rest of the goblins. Soon, we reach the top, where we find ourselves looking at a set of obsidian doors. They're carved with strange symbols that look rather like Viking runes, though I don't know that for sure.

[ShadowDancer: Hey, those look cool! We should try to translate them!]

[ChaosRider: I'll take a screenshot and start comparing it with the Internet Archive!]

[DarkCynic: Yeah, good idea! I'll help! Shoot me a DM, and we can do it together! I'm somewhat of an expert on this sort of thing.]

"Alright." I slowly step up to the doors and push against them. They don't open, so I grit my teeth and push a bit harder. Still nothing happens, which confuses me a good bit, but I suppose there's nothing I can really do about it. I start looking around for any sort of a door handle or secret entrance, but when I find nothing, I can only assume that there's nothing more I can do except wait on the chat to turn something up. There are a *lot* of runes, so it's almost certainly instructions on how to get through; I just have to wait until the chat is able to find something on them. "Well, it's hurry up and wait, I suppose. Bjorn, hop back into the pocket dimension. Burnie, you too."

My pets both accede to my wishes and slip back inside, and I sit down, letting my feet dangle across the open expanse below. Columbus sits down next to me, and for a moment, we look down at the battlefield.

"They got some good frozen ones," I comment. "That ought to keep GamerBro happy."

[GamerBro: Frozen goblins can thaw out!]

[ChaosRider: Then buy a freezer!]

I chuckle softly, then glance over at Columbus. He sighs deeply, then slowly nods. "Alright, alright. The stardust."

"Correct." I nod.

"The short answer is that I was hired to do the job." Columbus shrugs. "It was yesterday, I believe."

"Yesterday?" I blink in surprise. "What time?"

"I don't know. Morning, I think?" Columbus shrugs again. "Anyway, I—"

"Hold up." I lift a finger. "Let me get this straight. Yesterday *morning* you were hired to steal the stardust from me?"

"Yes." Columbus nods, frowning. "Why is that a problem?"

"Because I didn't even get the stardust until midnight last night," I answer. "I had just gotten back to my apartment. Ali had teleported away, and I was heading back inside, and then this portal opened right below, and . . .”

Columbus's eyes twitch, but I can't tell exactly what that means. Suddenly, though, my chat comes to life.

[DarkCynic: Jason! We know how to open the doors!]

[LunarEclipse: Yeah! Just go poke that triangle! That ought to do it! But *don't* touch the one that looks like a smiley face.]

[ChaosRider: Yeah . . . That would be bad.]

“Well, duty calls.” I puff out my cheeks and climb back to my feet. “I want to hear more about this. That's concerning, to say the least.”

Columbus doesn't say a word, but his face is thoughtful. I hope that doesn't affect his performance in the next room. Slowly, I walk up to the doors and push the triangle, and it lights up. With a rumble, the doors slowly open, and I step through.

Whoosh.

With the soft noise of flame igniting, torches burst to life all across the area. It's a small room, at least compared to the others, furnished with nothing but a few obsidian columns, a handful of obsidian pyramid things, and a set of doors at the other end. There's a large keyhole, making me suspect that we're going to have to locate the key somewhere in the room, though at the moment, I don't really see anything that looks like it could hold a key.

“Well. This is interesting.” Columbus walks into the room behind me, fidgeting with his machete. “Ever seen something like this before?”

“Not really, no.” I shake my head. “It reminds me somewhat of an antechamber I found in an ice dungeon. That one was . . . interesting.”

"Interesting in a good way, or not so much?" Columbus asks with a wry smile on his face.

"Take a guess," I murmur. "In this line of business, boring is always good."

Suddenly, one of the pyramids shudders. I frown, then slowly draw out my Dagger of Doom and start walking toward the thing. There are very few reasons that a pyramid would be shuddering. All of them are dangerous, and none of them could be considered boring. Slowly, I approach the thing, then raise my dagger.

Crack!

The pyramid dissolves into a cloud of obsidian dust—or maybe obsidian rubble; it's hard to say for sure—and attacks me. It forms a spear and hits me in the chest, knocking me backward across the room to slam me into a pillar. I groan and drop to my knees, and the thing disengages and flashes toward Columbus. He swings at it, but it simply wraps around his arm to form a cast of sorts, then twists sharply. He hollers in pain as the sprite slams him to the ground, then flickers and forms a small cloud of debris in the air once more.

"I. Hate. Sprites," I groan as I take a firmer grip on my dagger.

"How many have you fought?" Columbus stares up at the thing above him, not wanting to incite its fury.

"Three."

"And I've seen two of those. That doesn't fill me with confidence." Columbus lets out a long breath.

"Neither will that attitude. Come on!" I charge forward, gripping my dagger as hard as I can. I stab at the middle of the cloud, but it flashes forward, wraps around my wrist, and brings my arm down to strike at Columbus. I manage to stop it just in time, and I strain against the force that the sprite exerts. Slowly, I raise my arm back upward, gasping with the effort. Suddenly, it disengages and attacks my face, forming a stone mask across my eyes, mouth, and nose.

Of course, now I can't breathe for anything. Now, this isn't the first time that a sprite has done this to me, so I know how to handle it. I have yet to find a way to handle it without a great deal of pain, *but* . . .

With all my might, I slam my head forward into a wall, trying to shatter the mask. It disengages at the last second and flashes off into the distance, and I, naturally, headbutt the wall. Which hurts. Still, I'm upright, and that's more than can be said of a lot of people in this world.

[GoldenShield: Go, Jason! Fight through the pain!]

[FireStorm: What doesn't kill you makes you stronger, eh?]

[IceQueen: You've got this!]

I nod in agreement with the chat, then turn back to the sprite. Columbus steps up next to me, and we stare out across the room. Of course, the sprite takes this moment to dart to the other three pyramids in the room, causing them to dissolve into clouds of rubble as well.

"What do you think?" Columbus glances at me. "Four sprites, or one mega-sprite?"

"I don't know, and I honestly can't decide which would be worse," I mutter. "We've got to find a way to kill these things."

"If you have any ideas, I'm open to them."

"If I have any, I'll let you know!"

I charge forward, ready to do my best. All four sprites flash forward to meet me so fast I can hardly see them. One hits each limb, and I'm lifted off the ground and slammed back into the wall with enough force to send out a shockwave. The four sprites melt themselves into the wall, drawing out obsidian to form shackles that seal me to the wall. I groan as they detach a moment later, having successfully changed the shape of the entire wall to accommodate my form. With that, they all seem to turn toward Columbus, and slowly begin to draw together into one mega-sprite.

"Oh no, you don't!" I grit my teeth together and strain with all my might. "Come on . . . Come on . . . You're not John, but you've got it in you!"

A crack echoes across the room, and the mega-sprite seems to turn back around. I come crashing out of the wall an instant later, breathing heavily, and grab at several large rocks falling from my wrists. With all my might, I spin and throw the stones at the mega-sprite, which it simply catches and throws back at me. The returned stones hit me squarely in the chest, which *hurts*, but I stay alive. With that, I stagger forward, gritting my teeth.

The mega-sprite actually flinches backward, then forms into a large spear and flashes through the air at Columbus. The spear, I should point out, is almost ten feet long and as thick as a weaver's beam. Columbus dives out of the way, but it still hits him in the leg, spearing him clean through. He screams in pain, and with that, the mega-sprite dissolves and wraps around his entire body, forming a casing. I ball my hand into a fist and punch at Columbus's head, causing the mega-sprite to dissolve right as my hand impacts it.

Wham!

"Ouch!" Columbus hollers, working his jaw. "What'd you do that for?"

"I'm trying to keep you alive," I mutter as the stone forms back over his face. With nothing else to do, I pick him up and smash him to the ground. That makes the whole thing dissolve and return to its cloud-like form, leaving Columbus writhing on the ground in pain. Quickly, I open my inventory and snatch out one of the red crystals from the previous room.

The mega-sprite, though, isn't going to remain discouraged. It attacks me next, wrapping me in a thick layer of obsidian. I feel it pick me up and toss me into a wall, where it seems to actually fuse me into the stone, pushing me deeper and deeper, trying to bury me.

Thankfully, I pretty much knew that it would be doing that, which is why I grabbed the crystal. Hardly daring to breathe, I crush the crystal in my hand, letting pure heat explode outward.

Wrapped up in the stone like it is, the crystal goes off like a bomb. Smoke and fire roll through the room, and a concussive blast shakes the walls and foundations of the area. I stagger forward and fall to the floor, gasping for air, and slowly look around. Melted slag lies here and there and slowly starts to pull itself together even as I watch. I groan as the obsidian mega-sprite once more takes form in the air, though a bit more slowly than it's done in the past.

"Die, sprite," I mutter and throw the Dagger of Doom at the thing. It wraps around the weapon, forming a shell-like casing, and I hold my breath. Will it work? What is an obsidian sprite's weakness, anyway?

[Dagger of Doom has discovered a [Blast] weakness.]

Another explosion shakes the room an instant later, and bits and pieces of the sprite cut me across my whole body.

A normal human would have been killed instantly, but my Awakened body handles it well enough. As the blast dies down, my dagger falls to the floor, and Columbus whistles.

"That dagger is *way* too overpowered."

"Are you really going to complain?" I open up my inventory and pull out several Pumped! bottles. I toss one over to him, which he catches. After looking it over warily, he cracks off the top and starts to drink it. "That thing was mopping the floor with our pulverized bodies, and the only way I was able to deal a lick of damage to it was to blow myself up, just about."

Columbus shrugs. "I'm just saying." He slowly climbs to his feet, and the two of us start walking toward the doors at the other end of the room. They rumble open upon our approach, and I find myself looking at a long dark corridor. This one, unlike the caves, seems to be man-made. It's a hallway with a black carpet set upon obsidian floors, dark tapestries hanging upon obsidian walls, and black suits of armor standing between black pillars. A few torches light up the place as well as they can, but, as I hope I've conveyed, it's not the brightest place in the world.

"Looks like we're getting close to the boss," I comment. "Come on. Twenty bucks says that those suits of armor come to life as soon as we get close to them."

"Twenty bucks?" Columbus snorts and starts along after me. "How about twenty *million* bucks? I know how much you're worth."

"Twenty thousand."

"Uh . . . Deal."

As we approach the doorway, though, I hear a loud

eruption coming from behind us. We both turn around, looking out the way we've come, and I see what looks to be fire flickering off the walls.

"Any idea what that would be?" Columbus mutters.

"Just a few." I nod. "Brace yourself. I have a feeling we're in for a fight."

CHAPTER TWENTY

Columbus and I quickly step to the side of the room. Columbus crouches down behind a pile of rubble, and I decide to test out my new ability. "Skill: Innocence."

With a flash of light, a small glow surrounds my body, then fades away. I stand in the middle of the room, and, slowly, a figure appears up the passage.

It's a person, a girl with fiery red hair. And by fiery red hair, I mean that literally—it's actually on fire. Otherwise, she's wearing a black outfit that's quite at odds with her hair and has eyes that look as dead as a corpse. She's holding a sword in one hand—a sword that looks Japanese, if I had to wager a guess, though it looks like she might have something else in her other hand. She comes to a stop, and I give a nod. Bjorn emerges from the pocket dimension and bares his teeth, with Astrid following a moment later. The woman looks at them both, then gives me a nod.

"Where is he?"

"Where is who?" I hold up my hands. "Bjorn, the most powerful Frost Wolf this side of Ragnarok? He's right here."

"You know who I mean." The woman snarls softly. "I'll not tolerate flippant behavior."

"Then you're not going to tolerate me very well, I'm afraid." I have to laugh, crossing my arms, though very much keeping my daggers at the ready. "Now, why don't we talk about who you are, and why you're here?"

The woman snarls and moves to raise her sword but then pauses. Her face becomes annoyed, and her lip curls slightly. I can only assume that she's trying to attack me, but the system won't allow it until I attack her first.

"My name is Fuega."

"A feminine version of fire." I give a small nod of approval.

"You speak Spanish?" She raises an eyebrow.

"Enough to sound like an absolute idiot when talking to someone who actually speaks Spanish." I shrug. "So it depends on exactly how you define things. Now, if you don't mind, Fuega, I'd rather like you to explain why you're here."

"You know why I'm here." Her jaw sets. "Columbus has a hit on him, and I'm here to collect. One million for bringing his head on a platter. Five million for bringing him alive."

"And who's the buyer?" I ask. "Somehow, I doubt that your little Memento Mori club has the cash to offer such a hit. You're being bought by someone. Who?"

Her jaw sets, and she tenses up. An idea strikes me, and I slowly step forward.

"How about I offer ten million to join me on the rest of this dungeon?" I hold out my hands. "I'm good for it."

"Ten . . . million?" Her eyebrows lift.

"Ten million, and all you have to do is help me kill what-ever monsters are lurking in the rest of this place." I shrug. "Alternatively, I can beat you to a pulp and either kill you or tie you up for this whole dungeon tourism thing to gawk at."

"I'd rather die than go to prison." She lowers herself into a stance once more but still can't get herself to attack me.

"Then I know how I'll punish you." I nod. "Now, last chance! Join me!"

"I can't!" she snaps. "You have to know that if I don't fulfill my bargain, I'll be hunted just like him!"

"Ten million can get you a long way in the world."

"Not far enough," she murmurs.

"Great. Well, in that case, I look forward to hearing *all* about this mysterious buyer of yours." I shrug and draw out my daggers, holding my Seeking Dagger in my left hand and the Dagger of Doom in my right. I also stick the Dagger of Damage into my belt, ready to be pulled out at a moment's notice. She sets her jaw, and I nod.

"Just so we're clear, when you're beaten, you'll tell me everything."

"Never."

"Then I'll assume you understand me." I throw the Seeking Dagger with all my might and lunge forward with the Dagger of Doom. The Seeking Dagger curves toward her heart, and she struggles in vain to move. Suddenly, it hits her with a loud *smack* an instant before I throw the Dagger of Doom into her torso as well.

[Dagger of Doom has discovered an [Acid] weakness.]

The blade turns green and sinks into her torso with a sharp *hiss*. She screams in pain and doubles over, and I spring upon her. I almost feel bad as I kick her in the face, sending her reeling backward. Fiery hair flows all about as she staggers back into the hall, and she catches herself with a start.

Suddenly, her eyes seem to come to life, and she yanks the Dagger of Doom out of her belly.

"You're going to pay for that."

She flashes back at me, drawing her sword back. As she does so, her opposite hand flashes forward, and she throws several small stars at me. They blaze with electricity, hitting me all across my torso and sticking rather well. Lightning arcs across my body, which *hurts*, and I stagger. A moment later, she stabs out at me, and I'm only just able to twist the main part of my body out of the way. The sword pierces my left arm, making the whole thing flop uselessly at my side. I grit my teeth and punch her with my right arm, then snatch out the Dagger of Damage and stab at her several times, though I only land one or two.

"You think *that* thing will take me down?" She laughs and slowly backs away as I recover my stance. I stare her down, and her hair roars ever hotter. "You're never going to—"

"*Oooooooooooooooooooooooooooooooooooo!*"

Bjorn howls, and her hair suddenly dims in intensity. Astrid barks loudly an instant later, causing a blast of fire and gravel to erupt from underneath the woman. She staggers, and the two pups leap upon her, scratching and biting and howling. She flails backward under the combined attack, which gives me a brief moment to slap a bandage over the wound caused by her sword. That done, I face her down and charge forward, ready to put an end to the battle for good.

Unfortunately, that doesn't happen, as she suddenly

launches a lightning attack that knocks both dogs backward. They howl in pain, stunned, as I leap over them. The Seeking Dagger thwacks back into my palm, and I throw it again, this time behind me, and come up with my Dagger of Damage again.

"Stay away from me!" she shrieks. Her hair seems to lengthen, and flames wreath her an instant later.

"Do *not* try to play the victim here." I kick her in the torso, blasting her through the flames and out the other side. She hits the wall of the cave and slumps to the ground, and the Seeking Dagger flashes down toward her face. She's just able to bat it away with her sword, but it only clatters to the floor, spins, and launches itself back at her once more. "I gave you every chance to join me."

Before she can answer, I grab the scruff of her shirt, lift her into the air, and stab her several more times. The damage dealt by the Dagger of Damage rises up a bit more, and I spin and throw her into a pillar as hard as I can. She slumps to the ground, only to rise up once more, angry as a hornet. Her hair flickers green, and she snatches something else with her right hand and throws it at me. I dodge out of the way, only to see green magic flaring brilliantly.

Bzzzzzzzzzzzzzzzzzzt!

Green, necrotic magic explodes around me. It's hard to describe the type of pain, exactly. It just sort of deadens everything and makes your whole body ache with phantom pain. As it dies away, I find my body shaking, and I grit my teeth.

"I've just sucked some of your life away." Fuega smiles. "I've replenished my own health at your expense. Tell me, how does that fee—*urk!*"

Now, as everyone knows, "urk" is the Goblish word for "food" and is one of the most common ones you hear when fighting goblins in the dungeons. In this case, as everyone reading this likely assumes, the sound actually came from Columbus's lasso snapping around her neck. He pulls with all his might, and she's lifted off her feet and slammed back to the ground. I leap upon her an instant later, slamming a foot into her chest, and raise my Dagger of Doom once more.

She responds with a blast of kinetic energy that hits me in the chin, knocking me up into the air and sending me staggering backward. I stagger and get my footing, but by that time she's already burned herself out of the lasso. Columbus draws his machete as she turns to face him, but everyone present knows that he's not going to be able to defend himself.

Not for long, anyway.

"You know what?" Columbus spits on the floor. "I didn't even want to take the deal anyway. I didn't want to join this group, and I didn't want to get mixed up in all this."

"We all do things we don't want to do." Fuega starts walking toward him. "I've done more than my fair share. I don't want to be in the dungeon. I'd *rather* be tracking more interesting targets, but we don't always get what we want, now, do we?"

I take a deep breath and start drinking a Pumped! to recover the health that Fuega sucked away from me. As my health bar starts to creep back upward, I brace myself and take up my Dagger of Damage. Fuega raises her sword, and green energy begins to pulse up and down the length of it. Columbus uncoils his whip, then lashes out at her. It shoots past her head, and she laughs as it smacks onto something else.

"You're such a fool. You can't even—"

Of course, what she doesn't know is the fact that, instead of missing, Columbus's aim is perfect. His lasso wraps around my palm, sticking firmly. He then pulls, and I throw myself into the movement, allowing him to launch me at Fuega with a great deal of force. She had been listening for me, but as I hadn't actually moved my own feet—or really even let them touch the ground—she's utterly unprepared when I hit her.

Her hair burns my face, but I ignore the pain and slam her to the ground just as hard as I can. I grab her wrist and knock the sword from her palm, then knee her in the back with as much force as I can muster. She snarls and lets loose a blast of flame, then spins and kicks me.

Now *that* hurts. I look down and see blood and realize that she has some sort of blade that can pop out of her shoe. Still, I'm far from down, and I kick *her* before jumping to my feet. By that point, Columbus has readied his lasso once more, and as Fuega climbs to her feet, it falls down across her and clamps her arms to her side. This time it's made of un-meltable steel, and as she starts to fight against it, I step up and draw out my daggers.

This time the fight doesn't take long. The damage dealt by the Dagger of Damage compounds quickly, and the Dagger of Doom deals an immense amount of acid damage. Soon, Fuega is swooning, and I kick her in the torso, knocking her back into a pillar. She groans softly, blood flecking around her lips, and I press the Dagger of Damage up against her throat.

"How much health do you have left?" I hiss in her ear. "This dagger will deal almost ten thousand damage the next time I hit you with it. Make one wrong move, and even if you're somehow resistant to dagger wounds, I bet it'll take you out."

Fuega takes a deep breath, then nods slowly. "I . . . I yield." Her head falls back against the stone, and she coughs. "Kill me quickly. If you don't, *they'll* kill me slowly."

Columbus walks up behind me and gives a nod. "Come on. We do need to be moving. Kill her and let's get out of here."

"Not yet." I turn to Columbus. "I want to know exactly what's going on here. A million dollars on your head. Five million on your head when it's attached to the rest of your body? There's something you're not telling me."

"What can I say?" Columbus shrugs. "The stardust is powerful stuff."

"Yeah, so powerful that it can apparently induce time travel; you knew I had it before I ever entered that dungeon," I snap, then turn back to Fuega. "Start talking or I'll kill you."

"Do it," Fuega murmurs softly.

"Fine. Start talking or I'll leave you to be tortured." I'm getting impatient. "Now!"

There's a long pause, and Fuega spits out a mouthful of blood. "Fine. I'll talk. They're not going to show me any mercy."

"You're right about that." I nod. "Go!"

She glares up at me, then sighs. "Yesterday morning, the Memento Mori guild was contacted by a representative of Krak."

"He was still with me at the time!" I scowl.

"Yes, well, you've already established that he was a traitor. Not sure why that still bothers you." Fuega shrugs. "Anyway, he came to us and said that you'd be getting the stardust later that night and that we needed to steal it from you. After that, it was just a matter of deciding who was going to do it."

That gives me pause, and I slowly ball my hands into fists. "Who came to you in the first place? What representative of Krak? Was it a dark elf?"

Fuega nods. "I don't know his name, but yes. A dungeon portal opened, and he came out. Said he'd seen our livestream and thought that we would be useful. That's all I know. I wasn't actually present at the meeting, but I've seen the livestreams of those who were."

Columbus steps up. "I was contacted a few hours after that. I was given you as the target and told that I was to try and snipe the next dungeon you went to. The next dungeon *after* you got the dust, that is."

"And why was that so hard to say?" I snap, slowly turning to him. "I've been trying to get that information out of you for the whole dungeon!"

"Because—"

"Because of *why* he agreed to do the job!" Fuega starts laughing. I look down at her, confused, and she just sighs. "Look, I've said too much. I really do need to get out of here, and since you've given me time to heal, I need to leave."

Fire flares around her bonds, melting through even the fireproof steel, and she rises to her feet. Unfortunately for her, I've been watching her wounds get better. She grabs her sword and starts to swing it up at me, and I stab her with the Dagger of Damage. The weapon deals a solid 8,192 damage. She lets out a bloodcurdling scream as the damage pierces to her core, and she drops back to the floor with a resounding *thud*. I can't tell if she's dead or not, but she's certainly not going anywhere anytime soon. I stare down at her body, then glance at Columbus.

"So. Care to explain why you chose to come steal from me?" I raise an eyebrow. Columbus doesn't say anything, and I sigh. "Look, you're really starting to get on my nerves. I've been trying to help you, and I've been trying to be patient with you, but you're stringing me along. Eventually, we *will* get to the end of this dungeon, and when that happens, you're going to come back to the real world. At that point, you'll have to either take me to the stardust or try to survive on your own while a *great* many people try to kill you for it."

"What are you saying?" Columbus growls softly.

"I'm saying that you have to trust me." I push past him and stalk angrily toward the darkened hallway. The suits of armor begin to rattle as I approach, but I'm not worried. "If you don't, you're only going to doom yourself, me, and any-one else who happens to get caught in your wake."

Columbus doesn't say a word. At this point, I honestly can't decide if I think he's *actually* someone who's being manipulated or if he's a villain running a longer game than I can see, or what. What I *do* know is that if someone knew I was going to get the stardust ahead of time, I've been playing right into *someone's* hands, most likely Krak's.

If that really is the case, then . . . Well, it means that I have a whole lot of ground to cover if I'm going to somehow come out on top.

CHAPTER TWENTY-ONE

As I approach the doors to the darkened hall, I draw out my Seeking Dagger and throw it as hard as I can, straight down the middle of the hall. It curves almost instantly, slamming into one of the enormous black sets of armor. There's a loud *clang*, and the suit staggers backward while the dagger flashes back to my hand. It doesn't seem to have been affected at all, which is frustrating, though not necessarily surprising. Things like living suits of armor tend to be high on damage resistance and low on weaknesses.

Thankfully, I have a dagger that can seek out what few weaknesses it may happen to sport.

Four sets of armor clunk out of their alcoves as Columbus and I charge into the area. They're all armed with massive swords, clearly cut out for infantry fighting. Thankfully, I'm only one lone soldier, not an entire army. Not that such a fact inherently skews the odds in my favor, but . . . you know.

I charge at the closest one and pull out my Dagger of

Doom. The suit of armor swings down at me, intending to chop off my head, and I dodge the attack before slamming the dagger down into its chest plate.

[Dagger of Doom has discovered a [N/A] weakness.]

"What?" I dive backward as it slashes down at me. "It's resistant to *everything?*"

[GoldenShield: Actually, that doesn't surprise me. It probably has almost no health, like 100 hp maybe, but it's buffed against all attacks.]

[ChaosRider: Yeah, and I bet its damage threshold is set at a few points higher than its actual health, so you have to one-shot it in order to kill it.]

[ViperQueen: That's going to be epic! One-shotting something like this!]

I grit my teeth. That's not the way daggers work! Oh well. If that's what I'm given, that's just what I'll have to work with. Quickly, I switch out weapons, holding my Photonic Dagger in one hand and my Dagger of Damage in the other.

"Astrid! You're up! Burnie, you too!"

Columbus looks at me but says nothing. Instead, he simply wades into combat, slashing and hacking with his machete. I almost mention to him that he likely won't be able to hurt them, but . . . I'm a bit annoyed with his attitude, and he doesn't exactly look like he's in a lot of danger, so I decide to let him struggle.

As Astrid and Burnie emerge from the pocket dimension behind me. I rush forward, charging at the suit of armor I just attacked. It strikes at me again, and once more I duck beneath the blow, putting myself right up against it. Quickly, I strike upward with my Photonic Dagger, slamming the blade into the crack in the armor's armpit. The blade screeches loudly as it punches a small hole through, but still doesn't seem to really affect the suit. I yank the blade back out as the suit of armor bashes me with the hilt of its sword, and I stumble slightly to the left.

The suit of armor seems almost to rejoice for a moment, but its victory is short-lived. Burnie cuts in a second later and blasts the armor with an immense fireball. The armor staggers backward, glowing red under the attack, but remains standing. Burnie lets out an exasperated *squawk*, then lets loose another gout of flame. The blue fire rages against the black metal, and I watch it heat to orange . . . then yellow . . . then white . . .

With a great *hiss*, the armor collapses upon itself, transforming into a pile of molten metal on the floor. I smile and punch the air, then smile even more broadly as Astrid lets loose on two of the others. She's even less subtle than Burnie and simply growls until the floor breaks open and causes the two of them to fall into a fiery rift. Another growl closest the rift up, leaving a single suit challenging Columbus.

"I've got it." I run forward. "Switch out!"

Columbus nods and steps back, and I lunge forward, blade carving a long path through the air. This time I slam my Photonic Dagger up underneath the chin of the armor, aiming for a small gap there. My aim is perfect, and the blade slips right into the gap and locks tight. I grit my teeth as the suit of armor strains against me. I push upward, driving it deeper, and then . . .

Pop!

My dagger slams in up to hilt, and with a loud crash, the helmet is blasted clean off. It clatters to the ground a few feet away. The rest of the suit sways for a moment, then falls apart, collapsing into all the pieces that composed it. Columbus frowns, and I bend down and pick up the sword that the armor dropped.

[Weapon Acquired: Black Steel Sword]

[Level: C]

[Details: Ignores 75 points of damage resistance.]

"I'll take that." I give the sword a twirl, Burnie comes down to land on my shoulder, and Astrid steps up next to me. Down the hall, a great many suits of armor all start to rattle as they step out of their alcoves.

"Why don't I get one?" Columbus whines.

"Pick one up for yourself." I shrug. "Hold back if you're afraid. Astrid, Burnie, come on! Let's get to it!"

Columbus does indeed hang back as my pets and I run forward. Four more of the suits come clanking out, and Burnie and Astrid cut loose. Great gouts of flame pour forward, taking down two of them in a sweep of energy and heat, while Astrid sucks the other two down. We simply walk forward, tearing through them easily until we've made it almost halfway down the hall. There's still a good bit more space to cover, and I can see a large dark shadow that I'm pretty sure is a mini-boss at the end, but we're making good progress.

[DarkCynic: Yeah, that's the way to do it! Make it look effortless!]

[ViperQueen: You know, you could try a *little* harder to make it look like a challenge, Jason! This is almost getting boring!]

[Originalgoth: Yes . . . boring. Let's see you crank it up a notch!]

I roll my eyes but nod. "Alright, then. If we want it turned up a notch, let's turn it up a notch. Burnie, why don't you hold back for a moment?"

The chat goes wild, and I charge forward with the Black Steel Sword. Now, don't get me wrong, I'm not really a sword guy, generally speaking, but the thought of actually getting to beat these things up by myself is an appealing one. The closest suit of armor lunges at me, slashing across me with its sword, and I raise my own weapon to block it.

Clang!

Steel rings against steel, and we both come to a halt. I disengage and swing around, striking at its head, but it blocks. Then, disengaging once more, I strike at its torso. Once more, a block—or rather, a redirect. I spin out of the way as it bats me to the side, and then, suddenly, the flow changes.

The suit of armor lunges at me, using its bulk to push me backward, unleashing a blistering flurry of attacks. I bat them aside or block them and suddenly find myself in what looks to be a retreat. That's not really what I'd like to be doing right at this moment, so I grit my teeth and brace my feet.

"No, you don't!"

I lunge forward, sweeping upward with my sword, and bash its sword into the air. That leaves the suit's torso wide open, and with that, I spin and land a long strike across the gut of the armor. A long, white line is left on the steel, and it staggers. I don't know how much damage I've done, but I've hurt the thing, and I strike out once more.

Three more attacks later, I've broken through its guard and slammed the blade into the monster's chest. It doesn't exactly pierce the suit of armor, but a loud *crack* echoes through the hall, and the breastplate shatters into pieces. The rest of the armor clatters to the ground, and all the remaining suits turn to look at me. I set my jaw, then charge forward.

The dark blade shines in the light of the torches as I throw myself into the fight, striking here, slashing there. The suits of armor are blasted apart underneath the attacks, and as more suits lumber out of their alcoves, I simply cut through them.

[ChaosRider: Wow! Looks like something came to life inside of Jason!]

[ViperQueen: Yeah, he really looks alive!]

[DarkCynic: Go Jason!!!!!!]

As I reach the end of the hall, I find myself gasping for air, but I'm still standing. Behind me, the last few suits of armor creak and slowly topple over with loud crashes, and I lower my sword to my side.

And then, with a loud *whoosh*, torches blaze to life on either side of the massive suit of armor that I glimpsed earlier.

This thing is twenty feet tall, maybe more, and has a sword that's longer than my entire body. Slowly, it lifts the blade and gives it a few practice twirls as it steps down from the small platform on which it had been standing. Its head tilts down with a loud *creak* as it focuses upon me . . . And, with that, it lunges.

Swish!

Whoosh!

The blade is so big that it creates a breeze as it passes by me. I dive out of the way, knowing that there's almost no chance I can block or parry such a massive weapon. It swings three times, then lifts the blade and brings it crashing down. I leap backward, and the point of the weapon is driven deep into the stone. To my surprise and annoyance, the suit simply draws the blade right back out of the stone with the same ease it exhibited when it first attacked, and it lunges once more. It's not going to give me a moment of breathing room, that's for sure.

Foooooooooom!

Unbidden, Burnie swoops over my shoulder and lets loose a great blast of fire. The suit doesn't even bother to look at him; it simply absorbs the flame as though it were a bit of sunlight on a cloudy day. Its armor barely changes color at all and returns to black the moment that Burnie disengages and flies away. It's a tank, there's no doubt about that.

"Astrid?" I glance at her. "Why don't you give it a whirl?"

Astrid growls and lunges forward, giving a sharp bark that shakes the whole hall. The ground beneath the feet of the suit cracks and rumbles, but it simply plants its feet, and after a moment, the rumblings die away.

Master! It's countering my attacks!

That fact doesn't surprise me. Mini-bosses and bosses often have abilities to help them avoid being cheesed. It's still possible most of the time if you really know what you're doing, but it requires having that knowledge, which isn't always the easiest to locate in the middle of battle. No, I've got to defeat this thing the hard way.

And that means that I need to roll up my sleeves and get to work.

The suit of armor lunges forward once more and drives its sword into the stone. I take that opportunity to leap forward, raising my sword and bringing it down on the suit's wrist. There's a small seam in the armor there, where the gauntlet meets the arm. The sword hits it with a loud *whack*, and I see a familiar white damage line left on the metal. The suit of amor grunts, and I raise the sword and swing it down with all my might.

CRACK!

The sword smashes through the seam, cutting the gauntlet from the arm. The suit staggers back and looks down at its hollow wrist. A mist seems to drift out of the thing, letting out a soft *hiss.* I brace myself, and the suit of armor slowly raises its left arm and reaches behind its back.

The thing is drawing out another weapon, I'm sure of it. Now, there are dozens of different weapons it could be grabbing, but I don't really want to wait to find out. Instead, I charge forward as fast as I can go, sword flashing through the air, and strike at the closest knee I can reach.

CRACK!

This time, prepared for the blow, I swing with the proper force and angle. The blade smashes through the joint, and with that, the suit of armor tilts to the side and comes down with a *crash.* On the ground it suddenly doesn't seem quite so big, and I run toward its head. Hoping that it looks epic, I plant a foot on its chest, jump up into the air, then come down on its visor and drive the blade straight through the narrow gap into its skull.

Clang!

The sword simply passes through the empty space inside the helmet and hits the backside of it. Apparently, you have to actually cut through a joint in the armor to actually hurt the thing. It starts to rise, and I scowl. I really, *really* don't want this thing left alive for any longer. Quickly, I yank the sword out and toss it away, then open up my inventory and yank out the last few exploding crystals I have. I open up the visor and stuff them all inside, slam it shut, and dive out of the way.

KA-BUNK!

It's really, *really* hard to describe the sound of an explosion going off inside a metal helmet. If you've ever set off a firework inside a bucket or tin can, picture that. Smoke and fire explode out through the visor, the right arm, and the right leg, and the suit of armor falls silent.

"It's . . . dead?" Columbus asks, slowly approaching.

"Indeed." I brush off my hands. "And *that's* what a level twenty-nine warrior can do."

[ShadowDancer: Jason? We can see your levels. You're totally at Level 30 right now.]

"What?" I blink in surprise and glance at my stats, confirming that yes, indeed, I am at level thirty. "Apparently, I zone out during fights. Well, let's see if we can push that to thirty-one or thirty-two by the time we're done with this dungeon."

The chat seems to *love* that, and I slowly look for the way through to the next portion of the dungeon. Suddenly, though, the entire wall that the larger suit of armor was guarding seems to split open. It rumbles inward, revealing a *massive* chamber.

This is the boss room. We've made it. And now it's time to see what we can do.

CHAPTER TWENTY-TWO

As the doors swing open to their full extent, I slowly start to walk forward. Burnie lands on my shoulder, and Astrid pads up behind me. Suddenly, I notice Columbus hanging back, and I glance over my shoulder at him.

"Cold feet?" I raise an eyebrow. A thought suddenly strikes me, a problem with his earlier story. "You're not going to try making a deal with *this* dungeon boss too, are you?"

"It's not that," Columbus mutters.

"Good." I nod. "Because you still haven't told me every-thing, and we're getting close to the final bit of time where you'll be under my protection. Any last words you'd like to get out to me?"

"What more are you wanting to know?" Columbus sets his jaw.

"Why were you bringing the stardust to the spider if you were hired by someone sent by Krak?" I hold up my hands. "You said that you chose the dungeon because you were trying to snipe me, essentially. The more that I think about it, the more your stories aren't lining up, and I don't really like people lying to me."

That gives Columbus pause. I can't tell exactly what's going through his brain, but I'm sure he's working another angle, a way to explain away his mysterious conduct. More and more, I'm getting the idea that something deeper is happening. I just wish I knew what.

"Fine. Don't talk to me." I shrug and turn around. "Come help me beat the boss. I'm not letting you hang around out there by yourself."

Columbus crosses his arms, but Astrid growls at him, and he nods and slowly walks into the room. I lead the way, and we've soon completely entered. The doors slam shut behind us, and for a moment the room is plunged into total darkness.

That darkness doesn't last long, as enormous torches, large enough to be bonfires in their own right, all flicker to life. They hang around the edges of the room, which is quite simple as far as boss chambers go. No obstacles, no furniture. Simply a massive open space . . . And no boss that I can see to inhabit it.

"Come out, come out, wherever you are," I call out, slowly walking forward. The floor is obsidian, and I crouch down and put my hands against the stone. I can feel it trembling, but not as though a monster is going to show up immediately. "Here, bossy bossy bossy. Here, bossy bossy bossy."

"What are you doing?" Columbus snaps at me.

"Mostly trying to throw you off your guard." I shrug and stand back up. "Also trying to . . ." My voice trails off as I hear a whistling noise. Slowly, I tilt back my head to look upward.

It's at that moment that I realize there's not really any ceiling, just a long open shaft that seems to run upward for an immense distance.

That's not good. I catch a glimpse of something red moving *very* fast, and I jump up in the air as hard as I can.

BOOOOOOOOOOM!

A giant, forty feet tall, lands on the ground with a resounding blast. A shockwave rolls across the floor and flashes underneath me, but it hits Columbus squarely in the chest. It knocks him down but doesn't seem to do anything more than casual damage. With that, I regard the giant, sizing him up.

He's a beast, that's for sure, with four arms and as spindly as a spider. Spikes protrude out of his back, and his face is sort of stretched out like a lizard too. The only clothing he wears is a loincloth, which is quite tattered and seems to be made out of the hide of a bovine of some sort. He snarls and looks down at us hungrily, and I get the feeling that this is going to be a boss high on damage and low on words.

"Well, Columbus, if you've got any weapons in your inventory that can actually pack a punch, now's your chance to use them!" I throw my Seeking Dagger and charge forward. The dagger zooms around the creature and hits him in the back, where it mostly just sticks there. The monster twitches a bit, like a horse that was just bit by a fly, and charges at me.

His eyes are wild, and his tongue lolls out of his mouth. He screams and lunges forward, trying to hit me with both of his right arms. I duck underneath them and slash the Dagger of Damage across his leg. I manage to get in two more attacks before he spins and throws a massive uppercut at me, forcing me to jump backward once more. This time, though, I don't hesitate but immediately run forward and stab him in the leg several more times. The damage dealt by the weapon rises up a bit, though not enough, and he raises his leg to stomp on me. I'm forced to dive out of the way once more, and the creature lets out a powerful shriek.

I'm not exactly sure what tells me that an attack is coming, but something seems to flicker in the back of my mind, and I dive forward. A spray of darts—they look like spines fired from the giant's own flesh—flashes over my head and clatters against the stone. I come back to my feet and spin to face the thing, where I find Columbus clutching his arm, back near the door. Burnie has avoided the attack and swoops down to blast the giant with a ball of flame, while Astrid seems to have retreated into the pocket dimension. That'll work well enough.

"Jason!" Columbus calls out. "Help! I'll tell you anything!"

I would have saved him even without the encouragement, but I'm not going to turn down the opportunity. I run forward and draw out my Photonic Dagger, which I transform into a sword. The giant doesn't see me coming as I dash between his legs, slashing at his thin, spindly calf. He hollers and jumps backward, shaking the whole room, and I spin, turn the sword back into a dagger, and throw it into his face. The weapon sticks into his cheek right below his left eye, and the giant roars and thumps his chest.

"Columbus, I need your whip." I hold out my hand. "Trust me. Give it to me now."

Columbus grumbles, but he knows I'm not messing around. Quickly, he tosses the weapon to me, and I grab hold of the handle. With that, I charge forward and dodge-roll through another attack, then spin around.

"Alright, giant! Take this!" I lash upward with the whip, and it wraps around one of the lower spines. With that, I pull myself upward.

Or at least I try to.

Two things happen that prevent this from happening. First, the whip loses its grip. Second, with what little traction it does have left, it breaks the spine off. The giant howls and spins, and I sigh. I use my Dagger of Damage to stab him several more times while I dance around his legs and then use the whip once more.

This time it hits a larger spine, and I quickly pull myself up. As soon as I reach his back, I grab hold of the pointy protrusions and start climbing upward, hanging on for dear life even as the monster snarls and spins, raging and thundering against my presence there. Burnie swoops back and forth, hitting him with fireballs here and there, always making sure to attack the sides *not* closest to me. Soon, I reach the neck, where I grit my teeth and prepare to make my stand.

"Alright, giant. Take this." I lash the whip around the giant's neck, tie it up as best I can, and pull it tight. The giant chokes and staggers, and I pull even harder. Then, with my free hand, I continue to stab the monster with the Dagger of Damage. The damage count rises higher and higher. I hit eight thousand damage . . . then sixteen thousand . . . And then, without warning, the spines on the giant grow. New ones pop out all over the monster's back, while the existing ones grow longer. I take two spines to the foot and one to the leg, and with a scream, I fall back to the ground.

The giant spins around with glee, apparently having gotten a second wind of sorts, and kicks my dagger away from me. I don't know if that means that he has multiple health bars, or what. One thing that I distinctly *don't* like about this apocalypse is the lack of health bars on monsters, but there's nothing I can do about that. Anyway, the monster snarls and leaps at me, and I narrowly roll out of the way.

"*Oooooooooooooooooooooo!*"

Bjorn's howl cuts through the air, and the giant's right side freezes. Both of his arms are locked into a half-attacking position, and he snarls. I flash a quick thank-you to Bjorn, then run forward and draw out my Photonic Dagger. I don't know where my Dagger of Damage is, but in the chaos, I don't have time to look for it. Instead, I throw myself forward and hit the lower arm with my other dagger, throwing every ounce of energy I have into the strike.

Crack!

The arm shatters and breaks, making the giant stumble, off-balance. I press the attack immediately, slashing at the giant's legs with everything I have. My Photonic Dagger carves dozens of wounds across the beast, and he raises a leg to stomp on me. I dodge out of the way just in time, but then . . .

"Jason!" Columbus's voice is weak, and I glance over at him. He's fallen to the ground and looks rather green. "Jason, I think I . . . Poison."

I grit my teeth and take a step toward him, momentarily forgetting the giant. That's a mistake, as I'm suddenly blindsided by both of his left fists. The impact flings me across the room, where I hit a wall with enough force to send out a minor shockwave. Slowly, I pick myself up and find the giant stomping toward Columbus, intent on finishing the job. I see the Dagger of Damage over on the other side of the room, but there's no way I can get to it before the giant reaches Columbus.

Which means I have to improvise.

I draw out the Dagger of Doom and run forward. I don't have much hope that it'll do a whole lot. After all, even if it finds a weakness, it's still only dealing a base damage of forty or fifty, which just isn't enough to stop a monster of this size. That said, a critical hit is better than a standard hit, and if it can tell me the monster's weakness, I can exploit it.

Maybe.

The giant reaches Columbus and lifts all three of his fists, preparing to smash him into oblivion. I fling my Dagger of Doom as hard as I can, and it hits the beast in the side, just above the loincloth. That makes the creature howl with pain, and he spins toward me. A notification flickers across my vision telling me what sort of damage it dealt, but I have enough problems at the moment that I miss reading what it says before it goes away. Oh well. I have the giant's attention, and that means that Columbus is safe.

I suppose only time will tell if that's actually a good thing or not.

I dive underneath a blow, then spin toward my Dagger of Damage and charge for it. I hear the footsteps of the giant charging up behind me and realize that he's a *lot* faster than me. When I hear the telltale *whiff* of air, I drop to the ground, flat on my back, and a mighty fist passes right over my head. With that, the giant runs right over me, his feet coming within inches of hitting me, and I jump back to my feet and dive for my dagger. My hand closes over the hilt, and with that, I leap back to my feet.

The giant spins just as he reaches the wall. He looks down at me, fully and fiercely, and runs back toward me. This time I stand my ground, and as he reaches me, I slash upward with the dagger. The blow hits him in the fist as he tries to attack me, and with a great blast, the dagger cuts straight through the monster's wrist.

"YOOOOOOOOW!" the giant screams and holds up the stump of his wrist, then turns and rumbles toward me once more. By now, though, the fight is mine, and we both know it. I throw the dagger straight into his belly, and the weapon deals . . . I don't even know how much, but well over fifty thousand damage. It punches straight through the creature and out his back, leaving a gaping hole that a horse could have jumped through. Slowly, the monster falls to the ground, though he's still twitching and trying to rise as I slowly walk over and pick up my dagger.

"You shouldn't have come down from your ceiling," I gloat over the giant as he struggles to rise. I reach his head, and he turns and snaps at me. Carefully, I lean down and tap the giant's neck with the blade. The result cuts off the giant's head cleanly, and with that, I stand up and tuck my weapon back into my inventory.

[RazorEdge: THAT WAS EPIC!!!!!]

[LunarEclipse: Yeah! I want to see it again!!!!]

[FireStorm: We should totally be recording this and putting together a highlight reel so we can sell it as a movie once this apocalypse ends.]

I nod at the chat, but over by the door, Columbus is gasping and starting to turn rather purple. I'm no expert in the realm of poisons, but I *doubt* that it's a good sign. Still, wary of a trap, I don't make any great speed as I walk over to him.

I still have a lot of questions . . . and this time Columbus had *better* give me some good answers.

CHAPTER TWENTY-THREE

As I reach Columbus and kneel down, he gasps and looks up at me.

"Am I still alive?"

"For now." I nod. "Do you have any antidote?"

"No." He shakes his head, and I can practically see the gears whirling inside his skull. I know exactly what he's about to say, and he knows what he needs to do. "I need . . . the stardust."

"There *are* other antidotes out there," I point out. I still don't really understand the limits of stardust and don't want him to use it to defeat me and escape. Then again, if he could have done that, he likely wouldn't have hidden it in the first place.

"They'll take time to find. I can . . . I can take you there." His head lolls to the side for a moment before he's able to lift it back up. "Please."

[ShadowDancer: Come on, Jason. Surely your heart isn't *that* hard!]

[ViperQueen: Yeah! He's bad, but he seems genuine!]

[RazorEdge: Don't become one of the bad guys!]

It feels like I'm being played, frankly, but there's nothing I can really do about it. I need the stardust, and this is how he's going to get me there. Bjorn pads over to me, and I heft Columbus onto his back. That done, we strike out through the dungeon. I make a note that I'm up to level thirty-one, which is nice, but I don't have the time to accept my rewards.

Not yet, at least.

The moment we materialize back in the game shop, James—or maybe Felix?—is standing there, an annoyed look on his face. The portal closes the moment we step through, and he sighs.

"Look, I did the best I could." I shrug, then nod pointedly at the snake statues, as well as the tied-up lava cats. "Your business is still going to be booming. Maybe you can make your own dungeon, or something."

The man's eyes briefly light up, but I hear chopper blades outside, so I make my way through the shop and out into the street. The sun is setting, bringing an end to the day, but I have a feeling I'm not going to be getting to bed anytime soon. The helicopter lands on the street, and I climb up inside, setting Columbus as best I can into one of the seats. He groans but nods as the helicopter lifts off.

"Where are we going?" the pilot calls back.

"Head to . . . Head to Jason's apartment," Columbus answers. "Once we get there . . . I can tell you without alerting everyone who's watching him."

I nod to the pilot to confirm, then pull out my phone. It takes only a moment to ring up Mr. Wang, who sounds just as bright and perky as ever.

"Jason! Jason the Mason! Actually, I'm kidding, masons are scary. Plus, you're sort of a break-things-down person, not a build-things-up person."

"And you sound like you have *way* too much caffeine in your body." I raise an eyebrow. "Have you slept since I first met you on the street?"

"Once, for about two hours. Now, if you could please cut to the chase, as I have a meeting with the prime minister of Britain in thirty minutes." Mr. Wang still sounds just as pleasant as always, but I do detect some sort of stress beneath his exterior. "What's up?"

"I need you to contact Ali and John. Have them meet at my apartment immediately," I answer. "I have a feeling we're about to need all the help we can possibly get."

"I'll see what I can pull together," Mr. Wang says. "You just do you, and I'll do me!"

"Wonderful." I raise an eyebrow. An instant later, the phone call ends, and I turn back to the New York skyline.

It truly is beautiful as we flash over all the darkened streets. Above, the sky sparkles down with brilliant stars, but from below . . . Well, the ground almost looks like a night sky in and of itself, shining with enough intensity to block out many of the stars. Reds and yellows and greens all mingle together, a whole city of vibrant life weathering the apocalypse together. Soon, we start the final approach to my apartment building, hundreds of feet above the ground, which is one of the brightest pillars of them all. It really is a wonderful sight in so many ways, and as we come down on the helipad, I feel a sense of joy. I hop out, grab up Columbus, and we slowly make our way down into the living room. The chopper stands ready, but I don't think I'm going to need it. When Columbus clues us in, we're going to need to run just as fast as we can, and I doubt a chopper will be fast enough.

Carefully, I set Columbus on the couch. A moment later, an arrow shoots through the open door, and Ali and John appear with a flash. They both look tired, and John looks like he just went through a slime dungeon—either that, or he killed a giant by crawling inside its nose. That said, they're here, and they both walk over to Columbus.

"Alright." I cross my arms and look down at him. He's barely conscious now, or at least he appears that way. "Time to talk."

"Right . . . there." He raises his finger and points at my refrigerator. I raise an eyebrow, then shrug. "Alright. John, can you go grab him a Pumped! drink? He's probably thirsty; that last dungeon was hot."

"Do I look like a servant?" John jokes good-naturedly as he walks over to the fridge.

"Sort of, yeah." Ali nods. "I mean, more like a servant who cleans toilets, but—"

"Jason?" John freezes as he opens up the fridge.

"What?" I turn to him, then notice a shocked expression on his slime-covered face. Slowly, he reaches inside and, to my surprise and horror, pulls out the vial of stardust. It sparkles in the evening light, and Columbus smiles and nods weakly.

"I need some," he whispers, opening his mouth. "Just . . . Just a drop."

John hesitates. I walk up and pop the vial open, allowing the *tiniest* amount of dust to drift out onto my finger. Carefully, I walk over and shake a couple grains into Columbus's mouth, and the color returns to his cheeks almost instantly. As he gasps for air and starts to rise, John claps the vial shut and sticks it into his inventory.

"I'm so confused." I hold up a hand. "How exactly—"

"I'll explain later." Columbus waves to us and starts running back toward the helipad. "We need to go, and we need to go now. They'll be here in seconds."

"Who?" I draw out my daggers. "I'm ready to fight."

Suddenly, I start to hear thumps and explosions from below, and Columbus shrugs.

"Who? Everyone."

A blast of fire shoots through the window of my apartment and hits my couch. A moment later, something shoots past on a flaming flying carpet, and I gulp. I can see other winged creatures rising up against the backlights of the rest of the city. This is about to go *very* badly.

"We need a better place to make our stand." I run after Columbus. "Come on! Get to the helicopter!"

We all pile inside just about as fast as we can. The pilot takes off immediately and deploys several missile racks that pop out of the sides. He fires one instantly, hitting a pegasus racing toward us, then roars off through the sky.

"Alright! Time for answers!" I point my Dagger of Damage at Columbus's throat. "How did that thing get in my apartment?"

"You brought it there, actually!" Columbus shouts out. "When we fought the sprites in the park, remember? You didn't notice, but I reverse-pickpocketed you. Then, back up in your apartment, one of the servants, who I paid off, took it back out and put it in the fridge, ready for me to get later. The problem was, I had to actually get you to take me back here since security is so tight."

I nod slowly. I had thought as much. It was all a trick, every last bit of it. "Give me one reason why I shouldn't kill you right now."

A witch flies past on a broomstick—no, a whole squadron of witches. They begin firing wild spells at us, green blasts of magic that shake the chopper fiercely every time they hit. The helicopter spins and lets loose a machine gun blast, but they're too fast. I grit my teeth and pull the door of the helicopter open, then pull out my Seeking Dagger.

"Columbus, keep talking! Ali, help me knock these things down!"

Ali steps up next to me, whips out her bow, and fires an arrow into the darkness. It explodes brilliantly a moment later, taking out one of the witches. My Seeking Dagger flashes through the air and cuts a broom cleanly in half, causing the witch to fall from the sky, then snaps back to my palm.

"You're going to leave me alive because I have a plan to keep us alive. I don't *want* to die, after all." Columbus shrugs. "You can either land somewhere and face off against other Awakened, dungeon bosses, and legions of minions for the next week, with no food or rest, and *hope* that you'll come out on top—or you can listen to me and trust that I have a plan."

"I have to say, I don't really trust you at the moment," John mutters.

"And as for your other questions, the original plan was to give it to any old dungeon boss. Krak has his connections, and word of the dust hadn't yet spread through the whole dungeon world." Columbus turns to me. "None of them would have known what they were holding, so they would have just passed it along without question. You interrupted my deal, so I had to improvise."

"And how were you contacted before I even knew about the dust?" I snap.

"The dark elf king in possession of the dust was being watched by the queen. Originalgoth. I'm sure you've noticed her presence." Columbus shrugs. "It wasn't a coincidence that she acted so quickly. As soon as he would have tried to move the dust from his dungeon, he would have been slain. Thus, in an attempt to preserve his own life, he planned to pass it along to you, and then the dust would be taken from you and passed along to Krak. He didn't count on her vengeance being quite so . . . forceful, or so rapid."

"That answers a few of my questions," I mutter. I throw my dagger again, this time cutting two of the witches out of the sky before it returns to me. "My only question now is where we're headed. I suppose we're going to see good old Krak? A family reunion of sorts, where the two of us will shake hands and pretend that everything's all good between us?"

"Not exactly." Columbus leans forward. "He doesn't exactly trust you, given that you *did* try to kill him last time."

"It was a bit more mutual than that, if you must know." I glance over my shoulder. Ali takes down the last of the witches with an ice arrow, but I can see more rising up from the city below. Seems like just about everything with flight capability is zeroing in on us.

"And I'm sure the two of you will meet up again to talk it through. Regardless, we're heading to a zone where the dust will be passed off to a representative. If you give it over, no consequences will come to you. All these people attacking you now will have no reason to do so since you'll no longer have the dust, and Krak will have what he needs."

I set my jaw and shake my head slowly. "I'm not making that sort of deal."

"Well." Columbus shrugs. "We'll see if you're still singing that tune here in a few moments. Oh, right there! Nose down."

He points down through the darkness, where I see a nearly finished Pumped! factory. There are still a few things that seem to be going in, but by and large, it really looks to be mostly done. That was *fast* construction . . . or at least the appearance of construction. I suppose I can't see inside the structure to see what the inside of the thing looks like, but I have a feeling that I'll soon be getting a first-hand look.

The helicopter roars onward toward the building, dropping lower and lower.

"Fly us over the smokestacks!" Columbus calls out. "Everyone, get ready to jump!"

I hear a low rumbling noise and look through the back window of the helicopter to see a plane of some sort approaching *rapidly*. Horror shoots through me, and I shake my head.

"No time! Jump now!"

With that, I run forward and throw myself out. The pilot punches out as well, Ali fires a teleporter arrow, and John simply jumps. I don't really see what Columbus does, but the rest of us find ourselves tumbling down toward the ground below.

Above us, there's a brilliant flash of light as a missile is fired into the helicopter. The explosion hits me an instant later, and

I find myself launched even faster toward the ground. I have no idea how I'm going to survive . . . But I'm certain that I'm going to pummel Columbus into pulp if I ever get my hands on him again.

CHAPTER TWENTY-FOUR

Looking below us, I see that I'm falling toward the edge of the Pumped! factory onto a narrow strip of rocky ground between the building and the bay. Ali appears below us with a flash of light, and I nod in thanks. She's down safely. The pilot almost certainly had a parachute. John can survive almost any landing. That only leaves me to figure out how to stick the landing, and, unfortunately, I'm a bit clueless. Burnie doesn't have the wingspan to slow me down enough, and I don't have any items that will really be of use.

Thankfully, I'm spared from coming up with any sort of crazy MacGyvered contraptions. One of the witches flashes out of the darkness and hits me, her eyes going wide, and the two of us skew through the air wildly. She flails about, and I do the same—after all, having a broomstick slammed into your gut at two hundred miles an hour isn't pleasant—and the two of us go crashing through the windows of the factory. I find myself hurtling toward the concrete floor, and we land with a loud *smack*, tumbling over and over each other. When we finally come to a halt, we both rise shakily to our feet, and the witch readjusts the hat on her head.

"I'll get you, my pretty!" She slowly raises her hands, which begin to crackle with lightning.

I raise an eyebrow, and Bjorn dives out of my pocket dimension and flattens her. His teeth flash in the dim light of the factory, and with that, she's no more.

"What about my dog?" I walk past her corpse, glad to be rid of the monster. "Will you get him too?"

There's a loud *boom* as John crashes through the ceiling and lands not far from me and a *click* as Ali walks through the door. Now the only person we're waiting on is Columbus, but I frankly don't know if we'll ever be seeing him again. Meanwhile, I slowly look around the empty room, nodding as I begin to understand.

The inside of the factory is entirely empty. It's a hollow shell. Well, right underneath the smokestacks are furnaces that I imagine could produce the illusion of smoke or steam, but that's it. Otherwise, the place is void and barren.

Which leaves me confident that I know what's about to happen.

"This is weird." Ali slowly walks up to us. "Do you have a feeling like we're about to be attacked?"

"More than a feeling." I nod slowly. Suddenly, the hair on the back of my neck stands up, and I get the distinct feeling that I'm about to get zapped. I dive out of the way, and with an earsplitting roar, a rift opens up in the middle of the building.

The rift roars and churns with fierce lightning, and the three of us regard it warily. Rifts are nothing to sniff at. They tend to be larger than dungeons, far more deadly, and often have all sorts of traps. Oh, and they can spit monsters out at far higher rates than some of the others. Dark forms begin to swirl through the dark energy around the portal, and a shape slowly emerges.

Somehow, I'm not surprised to see Columbus. Of course, now he's not in his cowboy disguise. No, now he has skin as black as coal, pointed ears, and a small crown that sits upon his head. His facial features are otherwise the same, though; he's simply morphed from one race into another.

"Your Majesty," I snort sarcastically. "I should have known it would be you."

Columbus shrugs. "As I said, I was being watched. Do you *really* think I would have trusted you to get the stardust out of the dungeon without the queen realizing my plan? I had a body double step into my place, and he performed *admirably*."

"Was there ever someone actually named Columbus, or was that a complete fabrication?" I demand.

"Was there? Yes. He's rotting in peace in the sewers somewhere." Columbus shrugs. "His moral scruples about helping us didn't help him get anywhere in the world. Now, if you please, I'd rather like the stardust. I've gone to great lengths to get it from there to here, and it has been *exhausting*."

"What makes you think we'd give it to you?" I snort. "You obviously have plans for it, and I doubt that said plans involve the survival of the human race."

"Your skills of observation are impeccable," Columbus says, mocking me. "I don't expect you'll want to give it to me, but . . . well . . ." He shrugs. "If you don't give it to me, I'll destroy the city, right here and right now."

"How?" I demand.

"This rift is B-Ranked. That means that I can generate bosses up to level B and unleash them upon the city, one every thirty minutes." Columbus raises an eyebrow. "Have you ever fought a B-Ranked boss?"

I don't know that I have, but I'm not the best at paying attention to rankings. When I don't answer, Columbus puts his hands behind his back.

"Let me save you the pain. You haven't. You've fought a few C-Ranked bosses, and you've done well enough with them, but B-Ranks are another class entirely. If you don't give me the stardust, here and now, I'll be releasing one of them to go attack downtown Manhattan. No matter what you think, you won't be able to stop it and neither will the legions of warriors who may gather to try and knock it down."

"We'll be able to stop it." I grit my teeth. "We've stopped everything else that's tried to come through these portals."

"But how long can you keep doing that?" Columbus slowly walks forward. "How long can you keep this up, Jason? Somehow, I doubt it's as long as you think."

"All you're doing is offering me a chance to beat things up," I growl softly. "That isn't going to convince me of anything." A flash of inspiration shoots through my mind. "In fact, I think you're stalling. I think you're *desperate* to get this stardust and you'll do anything and everything to get us to hand it over." My hands ball into fists. "It won't work."

"Maybe not." Columbus's eyes darken. "Well, then, I'm afraid I have to resort to other tactics. I'm sorry, Jason. You're a testament to your world. I really will miss it when I burn it down."

With that, a creature lunges out of the portal, crackling

with energy. It looks like a giant crab, thirty feet tall at least, and is bristling with a great many legs. Before any of us can do anything, it lashes out with a mighty claw and snatches up John, then dives back through the portal. He breaks out of its grip before he passes through the barrier, but by then, his trajectory is set, and he flashes through the rift portal. Columbus gives me a nod and steps back through the portal as well, and I grit my teeth as lightning surges and the rift starts to close.

Suddenly, Ali's hand latches down on my arm. An arrow flies from her bowstring at the exact same moment, flashing through the portal. Suddenly, teleporter light blazes around me, and we're both sucked into the rift.

Now, I complain a lot about how I hate dungeon portals. Rift portals, as I hope I've explained, are *far* worse. Being teleported through a rift portal? Utter agony. Teleporting itself is a somewhat pleasant experience, less horrid than the dungeon portals, but it still involves being sucked down an interdimensional straw. Admittedly, it's a bright and colorful straw instead of a dark and gloomy one, at least ordinarily. Mixed with the dark and angry colors of the rift, it becomes a mass of fierce colors amidst flashing light that bombards my eyes—or maybe my feet; your organs get mixed up, so it's hard to tell exactly what's what—with a dizzying and chaotic array. Then, suddenly, I'm thrown out the far side and find myself on a small ledge overlooking the main portion of the rift's area.

Unfortunately, it's not a pretty sight. The crab and John are locked in mortal combat. The crab is pressing the attack, slashing at John with its legs and pinchers while John punches at anything he can reach. Suddenly, I catch a glimpse of Columbus behind him, and behind Columbus, a spider.

A big spider.

Flash.

I'm unable to do a thing as the spider flings a dart at John's back. It sticks firmly; I don't think John even notices it. Suddenly, though, he sways and falls, landing facedown. The crab rises up and brings both claws slamming down on top of his body, shaking the cavern, and Columbus holds up a hand.

"Whoa, whoa! None of that! We've got him down. We don't want him dead! Yet."

The spider crawls past Columbus and starts to tie up John, and I brace myself. Ali puts her hand on my shoulder, and my chat really kicks up.

[RazorEdge: GO SAVE HIM, JASON!!!!!!]

[IceQueen: You've got like three seconds before he's spider soup!]

[FireStorm: Jason! Are you really the type of friend who would let his best bud die?]

[Originalgoth: This is an . . . interesting turn of events. Perhaps I need to watch this dungeon more carefully as well. Could someone please get me the Dungeon ID of this rift?]

[ViperQueen: Go away, scary lady!]

[FireStorm: Yeah! You're the cause of all of this, and I hate you!]

[Originalgoth: Without me, all of you would be stuck watching pointless cartoons on the internet instead of actively involving yourselves in this epic struggle. You should thank me.]

"I have to get down there." I start to rise, but Ali pulls me down once more.

"No. If you go now, they'll just kill him and extract the

stardust from his corpse!" Ali hisses. "They want him alive for some reason—probably to question him. We can save him if we're patient!"

"We're going to lose him." I grit my teeth as the spider starts to rise up, picking up an ensnared John. "We have to go *now!*"

"No!"

Columbus freezes and looks around, and I jump, ignoring Ali's warnings. With a loud *boom*, I land in front of the exit, fierce determination in my eyes. At least, I hope that's what I'm conveying.

"I have to admit, I'm impressed." Columbus raises an eyebrow. The crab turns to face me, and I brace myself. The thing is huge and has armor everywhere. I have very few doubts that this is the B-Ranked boss that Columbus was planning to unleash. "Still, you're only making my job easier. We closed the entrance, which means—*tha-ack!*"

Now, "tha-ack," when translated into dark elven speech, means something. I don't really have a clue what, but I saw it once in a forum online. At this moment, I don't really care if it means "I surrender" or "Die like a dog." All I intend to do is save John, and the fact that Ali has just fired an arrow through Columbus's throat makes that task at least somewhat easier. He doubles over, turning green, and another arrow hits the spider, exploding violently. Ali may not have wanted me to engage with them, but now that I'm here, she's not going to let me down.

"Get him out of here!" Columbus waves his hand. "Now!"

The spider hisses and rushes forward, up onto the claw of the crab. With a flick, the crab launches the spider up to the ceiling, where it catches hold of the stone and scuttles through a hole there. Columbus, meanwhile, yanks out a dark crystal and gives it a squeeze. He vanishes with a blast of dark portal energy, leaving me alone with the crab.

A B-Ranked boss.

The crab looks down at me, and I look up at it. Suddenly, it raises both its claws and brings them crashing down on top of me. Shockwaves explode outward from the point of impact, and dust shoots upward. I hear Ali scream, but I don't dare say a thing. Slowly, the crab raises its claws, and all its eyes—fun fact: crabs have a lot of eyes; they're compound, like a fly's—seem to blink in shock. I'm still there, having positioned myself between the two claws. The shockwaves cancelled themselves, and I'm entirely unhurt.

The same won't be true of the crab, soon enough.

I fling the Seeking Dagger, which flies up and slams into one of the eyes, making the crab shriek and draw back. With that, I leap up onto one of the claws and charge for its back, while Ali pelts it with dozens of arrows. Some are explosive, some acidic. None seem to deal an immense amount of damage, but I suppose that's just what we have to work with.

As I jump up onto the back of the shell, it sweeps one of its claws back at me, raking over the shell rapidly. I dive over it, coming up just behind the head, and drive my Photonic Dagger through a small chink in the armor there. I then transform it into a sword and hear a rather satisfactory crunching noise. The crab doesn't seem terribly annoyed by it and simply tries to rake at me with its claws once more. I'm forced to dodge again, and, though I try to stay on its shell, I fall to the ground instead.

As soon as I land, it turns into a fight for survival. Crabs have a lot of legs, and it uses every single one to try and stomp on me. I duck underneath the body of the monster, trying to hide from the legs, and it simply drops, trying to crush me underneath. I only narrowly dive out of the way in time and glance up at Ali.

"How much damage are you dealing with those arrows?" I call out.

"I don't know, but not much!" she answers. "We need a better plan!"

"I have one!" I nod. "Target the ceiling! Now!"

Ali gives me a brief return nod, and I once more dive out of the way as the crab turns and tries to beat me into the ground. A moment later, the first arrow hits the ceiling of the cave at the base of a great stalactite, and the spire of stone comes crashing down, hitting the monster dead in the middle of the back. It's knocked to the ground, and I run to the wall and start climbing up toward Ali.

"Keep it up! Astrid, see if you can help!"

Astrid materializes on the ledge next to Ali and howls. Cracks spread through the ceiling, and Ali fires one more arrow. It hits in the exact center of the cracking area, and the blast shakes the entire cave. When it all dies away and the dust clears, I find that a massive pile of stone and rubble has buried the crab, and on top of that, the little hole that the spider went through has been opened up a bit, revealing an alternate passageway.

"Get us through that." I point to Ali. "Now."

"Don't we want to kill that thing first?" Ali points down at the crab.

"We'll get it on the way back out." I shake my head. "For right now, we've got to get out of here. John is in danger, and every second is going to count. I don't know what they're planning to do to him, but . . ." I shudder. "Just go."

Ali nods and fires a teleporter arrow, and a moment later, we're up in the darkened passage above. Below, the pile of rubble shifts, and I grit my teeth. I want so badly to just kill the crab, which would provide me with much-needed experience to raise my level and maybe even make saving John easier, but . . . it could take hours to punch through that much armor.

No, we have to get moving. Ali and I turn toward the darkness and slowly take off down the darkened interior. We have a friend to save, and that's the simple reality of the matter. Once he's been rescued, well . . . maybe killing the crab can be a fun celebration we all do together when we're all a bit safer.

CHAPTER TWENTY-FIVE

Ali and I slip along through the dark passage. I pull out my Photonic Dagger, which gives a bit of light, and transform it into a sword to allow for more illumination. It helps, but not by much. Soon the tunnel turns sharply downward, dropping off into the depths of the Earth—or whatever interdimensional planet we happen to be standing on. Both of us pause, and Ali shudders.

"This tunnel wasn't meant for us, I think. We were supposed to go the main way."

"At least we can be relatively certain that Columbus hasn't booby-trapped this way. He might not even know we're on our way at all." I let out a long breath, then sit down and swing my legs over the edge of the pit.

"Are you just going to drop in there?" Ali asks. "You don't know how deep it is!"

"We don't have time to find another way, and I don't see any other options." I shrug. "Unless you happen to have some rope?"

Ali shakes her head, and I slip off the edge and drop into the darkness. Invisible walls flash around me, cloaked by the intense darkness. Down, down I fall . . . Until, with a *thwack*, I hit stone. My body isn't quite ready for it, and I fall backward to recover. My head whacks the side of the shaft, but not so hard that it knocks me out, and I slowly climb back to my feet.

"You're good!" I hiss upward. I don't really want to say anything too loud, for fear of some monster hearing me. There's no response, and I sigh. "Alright. Can someone in the chat please tell Ali that it's s—"

Wham!

Ali, who had indeed heard me, lands right on my head. Thankfully, I'm braced enough that I don't fall, and my reflexes kick in to catch her before she hits the ground. She gives me a nod as I set her down and take a step back.

"You almost stabbed me," she mutters.

"I didn't know you were going to jump right on *top* of me!" I retort.

"I didn't know you were going to stand right underneath me!" she shoots right back. This blame game could go on for quite some time, so I turn and start walking down the hall once more. The tunnel is broad, which is nice, but the stone around me just seems . . . gloomy. It's all jagged and broken— uneven, like even the ground itself is angry about being there.

[GoldenShield: Hey, Jason! Make sure to level up!]

[ViperQueen: YEAH!!! DO IT!!!]

I chuckle, then nod and open up my interface. I have two level ups, for going from level twenty-nine to thirty and from thirty to thirty-one. Quickly, I hit the button to choose the reward, and light flares through the air in front of me. Belatedly, I hope it doesn't alert anyone or anything further down the shaft.

[Skill Acquired!]

[Level: C]

[Speed: Will make you move faster. Levels up with use.]

[Pet Acquired!]

[Living Bomb. Abilities: Explode, Flight.]

"Whoa!" I blink in surprise as a little green blob appears in my hand. It looks sort of like a pufferfish, with two big, expressive eyes that remind me of a puppy. As I stand there, it swells up to the size of a baseball and floats up into the air. Now that it's expanded, it has some odd, checkered patterns across it: little spots of blue that I couldn't see earlier.

"What's your name, little fellow?"

Blub!

The word echoes in my mind, and I chuckle. "Alright, Blub. What are you exactly?"

Blub blub blub blub-blub.

"Your vocabulary is incredible." I raise an eyebrow. "Well, then, Blub, why don't you head inside and make yourself at home."

The pocket dimension opens, and Blub floats through. As it closes, I glance over at Ali, ready to get on with the dungeon.

"So, what do you think this is, really?"

"What do you mean?" She frowns in thought.

"This rift," I answer. "They built a Pumped! factory shell around the spot where they planned to open up the portal. There has to be a reason for that, right?"

"It's a good place to plan an invasion of the city," Ali

answers. "I mean, you open it up, you drop a boss inside, and boom! No warning, lots of carnage."

"Yeah, but there are plenty of places you could do that." I shrug. "Just open it anywhere in Jersey. No one goes there anyway. You'd be perfectly—"

Ali slugs me in the arm. "*I'm* from Jersey."

I laugh a bit. "I'm not even from New York. I just hear lots of Jersey jokes. Thought it would make the situation a bit better." I sigh and shake my head. "My point stands, though. There are abandoned warehouses across the city. There are old skyscrapers, basements . . . I mean, if *all* you wanted to do was create a secret place to spawn a rift portal, there are loads of others. Besides, just open one up in Times Square and dump out a boss if that's what you want. There'd still be no warning."

"There's probably a length of time they have to wait before they can spawn a boss," Ali points out. "A cooldown timer after opening the dungeon."

"Still, you get my point. It doesn't make sense. There has to be something that we're missing."

As if to confirm my point, I suddenly hear muffled voices in the distance. I quickly sheath my dagger, and the two of us creep along in silence and darkness. Thankfully, I only whack my head on the stone walls once, though it hurts enough to make me a bit more hesitant as we move forward. Soon we see a bit of light ahead of us and creep up to a small, rather jagged opening that overlooks a larger dungeon cavern.

There are large caves on both sides of the cavern, one leading back in the direction we came, and one leading the other direction. Around the former is a small contingent of elven warriors, all dark elves, armed with spears and swords and bows. They certainly seem to suspect that we'll be coming from that direction. On the other end, the spider can just be seen scampering off into the tunnel with Columbus marching alongside.

However, the middle of the room is something that's a bit different from anything I've yet seen. There are half a dozen portals along the edges of the chamber, all flickering with a purplish lightning that looks rather painful. Walking out of the portals, at a rate of one or two a second, are elves.

A lot of elves.

I see dark elves, red-skinned blood elves, bluish sea elves, a few charred-looking flame elves, and some others I can't immediately place. In any case, all of them are walking toward a long row of tables in the middle of the room, where they're all picking up uniforms that are labeled with the Pumped! logo. To my *immense* astonishment—I really can't describe just how flabbergasted this makes me—they don blue aprons, blue hats, blue shirts and shoes, and blue weapons; there's a whole array of licensed swords, spears, shields, bows, staffs, and more. It's a whole Pumped! army . . . And as they get dressed, they're all marching toward the opposite side of the room, following Columbus and the spider.

"Are you seeing this?" I whisper to Ali. "I seriously can't decide if this is real or not, or if I was knocked unconscious by that crab, and this is some sort of fever dream."

"No, this is real." Ali nods her head slowly. "Doesn't make a *lick* of sense, but I'm starting to think that you're right. The Pumped! factory shell wasn't put up by accident."

"But . . ." I shake my head. "*Surely* they're not planning on actually . . . opening up a fast food joint. Right?"

Ali only shrugs, and I bite my lip.

"Well . . . Should we go wreak some havoc?"

"Sounds like a good enough plan to me." She nods. "You go down in the midst of them, and I'll cover you?"

"I . . . Yup. Yeah."

I take a deep breath, then slowly slip out of the tunnel and drop down quietly to the floor. By this point no one has noticed me. I snap my fingers and open my pocket dimension, and Bjorn, Astrid, and Burnie all come out to join me. It might be overkill, but there are a lot of elves, and I'd rather not take chances. Ali fits an arrow to her bow, and I take a deep breath.

"Alright! It's time to inspect this joint!" I start walking forward and cross my arms behind my back. Elves turn to look at me, and I make my eyes hard. "Are your fryers heated to the proper temperature? Burgers cooked correctly? Are the soda bottles being thoroughly cleaned? And, most importantly . . ." I stare out at them. "Are all your uniforms being worn correctly? Failure to satisfy any of these criteria will be met with instant consequences!"

The elves all stare back at me, and I enjoy a brief moment when they're just as dumbfounded as I am. Ali breaks it, though, when she fires an explosive arrow into the table. Fire and smoke erupt outward with a resounding *whoosh*, and the elves finally realize that they're under attack.

"I hereby announce that this factory is being shut down!" I charge forward, drawing out the Dagger of Doom alongside the Photonic Dagger. "Please turn in your uniforms and see yourselves out!"

With that, we come clashing together, and chaos explodes

throughout the room. Ali unleashes a swarm of arrows that pour down across the area. Flashes of light and brilliant explosions shake the foundations of the room, and I see dozens of elves being thrown high into the air. Bjorn howls and freezes many of the elves, while Astrid growls and causes gouts of fire to erupt from cracks that open up in the ground. Burnie swoops overhead and lets loose a great torrent of flame, burning up a great many other elves, which, all things considered, doesn't leave me with a whole lot of them to fight. Disappointing, but I'll live.

The elves won't, though.

Several dark elves charge at me, brandishing their Pumped! weapons. One of them raises a staff, and dark magic flickers around the head of the weapon. Suddenly, a bolt of dark lightning erupts to hit me in the stomach, making me feel queasy. Another dark elf choses that moment to lunge at me with his sword, but I block it with my Photonic Dagger and stab him through the neck with the Dagger of Doom. He lets out a gurgle and falls to the ground, and I spin to the next one.

"You're not getting me down that easily." I leap backward and dodge another blast of lightning, then throw the Dagger of Damage into the dark elf's chest. Ice creeps across a good deal of its body, and I flash forward, pull it out, and punch the elf in the chin. The blow shatters his skull, killing him instantly. With that, I spin to the mage, whose staff has suddenly lit up with a roaring green fire.

"Haha!" the mage cackles. "Withstand this, if you can!"

The fire emits a great *whoosh*, and it ripples through the air, crackling and raging and swelling and growing. I leap backward, and Bjorn takes a moment to cast a bit of his ice magic in my direction. The flames fade away almost instantly, and I lunge forward. Before he can work any more dark magic, I rip the staff out of his hands, spin, and smash the weapon across the side of his head. He drops like a rock, and I throw the staff like a spear through another elf who's charging at me.

Snip!

An arrow flashes past my head, and I spin to see a wood elf shooting at me. His arrows seem to simply grow from his hand as he pulls the string back, which is annoying because I can't outlast him. I charge forward, dipping and diving, but he only springs back, climbing up on some boulders. I grit my teeth, then yank out my Seeking Dagger and throw it straight at him.

The next shot is so flawless that I never could have planned it. Both of our aims are perfect, and the arrow hits the dagger dead-on. It splits down the middle, and the two halves flash on either side of me, striking down a flame elf and a blood elf. The dagger hits the wood elf a moment later, and all three fall to the ground.

I spin around as the Seeking Dagger snaps back to my hand. Several blood elves are advancing toward me from one side, while several flame elves are coming from the other. Quickly, I throw the Seeking Dagger once more, which begins to circle in a wide, whooshing path. It dips inward and strikes down one of the flame elves, then flashes back away, and I nod. A moment later, the other elves have arrived, and I'm in the fight of my life.

The flame elves, just like their name suggests, create long tongues of fire that rage down their swords. The blood elves, meanwhile, have their own weapons, which begin to glow with a blackish energy that almost makes me woozy just looking at. They're all vile creatures, not worthy of the noble title of elf, but I suppose that's just life sometimes. They all come toward me, and I'm suddenly locked into a desperate fight, blocking and parrying. Half a dozen blades all come at me at once, but I spin and dodge and strike, managing to avoid being hit except for a few minor flesh wounds. My Seeking Dagger continues to flash about, swinging in a broad circle around us, darting in here and there to hit the last of the assailants.

As the last of those attackers fade away, I spin toward the exit, where a small handful of elves, all mages holding staffs, have formed a blockade. Magic pulses up out of their staffs and forms a dome over top of them, while the remaining ones all form a circle and begin to combine their magic. I grit my teeth as I look at them all. Burnie flashes overhead and launches a fireball at them, but it only bounces off the shield and hits the wall. Bjorn and Astrid's attacks all end at the shield as well. I nod as I think it through, then hold up my hand. The Seeking Dagger smacks back into my palm, and I sheath it quickly.

[DarkCynic: What are you going to do, Jason?]

[ViperQueen: He's about to go *ham* on these guys!]

[LunarEclipse: I can't wait to see it!]

I nod grimly, then charge forward. I have a friend to save . . . and I'm not going to let these annoying mages stand in the way.

CHAPTER TWENTY-SIX

My feet pound across the ground as I race toward the mages. My pocket dimension flickers and Blub pops out and lands in my hand. He swells up to his full size, and I grip him just as if I were pitching the opening throw for the Mets. He gives a small squeak as I reach the shield. With all my might, I lower my shoulder, plowing straight through the shield.

Apparently, it was only designed to stop energy attacks. My—very physical—body whooshes straight through without obstruction, and I knock over several of the mages upholding the shield. The other mages all spin toward me, and a great torrent of energy begins to swirl. Before it can be discharged, though, I throw Blub straight into their midst.

KA-BOOM!

The blast hits me in the chest and knocks me backward. The elves are tossed asunder, and the shield breaks. As I rise to my feet, they start to gather themselves, and I whisper under my breath, "Skill: Speed."

The world around me slows, and I dart forward, blades flashing. It takes mere instants to cut them all down; they lay on the ground, bleeding upon the stone, dead as the Pumped! gear they're all wearing. I slowly take a deep breath as the skill wears off, and I look around for Blub.

It takes me a moment to locate him. As it turns out, he's flopping about like a fish, not far from me. As I pick him up, he slowly starts to inflate, and I smile. He's not able to inflate very far, though.

"And just how long does it take before you can do that again?" I ask softly.

Blub!

"If anyone out there is fluent in blub-speak, I would happily pay for a few quick lessons." I smile and pass Blub over to Bjorn, and the two of them slip back into the pocket dimension. Burnie and Astrid do the same, and Ali jumps down to come join me. We both turn toward the exit and start making our way in that direction. I don't see any other warriors, and the portals have all closed, but it's hard to know how many may have already come through.

"So, what is this?" Ali kicks one of the Pumped! swords. "I've never seen anything like this before. Never even heard of it."

"Trust me, I'm working through every possibility I can think of, and I've got nothing." I shrug as we slip into the next tunnel. Ahead, I can hear the steady clank of machinery. "All we can do is keep fighting our way forward and hope that we find s—"

I stop as we reach the next junction and look out into the third cavern of the rift. Now, it should be noted that a lot of rifts have paths that are far less linear to follow than dungeons, and this seems to be where this rift in particular breaks from the simple cavern-to-cavern setup. The area is massive, with dozens of caves branching off this main cave. Now, all that is more or less par for the course, but what absolutely shocks me are the dozens of conveyer belts running into and out of the caves. As we watch, elven workers, all wearing their official Pumped! uniforms, load up wooden crates onto some of the conveyer belts, which are then sucked along into the caves while they unload other crates coming out of the caves in return. It's all quite . . . odd; there's simply no other word for it. The crates returning from the caves seem to be full, while the crates sent out seem to be empty, or at least not *as* full. I can see elves loading glass bottles onto some of the belts, and unassembled burger boxes onto others, and . . .

"This is a shipment facility," Ali whispers. "Like . . . this is seriously a Pumped! production facility."

I nod slowly. A large pile of filled crates is slowly growing. Suddenly, a portal opens above, and a small black dragon drops down to land in the middle of the floor. Workers rush forward and begin to load the crates onto a number of straps hanging off its back, and within a few moments, they've saddled the thing up almost like a pack mule. As soon as it's full, the thing flaps its wings and shoots up through the portal. The portal then snaps closed, and the workers go back to loading and unloading.

"Well, then." I shrug. "Shall we shut this place down?"

"I'm perfectly okay with that." Ali nods and fits an arrow to her bow. "Give me two seconds."

"Two seconds?" I chuckle as I stand up and draw out my daggers. "You're going to shut this place down in two seconds?"

In answer, she fires an arrow. It streaks through the air, flashes across the whole of the room, and slams into a small control panel on the far side of the cavern, clearly marked *Authorized mini-bosses only.* I can't see what it hits, but the moment it impacts the panel, all the torches around the area turn red and an alarm begins to blare. Conveyer belts grind to a halt, workers look around, and a voice cries out loudly through the facility.

"Attention, workers! An emergency has been detected. Please evacuate the area until a competent team has been dispatched to assess the situation."

The workers all let out a cheer and start walking toward a cave labeled *Off-duty.* I chuckle, then nod to Ali and slip out of our hiding place. She follows, and the two of us march across the middle of the floor.

"Your eyes are better than mine, looks like. Now, all we have to do is figure out where to—"

Pzzzzzzzzzzzzzat!

A great flicker of lightning explodes across the middle of the room, and a portal opens. I grab Ali and pull her behind one of the conveyer belts and peer out from behind a box as a creature slowly emerges from the darkness.

It stands a good head taller than some of the elves and has black scales instead of skin. It *is* humanoid—at least mostly—though it has reptilian frills sweeping down from the base of its skull to its shoulders. Its eyes are piercing and yellow and have a dark sort of magic set within them. Long claws come down from each finger. A low clicking sound emerges from the creature, and it slowly begins to look around. I duck back out of the way, hoping that it didn't see me.

[FireStorm: WHOA!!! Never thought I'd see one of those in real life!]

[IceQueen: Donald Davidson fought one of those just a few days ago and got *creamed.*]

[ViperQueen: Yeah, but I'm sure that Jason will be alright!]

[Originalgoth: Don't be so sure.]

Ali glances at me. I can see her eyes darting back and forth as she reads her own chat, and her face grows rather pale. I lean close to her, and she whispers a single word.

"Dragonspawn."

I gulp, then draw a deep breath. "On three?"

She nods and fits an arrow to her bow. I draw out my Dagger of Doom and my Seeking Dagger, nod three times, and we both stand up. I throw my Seeking Dagger as hard as I can . . . and it flashes straight through the space where the dragonspawn was just standing. To my annoyance, it turns around, then whirs straight back at me.

"Come on. Go find the—"

Realization hits me, and I dive forward over the conveyer belt just as a blast of green vapor shoots through the space where I had been standing. The metal melts into slag, and Ali screams as she dodges as well. I stand back up to find the dragonspawn standing there, mocking me. It catches the Seeking Dagger with its right hand, then tucks it into its own inventory.

"Kill me and get it back." Its voice is deep and rumbles darkly. "If you can, of course."

It stands nearly a head taller than me, maybe two. It takes

a deep breath. Ali rapidly scrambles away, limping a bit on her left side, and I dive to the side. With that, the dragonspawn exhales a massive blast of searing, acidic flame. The conveyer belt in between the two of us is transformed into a little pool of metal gunk, and I barely escape; my own legs get hit with a bit of the fire, which hurts a lot more than I might have expected. Anyway, I come out of the room and throw my Dagger of Doom at the monster, but it catches that one too and adds *it* to its inventory.

[ChaosRider: You're not doing so hot, Jason!]

[Originalgoth: This *is* entertaining!]

[ShadowDancer: Come on, Jason! Pull it together!]

I grit my teeth and draw out my Photonic Dagger, and the dragonspawn simply chuckles.

"Getting desperate yet?"

"No." I give my head a small shake.

"Well, then." The dragonspawn slowly reaches behind its back and draws out a dragonbone sword. It's a massive weapon, carved with a great many evil-looking runes, and seems to exude an evil sort of magic. "When this sword wounds you, it will absorb some of your life force. Your essence. Your blood will make it more and more powerful, lending itself to your defeat. Fight me and die, boy."

I glance at the sword. I don't really like the look of it. It has a *long* reach, and evil runes are never something to mess around with. That said, I have to get to him, and if that means going through the sword, I'll just have to go through the sword.

I quickly draw out the Dagger of Kings and throw that one. Unsurprisingly, the dragonspawn catches it and tucks it into its inventory almost without blinking. I add my Dagger of Damage to the mix, and the dragonspawn again catches it and tucks it into its inventory. Then, with one final toss, I fling Blub at it. It's a slick move, and the dragonspawn snatches the little exploding pufferfish out of the air as it slowly stalks toward me.

KA-BOOM!

Seemingly understanding the urgency of the situation, Blub explodes with a good deal more force than he did last time. Admittedly, I don't have a large sample to draw from, but it looks good to me and it knocks the dragonspawn sideways, allowing me to charge forward and leap at the monster. It recovers almost instantly and slashes upward with its sword, and I parry with my Photonic Dagger. That makes it stumble—not much, but slightly—and I transform my Photonic Dagger into a sword and stab it in the chest.

At least, I try to. The thing is *fast,* and it spins out of the way before I can land more than a simple scratch on its scales. It uses the spin to hit me with the flat side of its sword, knocking me flat on the ground. As I struggle to rise, it stands above me and stabs downward. I roll to the side, and the blade slams into the stone floor, driving down several inches into the black rock. I try to stand back up, but the monster simply kicks me, sending me rolling across the floor once more, and lunges. The sword grazes my arm this time as I stand back up, and I witness a small amount of my blood get sucked down the length of the sword. The runes on the blade start to glow, and I suddenly feel weak.

"You see? Now, behold my power!"

The dragonspawn opens its mouth and exhales another

blast of acidic damage, forcing me to dodge-roll one more time. As I stand back up, it attacks, its sword moving faster than ever. I use my sword of light to block desperately, but this monster is good. Two more strikes hit me in the arm and torso, and a bit more of my blood is sucked down into the sword. Not good. Not by any stretch of the imagination. I brace myself, then lash out, catching its sword with all my might. We lock blades, and I grit my teeth.

"Alright, dragonspawn," I mutter. "What's your name?"

"It would be incomprehensible in your tongue," the dragonspawn retorts. "You are a lower life form, and I will not share such secrets with the likes of you."

"Then I'll just have to call you incomprehensible," I sneer back. "Doesn't roll off the tongue, but it'll work well enough."

"What game are you playing?"

I take a deep breath. "The only type worth playing. The type that dis—"

Boom!

An arrow flashes through the air and hits the great sword, breaking the deadlock. Thankfully, I was ready for it. I lunge forward, and this time I land a good hit on the dragonspawn's torso. Once more, it pivots out of the way, but it's enough. Ali lets loose a barrage of arrows, one a second at least, and the dragonspawn turns toward her.

"Pathetic ranged warrior!" It lifts its hand, and a reddish magic begins to swirl about its palm. "You will feel the wrath of—"

"Skill: Speed," I murmur. The world slows, and the dragonspawn looks over its shoulder. I mentioned it was fast, right? The spell activates in its palm as I lunge forward, and it turns toward me. I slash upward with my sword, feeling as though I'm fighting against a warrior who simply . . . I don't know, just got out of bed or something? Slower than usual, maybe, but not by much. Thankfully, it's *just* enough, and I cut off the dragonspawn's wrist just as the red magic leaps from its palm. That causes the spell to discharge down into the ground instead of up at Ali, which, of course, causes a rather horrid effect.

Instead of exploding, a black hole seems to form, with red magic sucking in everything around it—stone, boxes, and a few bottles of Pumped! all get sucked inside. I scream and jump back. The dragonspawn isn't so lucky, and its left foot gets caught in the swirling magic. It snarls and cuts the foot off with its blade, then jumps away. Time chooses that moment to return to normal, and I brace myself.

As everything speeds back up, I find myself sliding toward the hole, while the dragonspawn leans up against the remains of the conveyer belt and digs its claws into the metal. After a few seconds, the hole collapses on itself, and I let out a gasp of relief. The dragonspawn, now missing both its left limbs, looks at me and nods. I notice that the runes on the sword are now swirling with a dark energy, the sort that likely comes from absorbing the dragonspawn's very own life force.

"You . . . You win," it whispers softly. "Give . . . my regards . . . to Krak."

With that, it sets the blade down on the ground and falls upon it. The tip punches up through its back, and it screams. Darkness flows up from its body, flashing into the sword as if it's being eaten, and the dragonspawn's whole body dries up as it gets desiccated by its own weapon. A few moments later, the corpse is little more than a husk that crumbles as the sword falls over and lands on the ground with a clatter. I see all my stolen daggers laying in the dust and Blub floats through the air to me as the dust settles.

"Ugh . . ." I grimace and step toward the sword, only to pause as I hear a chuckling noise. A portal opens nearby, and the sword slowly rises up, points itself at me, and then flies through the crackling energy hilt-first. Somehow, I have a feeling that I'll be seeing it again, and I can't say that I'm looking forward to that meeting.

"Well, that's done." Ali slowly walks over through the ruins of the conveyers. The Pumped! factory is rapidly being torn apart, and I have to say that I'm a bit saddened at the prospect of tearing apart something so unique, but . . . Well, I have more important things to think about than the minimum wages of dark elf warriors. "Shall we get moving?"

With a flash, the portal on the ceiling opens, and the small black dragon from before falls down to land with a crash. At the same moment, all the on-break workers come back out, and a great many eyes stare at us. Slowly, the dragon flaps back up through the portal, and all the workers turn around and walk back into the break room. Apparently, we're above their pay grade.

"Yes." I finally turn to Ali, and nod firmly. "Yes, I think we should."

CHAPTER TWENTY-SEVEN

We spend a few moments looking around the room, trying to figure out where to go next. I don't think I need to point out that there are *many* different paths that the spider, and Columbus, might have taken. The issue is figuring out which one, and I unfortunately don't have a good way of doing that.

"Alright, my favorite chat-people." I slowly turn in a circle, looking at the assorted paths. "Does *anyone* have a clue where we should go?"

[FireStorm: Not a one, Jason! Sorry!]

[IceQueen: Beats me!]

[ShadowDancer: I . . . actually might.]

[RazorEdge: Really? How???]

[ShadowDancer: Simple mathematics. Give me just a minute.]

I stand there observing the destruction and carnage for several long moments. Suddenly, the chat comes back on.

[ShadowDancer: Take the middle one. The conveyer belt with all the green lights.]

I nod and turn in that direction. Each conveyer has slightly different markings, and this one, as mentioned, has some green lights flickering up and down the length of it. Ali and I take off in that direction, and I ball my hands into fists. Whatever's down here, I'm going to be ready for it.

I hope.

The tunnel we enter is narrow, and the conveyer takes up the majority of it. I can see light in the distance, a fiery sort of light, and gulp. What exactly are we heading into? I glance at the conveyer to check and find a number of boxes of . . . French fries? They smell quite wonderful, actually, and have a fresh goldenness that makes my stomach growl. Frankly, I'd probably grab one if not for the unusual circumstances of their existence.

A moment later, we reach the end of the tunnel . . . and at that point, my appetite dies away entirely.

The room is a lava one, not unlike many other such rooms I've seen throughout the assorted dungeons and rifts I've visited. This one, though, has a massive upside-down lizard skull suspended over the lava, held in place by giant chains that seem to be connected to a large crank on the wall. The inside of the skull is hollowed out, with an immense amount of cooking oil bubbling and churning where the brain should be. There are, of course, massive wire racks that are being raised and lowered into said boiling oil, frying up the French fries. Several flame elves march around, checking on everything, while an obese half-giant marches around supervising. He holds an enormous meat cleaver in his hands and chuckles darkly.

"There we go! Fry 'em up, send 'em out! I hope they get this conveyer back online soon. Dragon must've knocked it loose again. Beats me why they don't just cook the thing and get a half-decent griffin to do the work for us, but that's corporate for you, I suppose! Only care about the bottom line."

My jaw drops, and Ali reaches over and pushes it back up. I grit my teeth, angry that this isn't the right way . . . until I spy a small cavern on the other side of the room, which leads onward into the facility. I take a deep breath, then nod to Ali.

"You stay here. I've got a plan. Give me one of your teleporter arrows."

Ali nods and pulls one of them out of her inventory, which she hands to me. I then use Innocence to cloak myself, at least somewhat, and slowly walk out into the room.

"Ah-ha! There we go! Finally, some new blood around here!" The half-giant laughs and claps his overweight belly. "That no-good boss of ours was supposed to have a whole new shipment of workers coming in! Did you happen to see 'em?"

I nod slowly. "Yeah, I saw them."

"Are they 'eaded this way?"

"Not . . . exactly." I wince.

The half-giant lets out a string of curses that would peel the paint off the hull of a ship. When he calms down, he starts swinging his cleaver in anger.

"Well, they need to get down here *pronto!* I've lost thirty workers today alone, and I'm not going to be able to make quota if I don't get more people! Go on, get to your post, and *please* tell someone that we're short staffed around here!"

I nod and scamper past the lava pits and the oil, then pass through the tunnel and into the next room. There, as I come out, I find myself facing . . . Well, essentially, in the middle of the room there's a massive machine that seems to be a mass of spinning gears and belts. The top of it has a funnel, just below the edge of a small cliff. The bottom of it has a number of conveyer belts leading out. As I watch, elven workers herd a great many cattle, pigs, sheep, goats, and other such farm animals off the cliff and into the machine. Red spray drifts up from the top of the machine, while pressed hamburgers come out the bottom. The burgers are then carried to a number of grills—heated by more lava pools, of course—where goblins fry them up and toss them into boxes to be shipped out. As the last of the pigs go stampeding over the cliff, two of the workers slip and fall in after them, and the half-giant's lost worker total rises to thirty-two. It then shoots up to thirty-three as the uniform of one of the goblins catches on fire from getting too close to the lava pool.

"You know what? I don't recognize your race." The half-giant thumps up behind me and puts a hand on my shoulder. "For that matter, you look like a 'uman. I don't like 'umans, if you get my drift."

I turn around and look up at him. "Maybe I'm a better human than usual?"

"No, don't think that's it." The half-giant leans down and scrutinizes my face. "There's something funny going on here."

I wince, then draw out the Dagger of Doom and stab the monster in the chin. His jowls quiver under the impact, and his eyes seem to suddenly come into focus.

WHAM!

As it turns out, half-giants can pack *quite* the punch, and his blow sends me flashing across the room to slam into the meat machine. The arrow falls to the ground and vanishes as Ali is teleported to my side, and she looks about.

"Are we safe?"

Clang!

The meat cleaver slams into the machine in between our heads, sticking solidly in the steel. The half-giant snarls and jumps down into the room, then stomps toward us, drawing out another cleaver at the same time.

"Nope. Objectively not," I answer. "Anything you could do right now would be appreciated."

I grit my teeth and charge forward at the mini-boss. Ali fires an arrow over my shoulder. It hits him in the gut but doesn't seem to affect him at all. Three more find their target, and he starts to look a bit like a pincushion, but he doesn't seem to mind. Instead, he simply slashes at me with his cleaver, which I dodge only to lunge in close and stab him with my Photonic Dagger. It transforms into a sword as I drive it deep into his gut, and he grunts in pain. The distinct problem with this arrangement is that I'm now *very* close to him, and he grabs me around the neck.

"I'll 'ave you pay for this," he whispers. Suddenly, he flings me up into the air, and I land solidly on the cliff overlooking the meat machine. At the far end, a portal flickers to let out a herd of cattle.

No. A herd of bulls.

"Bring 'em home!" the giant calls out from below. "Run 'em in!"

Dark elves charge out of the portal as well, driving the cattle frantically along the cliff. Two of the cattle slip and fall off early, but the rest seem mad with fear—which, all things considered, is totally understandable—and charge headlong at the meat machine . . . and, by extension, at me.

I look around for any way to escape but see none. With no other option, I charge forward and try to slip between the charging animals. No such luck. The lead bull simply turns and hits me with his horns, knocking me sideways. I brace myself, and three more of the animals lower their heads and charge at me. My feet slide backward as they hit, and I gasp with the exertion. There simply isn't enough friction to hold them back! They're pushing me toward the horrid machine, and I don't know what I can possibly do to stop it.

"Jump!" Ali calls out from below. "Jason, jump!"

I nod, though I know she can't see it, and leap upward with all my might. Suddenly, I find myself running on top of the bulls. A wide smile spreads across my face as I leap above the great heaving mass of black cattle . . . at least for a split second.

If you've never tried to run across the backs of a herd of cattle, save yourself a great deal of pain and never, *ever* try it. I fall flat on my face almost instantly, and the herd of cattle thunders over me like I'm a welcome mat in front of a retail store on Black Friday. It *hurts,* but on the flip side, they're not pushing me off the cliff anymore. When the last one runs past, I slowly peel myself off the ground and stand up, and the dark elves—who are all wearing Pumped! chaps and leather cowboy jackets, I should point out—all turn and look at me like I'm a zombie come back to life.

"If you know what's good for you, you'll turn around, walk back through that portal, and leave this dimension *far* behind." I take a deep breath, then grab a bottle of Pumped!

out of my inventory to heal from the herd of bulls. Just to show them how much business I mean, I bite the bottle cap off with my teeth, then spit it over the edge of the cliff into the meat machine. The elves get the idea, and they turn around and walk away. I let out a long breath . . . only to hear a loud *thunk* behind me.

"Looks like you and I have a bit more business to deal with." The half-giant stalks toward me, twirling his meat cleaver. He's standing between me and the meat machine, and an idea pops into my head. Of course, I don't have the faintest idea how I'm going to execute said plan, but tossing him into the meat machine seems like the best way to kill him. "Any last words?"

"Not yet, but I'll make sure to make them epic when the time comes." I puff out my cheeks and ready my sword of light. "What about you?"

The half-giant chuckles. "I was thinking the same thing. Come at me whenever you're ready."

He plants his feet and readies his cleaver, and I take my own stance. Waiting for me to come to him is probably a good plan. He looks like the patient type, and with the amount of health he has, he can withstand a few hits from my daggers. That means I have to come up with something, and—

Snort.

As it turns out, one lone bull was left behind, and it comes charging out of the portal. The dark elf workers scream and dive out of the way, and the thing comes charging straight at me. I glance over my shoulder at it, and the half-giant moves to attack as I find myself distracted. I'm caught between a rock and a hard place, and that means I have to do something clever.

I jump.

Alright, so it's not the *cleverest* thing in the world, but as I jump over the head of the bull, I grab its horns and sling it in the direction of the half-giant.

"Rock, meet hard place!" I let go of the bull and land on the ground once more as the mighty beast slams into the monster. They both let out startled gasps of air, and the half-giant raises his cleaver. Before he can cut it down, though, an explosive arrow flashes through the air and hits him in the chest. The combination of bull and dynamite sends him reeling backward, and I rush forward to add my own trademark attack into the midst.

As it turns out, there is no need. A second explosive arrow hits the cliff beneath his feet, making the whole thing crumble, and the half-giant and the bull both tumble backward into the machine. I grimace as I draw up short by the edge of the cliff, looking down into the wide mouth of the machine. There are more spinning blades and compacting gears than I can wrap my brain around, and I let out a long breath. Just looking down into it makes me queasy, and I slowly turn back.

Which is when I come up against the dark elf cowboys. They all have sneers on their faces, and before I can react, one of them raises a bow and fires an explosive arrow into my chest. Alright, maybe it *wasn't* Ali that fired the arrow. I'm knocked backward and feel the ground give way beneath me. Suddenly, I'm falling, and the whir of blades and gears echoes in my ears.

I'm falling into the machine, and I don't have a *clue* how I'm going to come out alive.

CHAPTER TWENTY-EIGHT

B*ZZZZZZZZZZT!*
Grunk-unk-unk-unk-unk-unk-unk-unk-unk-unk!
PZZZZZZZZZZZEW!

I bounce once off the metal funnel and fall into the machine. Now, I know what you're thinking. Blood! Gore! A rather tragic and gross end for the wonderful hero, Jason Lee. Thankfully, that's not what happens. Instead, as it turns out, the blades on the machine have a base damage of three, which they deal out about a dozen times every second. Now, I'm not a tank, but my damage threshold is higher than that, which means that I come through it alright.

Well, not alright. It hurts worse than a root canal, and it doesn't look like the machine has been cleaned in years, so as I'm sucked through the guts of this thing—breaking all the whirling saw blades, bending the axels, snapping all the belts, and ruining all the meat presses—I also get coated in the hair and blood of countless different types of animals. I have feathers stuck in my teeth, hoof particles in my ear. It's . . . it's really gross. That said, when the machine spits me out the far side, I'm alive, and that's more than can be said for the half-giant. I groan and sit upright once I reach the goblins, who all decide that cooking me is above their pay grade and turn and walk away without a fight. I swing my legs over the side of the conveyer belt and stand up, casting a single look at the smoking ruins of the meat machine.

"Jason Lee." Columbus's voice echoes through the air, and I ball my hands into fists. A portal opens just in front of me, and he slowly emerges, shaking his head. "I have to admit, I'm impressed! Getting sucked through a meat grinder? Now *that's* the sort of thing you don't hear about every day. Beating up monsters? You can do that in spades. But *that?*" He points to the smoking machine. "Were it in my power, I'd give you a thousand experience points just for the entertainment of seeing you get sucked through it."

"You're all heart." I pluck a broken saw tooth out of my palm, then use it to start picking chicken bones out of my teeth. "Now, what have you done with John?"

"I *was* going to dangle him above the meat grinder to threaten you, but . . ." Columbus shrugs. "The long and the short of it is that I have something far better. Widow? Bring him down."

I glance up at the ceiling to see the massive spider, who lowers down a bundle of webbing. It lands next to Columbus, who puts his hands behind his back. I can't see any of John, not so much as a hand or foot, nor do I know where Ali has gotten to.

"Is he alright?" I demand.

"He's alive." Columbus looks down at the bundle as it gives a twitch. "Oh! Look! Here he is now."

As if in response to his voice, a great spider leg shoots out through the webbing. The chitin on the end has been sharpened into a deadly blade, and I ball my hands into fists. Several more of the insectile legs come shooting out and start working to carve away the webbing.

"What did you do to him?" I demand, stalking toward Columbus. The dark elf, though, simply raises a hand, and I slam into a force field that appears around his body.

"What did I do to him? The very same thing I'll be doing to thousands of humans across your planet," Columbus snaps. "Watch and learn, Jason Lee, why humanity will *never* defeat the dungeons."

A loud howl echoes from within the webs, and the last of it falls away. I find myself looking at John . . . except not. It's his body, mostly, but he has two spider legs coming out of each shoulder where his arms used to be and large cricket legs where his ordinary legs once were. His eyes are compound, unfocused, and his mouth seems to have mandibles tucked away inside.

"But how did you . . ." I pause. "The food. The Pumped! factory. You're going to distribute this curse through the food chain."

"Yes, indeed." Columbus nods. "It's actually been a work in progress for some time. You've probably eaten infected food yourself. But without augmentation, the best results that we've been able to produce have been mild irritation, maybe a bit of general frustration, sometimes mild anger. However, with something to give a boost to our abilities . . ."

"The stardust," I whisper softly.

"Yes, indeed. For what it's worth, he didn't surrender it willingly, but he's only a level twenty, and we have some *very* powerful pickpockets on our side." Columbus shrugs. "Now the stardust is in our possession, and we'll soon be shipping out a load of food that will turn somewhere around a hundred thousand humans into uncontrollable monsters. Nothing your world won't be able to weather, I'll admit that much, but it will cripple you even more than you already are, stretching your lines thin, and *that* will make it even easier to crush you." Columbus starts walking backward. "Wars aren't won by a single crushing victory, but by many little ones spread out over time. This is our next step. I wonder who will come out on top, you or John? Can you bear to kill your friend? Can you even manage it?"

I grit my teeth. Suddenly, an arrow flashes out of nowhere and hits Columbus in the heart. He gasps as a layer of ice starts to spread across his body, and he staggers backward. John, though, suddenly seems to focus. He turns to me, and a low snarl emerges from his lips.

"John, this isn't you. This is—"

WHAM!

If the half-giant could hit hard, John hits me like a freight train being powered by a lightspeed engine. I'm thrown across the room like a cannonball and hit the wall with *immense* force. When the dust clears, I find that I've been pressed into the wall several feet, stuck inside a large crater that I seem to have created upon impact. John is stalking toward me, moving slowly and purposefully, his insect legs waving about, his eyes locked upon mine.

"Alright . . ." I groan and pull my arms out of the stone. My vision blurs, and I force it back into focus. My health is hovering down in the black, only a few points above death, and I quickly chug several bottles of Pumped! before peeling myself out of the stone and dropping back to the ground. John is approaching rapidly, and I frankly don't know how I'm going to stop him. "Time . . . to get . . . to work."

I grit my teeth and charge forward as fast as I can, leaping across the ground in great bounds, and draw out the Dagger of Damage as well as the Seeking Dagger. I fling the Seeking Dagger as hard as I can, aiming behind him, and watch as it shoots off into the distance, curves around, and comes back. John, not surprisingly, sees it and spins, then batters it to the ground. In that moment, I activate Speed and rush forward.

The Dagger of Damage blurs in my hand as I stab him half a dozen times in the blink of an eye.

[Damage Dealt: 2]

[Damage Dealt: 4]

[Damage Dealt: 8]

[Damage Dealt: 16]

[Damage Dealt: 32]

It almost hurts me to do, but it doesn't seem to bother him in the slightest. He starts to turn around, and I stab him two more times before I dive out of the way. Time goes back to normal, and with a great *crack*, all four of his arms lash out at me. The sharpened tips smash into the stone all around me, and he growls as he starts to crush the stone into rubble.

"John, this isn't you!" I kick him in the face. It's rather like kicking a mountain. His mouth opens, and the mandibles emerge, snapping down toward my face. I grit my teeth, then hold out my hand. Blub falls into my palm, responding to my mental command, and I throw him straight into John's mouth.

Now, invincible or not, having a Living Bomb explode in your mouth isn't pleasant. His head snaps back, and he's knocked backward into the air and comes down several feet away. I'm blasted back into the stone as well, and, head swimming, I climb to my feet and try to measure my next actions.

"Bjorn! Astrid! Burnie! Anyone who can help, I could use your assistance."

My pocket dimension opens, and my whole array of pets emerge. Well, all the ones that would be at all useful in this situation. John climbs back to his feet and lets out a hiss, and Burnie launches himself into the air.

FOOOOOOOOOOM!

A great blast of flame pours down around him. I can see John taking damage, but it's not nearly enough nor nearly fast enough. He simply ignores the pain and stalks through it, heading straight for us.

"Bjorn!"

Burnie lets up the attack, and Bjorn howls. A great blast of ice explodes across the ground, coating John in a thick layer of the stuff. It makes him pause for a few seconds, still as a statue, until he smashes his way through and keeps coming. Astrid howls, causing a rift to open in the ground and swallow him. As the stone slams back shut over his head, I let out a sigh of relief and pain . . . only for the insect arms to smash back upward from the stone, pulling him back to the land of the living. He lets out an angry hiss and gets to his feet, which rapidly reduces my options.

"I've got you, John!" Ali runs up from the side, bow twanging in her hand. She fires bolt after bolt after bolt into his body, making him stagger. Some of the arrows explode, some of them seem to burn him with acid, some of them cause ice to grow across portions of his body, but none of them stop him, or really even slow him down. "Maybe!"

I sigh, then nod and run forward. There's only one option I can see, and it's going to be a tough one. Still . . . desperate times, desperate measures, and all that. John snarls and jumps at me, and I duck under the blow, landing another slash along his lower torso.

[Damage Dealt: 256]

As I come out the other side, I spin to face him, and John spins and lashes out at me with all his legs in a whirling cyclone attack. I wait until it dies down, then lunge forward and strike him once more.

[Damage Dealt: 512]

The attacks seem to be wounding him but aren't doing nearly as much as I might have liked. I grit my teeth, and the two of us fall into a deadly dance. I hit him when I can and avoid being struck by him at all costs. Even a single scrape will probably kill me. I just have to get the damage from the dagger up to a reasonable level. As I battle onward, the damage climbs higher and higher, and he still just . . . takes it.

[Damage Dealt: 1,024]
[Damage Dealt: 2,048]
[Damage Dealt: 4,096]
[Damage Dealt: 8,192]
[Damage Dealt: 16,384]
[Damage Dealt: 32,768]

[Damage Dealt: 65,536]

[Damage Dealt: 131,072]

With that last strike, he's breathing pretty heavily, and a lot of blood is dripping down from his body. I brace myself and prepare for the next attack. Surely the next one will take him, right? I still don't *want* to kill him, of course, but he's *way* too powerful to subdue. I'm left without options, without possibilities, and as he swoons, I lunge forward one last time.

WHAM!

He blurs forward one last time, catching me under the chin. I'm blasted up into the ceiling of the cave so hard that I stick there for a moment, then fall down to the ground once more. I land right in front of him, and he makes a clicking sound and leans forward. Ali shoots two more arrows into his shoulder, but to no avail.

"I'm sorry, John," I whisper. "I . . . You're my best friend."

John's expressionless eyes stare down at me as he raises his legs for one last strike. And then . . . And then the Dagger of Damage, which had gotten stuck in the ceiling just like me, detaches and falls down.

[Damage Dealt: 262,144]

John screams a real human scream and collapses in a puddle of blood. I grimace and slowly rise, my health blinking at a point or two remaining, and look down at my friend. He's motionless, and I slowly walk over and kneel down at his side. With a loud *shlunk,* his insect body parts are transformed back into his human parts, leaving him human once more, though dead.

"I . . ." I can barely speak, and I look up at Ali. Even my chat has gone silent, which is the first time since the apocalypse started. "I had no choice. I . . ."

My eyes suddenly narrow. Down by his pocket, something glitters. Stardust. Only a grain or two, but it's something. I lick my finger, getting it wet, then wipe it across his clothing. The tip of my finger glitters, and, hardly daring to hope, I dip it into his mouth.

Nothing happens.

I sigh, and I slowly rise back to my feet. Ali joins me, and, leaving John in the puddle of blood, we start walking toward Columbus, who is frozen like a statue on the other side of the room amidst the ruins of his scheme. As I approach, I grab hold of the arrow embedded in him and yank it out, and he thaws and drops to the ground, gasping for air.

"I don't know how much health you have left, but I'm about to take the last bit of it," I hiss. "I'll throw you in that boiling skull. I'll fix the meat grinder and throw you in. I'll do something, anything, just to be rid of you and to make it painful at the same time."

Columbus chuckles, then shakes his head. "You're too late," he whispers. "The shipment has already gone out. The rest of this operation—it was nice, and I would have loved to continue it, but . . . at the end of the day, it was all geared toward this moment. The stardust has been processed into poison and the poison inserted into the food: Pumped! bottles, hamburgers, French fries. We didn't need long, and we didn't need to infect the whole shipment. Right now, as we stand here, people will be transforming. You're. Too. Late."

"We're never too late." John's hand stretches between the two of us and grabs hold of Columbus's shirt, hefting him into the air. Ali and I both cry out in surprise and delight, and we turn to find John standing there, tall and strong—though missing his shirt sleeves and pant legs, of course—with fire burning in his eyes. "And we're not going to stop until we've driven every last dungeon from the face of planet Earth."

Columbus sneers, though I see fear in his eyes. A moment later, John punches him in the chin, sending him flying back across the room. A portal opens just before he lands, and he vanishes with a crackle of energy. The portal then closes, long before we could have gotten there, and John lets out a long breath.

"You're alive!" Ali flings her arms around John, and I hold out my hand. He shakes it and sighs.

"I am. No thanks to you." He nods at me, though he has a smile on his face. "Do me a favor, will you? Keep that dagger of yours *far* away from me. A little paper cut with it would deal me . . . way more damage than I'm prepared to handle."

"You've got it." I nod with a smile. "I'm just glad you're back."

"Me too." John chuckles, then frowns down at the ground. "What's this?"

I glance down as well, and I find a glittering crystal. It's not one I recognize, and I quickly bend down and pick it up.

[Rift Crystal]

[Level: S]

[Details: Connected to Rift Number 197.62. Can open and close the main rift entrance and open portals into nearby dungeons.]

"Now *that's* useful." I whistle softly, then tuck the crystal into my inventory. "I think we control our own rift now. Open!"

Nothing happens, though I hear a distant crackle of energy that *might* be the rift's distant portal turning on. I sigh, then shrug.

"Do you think we'll see Columbus again?" Ali asks as we all start walking back toward the entrance.

"Somehow, I doubt that Krak is going to leave him alive." I chuckle. "He succeeded, but only *technically*, and we did manage to tear down his facility and expose his cover. More importantly, I think—"

The ground suddenly rumbles, and I blink in surprise. Ali freezes, and John glances at us.

"What's that?"

I shrug. "We might have bypassed a small boss fight to get to you quicker. It's probably still waiting to be defeated."

[GoldenShield: Actually, it just escaped into the city!]

[IceQueen: Yeah! The rift just opened and spat it out!]

[Originalgoth: I *wonder* who did that?]

I feel heat rise in my cheeks, and I cough. "Well, I'd sure hate to play the blame game. Everyone?" I glance at John and Ali. "I think we've got one more adventure together before we can call it quits for the day."

CHAPTER TWENTY-NINE

The three of us race back down the desolate halls of the Pumped! factory, winding our way through the ruined conveyers and over the bodies of dead workers. We take the spider's route back to the main cavern—the ceiling collapse blocked the primary entrance—and find ourselves looking at the enormous rift portal. The lightning crackles angrily, and I look down at the pile of debris. Sure enough, it's a whole lot smaller. The crab escaped. I was sort of hoping that it was just an elaborate prank on the part of the chat members, but . . . this will work.

"Should I teleport us through, just like last time?" Ali unstrings her bow.

"What? Not a chance." I jump down and start running over the debris. "You couldn't pay me enough to do that again!"

"Are you kidding me? It was fun!" Ali calls down.

"Yeah and getting sucked through the meat grinder was

fun too!" I grit my teeth and dive forward through the portal. As per usual, it's fantastically unpleasant, and I roll out the far side and stand up. The crab has just crashed through the wall of the Pumped! factory and seems to be contemplating jumping into the bay. Ali appears next to me with a flash, and John swoons.

"Yeah, I'm with Jason on that one." He puffs out his cheeks. "It's like getting thrown into a blender and then shot through a garden hose and sprayed onto a cactus garden."

"What? All the lights, the colors?" Ali seems flabbergasted. "You two are actually serious?"

"Yeah. Worst experience *ever*," John confirms.

"Worse than getting your butt kicked by yours truly?" I raise an eyebrow. "I can pack a pretty good punch."

"I could say the same in reverse." John raises an eyebrow.

"Yes, yes. You're both very impressive." Ali steps forward and raises her bow. "Shall we get on with killing this monster?"

John balls his hands into fists and gives a small nod. "Let's do it."

Ali lets the arrow fly, and it flashes through the air to slam against the rear shell of the monster. There's a small explosion—I mean, it's technically a decently sized one, but set against the *massive* crab, it looks rather pathetic. The monster freezes, then slowly turns around and snaps its pincers.

Against the gloom of the night sky overhead, I can barely see the thing, and I sigh.

"Alright, let's get this started. Portal, close. Mr. Wang, is there any way you could get us some light?"

The portal snaps shut with a *zap*, and several spotlights flood the area. The crab winces, and I nod.

"Let's go!"

The three of us charge forward, racing onward toward the crab. Ali drops to one knee and starts shooting arrows, fiery darts that lance through the air to hit the crab's eyes and mouthparts. John catches hold of an immense I-beam, swings himself up into the rafters, and smashes through the front of the factory like a wrecking ball. He comes down on the upper shell of the crab with an enormous *boom* and blasts the thing down into the sand of the shore. I reach it a moment later and whip out my Dagger of Damage. After all, why not?

[Damage Dealt: 1]

[Damage Dealt: 2]

[Damage Dealt: 4]

The familiar pattern begins, and I leap up onto the back of the thing, stabbing as frantically as I can. John punches the shell of the monster once more, cracking it down the middle, and the crab seems to howl with pain. Suddenly, it reaches up and grabs John, only to fling him off into the distance. I see him crash against one of the immense smoke-stacks, but then he's lost in the darkness, and I turn my attention back to the crab.

Whack!

Another claw hits me from the side, and I'm thrown down to the gravel beach below. I grit my teeth and roll out of the way as it tries to squash me, then jump to my feet. Quickly, I draw out my dagger and stab upward, only belatedly realizing that it's not the Dagger of Damage.

It's the Dagger of Doom.

I haven't tried employing it against the crab since I tried and failed to use it against the suits of armor. After all, if something's covered in armor, you just assume it's immune to all forms of damage. As the dagger strikes home, though, a message appears.

[Dagger of Doom has discovered a [Lightning] weakness.]

A little bit of lightning flickers from the blade, and the crab seems to jump away in response to it, but it's too little to really do a whole lot. That said, it gets my brain spinning.

"Lightning?" I frown in thought. "That's interesting."

The crab spins and lashes out at me with a claw, and I'm forced to dodge out of the way. In the distance, I hear something crack, which I can only assume is John's handiwork. I backpedal across the street as Ali continues to pelt the thing with arrows, and I call out to her.

"Ali! Do you have any electric arrows?"

"No!" she returns. "I had a few, but I've used them all up! Why?"

"We need electricity, and a lot of it." I frown. "Where's the closest power station?"

[ChaosRider: There's a power station at the corner of Maple and 232nd.]

[IceQueen: Ooh! And another at Oak and 323rd!]

"Pretend I don't know how to navigate this part of New York," I snap. "I need directions. I need . . ." My voice trails off as a thought strikes me, and I glance over at Ali. "Have you ever wanted to stay in a fancy hotel?"

"Uh . . ." Ali raises an eyebrow. "Not that I *dis*like you, but I don't think this is really the time to be asking me on a date."

I let out a puff of air. "It was *supposed* to be an epic punch line, but I suppose we'll just have to go for it. John! I need—"

CRASH!

One of the Pumped! factory's smokestacks flashes down out of the sky and hits the crab dead-on. It explodes into an immense cloud of rubble, covering the entire beach in dust. Silence seems to fall . . . And then, with a thunderous roar, the crab comes charging out of the darkness, claws flashing, ready to destroy us.

"Mr. Wang! Get John and Ali into position!" I race down the street, and Lightfax explodes out of my pocket dimension. As she runs past me, I catch hold of her mane and swing up onto her back. "Crabby, you're on me!"

The crab snarls and spins, confused, but as helicopters swoop down and carry away the other two attackers, the crab decides to go ahead and come after me. Just like planned. I charge down the middle of the street, Lightfax's mane streaming out behind her, as the crab thunders along behind. Cars swerve wildly out of the way as we start to get to more populated areas. I even catch a glimpse of a few smaller bosses, just emerging from their portals, turn and dive back inside as they glimpse the great beast.

I should note that the crab is small enough to fit between buildings, but only *just*, and more than a few fire escapes are knocked asunder by the jagged edges of its shell. As we draw near to Mr. Harrison's hotel, I make Lightfax run faster, outdistancing the crab. By now, despite being surrounded by a *great* many things that it would almost certainly enjoy crushing, it's become so focused on me that it follows along with laser precision. Overhead, helicopters flash back and forth, but no one engages.

Good. Maybe that means we'll actually get a chance to win.

In front of the hotel, guests stream out as I approach. The

crab tears around the final corner and rages toward me, smashing dozens of cars along the sides of the street. Suddenly, I catch a glimpse of Ali in the doorway, complete with an arrow attached to a long, thin cable. Good. I come to a stop just in front of the door, and she raises her bow.

"Now!"

There's a sharp *twang*, and her arrow flashes across the distance and sticks in the shell of the monster. At that very moment, someone down below throws the switch, and the full capacity of the nuclear generator is sent through the cable and into the crab.

It's hard to describe just what the crab looks like in that moment. Lightning arcs from shell to flesh, from eye stalk to eye stalk, from mandible to mandible. Sparks explode from the top of the shell like a fountain firework, and flames explode from the places where the legs touch the street. It's an incredible pyrotechnic display, and all I can do is whistle and shake my head at it.

"There's nothing quite like a good—"

BOOM!

John, having leaped off the top of the hotel, falls almost thirty stories and hits the shell with the force of an asteroid. This time he punches clean through and lands on the street below in a perfect superhero pose, then climbs back to his feet as the crab sways. The electricity stops sparking as the cable overloads and melts, and the crab is left charred, zapped, and cored. I slowly walk up to the thing and draw out the Dagger of Kings, then give it a twirl in my hand. I have to admit, it *does* look quite spectacular, especially in the low light of the night.

"Alright, Mr. Crab." I look up at the immense beast and take a deep breath. "Time to die."

With that, I jab the weapon deep into the bottom of its head. That blow serves to take out its last few remaining health points, and the monster slowly topples to the side and lands with a resounding *crash*. Of course, doing so crushes several cars and knocks a fire hydrant over, but . . . I'm too excited to be held back by such small details. I grin from ear to ear and turn to my friends, who both walk over and pat me on the back.

"A job well done." Ali nods with a smile.

"Indeed." I look over the charred corpse. "And a fitting end to a *very* long day."

"Hey! I got five levels from killing that thing!" Ali suddenly grins.

"I got two." John scowls. "Lucky."

"Hey, I'm way lower than you are. It makes sense that I—"

I chuckle as the two of them argue and open up my own interface. There, I find that I have earned four levels, bringing me up to a solid thirty-five. Not too shabby. I make a mental note to choose my rewards once I get back to my apartment. Suddenly, I realize that I've been awake for a *very* long time, and my weary body starts to sag.

"Alright." I turn and start walking down the street. "I don't know about the two of you, but I'd love to sit down and have an ice-cold Pumped! while kicking my feet up. I need to rest, and I think I know just where to do it."

CHAPTER THIRTY

As it turns out, I do *not* actually know where to do it. Remember that giant fireball that tore through my apartment back when Columbus revealed that he had hidden the stardust in my refrigerator? Yeah, well, as it turns out, while we were fighting our way through the Pumped! rift, a whole crew of firefighters was fighting the blaze that had kicked off there. They managed to salvage everything below the top three floors . . . but my penthouse went up in smoke, along with the spare penthouses that Mr. Wang had purchased just in case the upper ones were blown away.

"And you're sure we can't just buy the penthouse right below the damage line?" I ask on the phone as the helicopter hovers near the place where the helipad had once been.

"I'm sorry, but our insurance premiums have already gone through the roof," the secretary says. "If you buy another room in our building, we'll have to pay. There's just no way it's happening. I'm sorry."

I sigh, and the line goes dead. Slowly, I turn and look at the others, and Ali shrugs.

"If you want, we can all crash over at my place."

Soon, Mr. Wang's helicopters deposit the three of us in Central Park, just across the street from the large apartment complex that Ali has been putting together for displaced dungeon crawlers.

"Come on!" Ali waves her hand. "It's not the Ritz, but it'll do well enough."

I nod and follow, and John comes along as well. We walk through the front doors, and Ali waves at the sleepy-looking nighttime receptionist. The walls are all made of plywood and Sheetrock, at least the walls that are actually anything more than simple wooden frames. We make our way down into the basement, where a few slightly more solid rooms are put together, and soon find ourselves in a cramped room with two beds and very little floor space. I sit down on one, and John sits down next to me, while Ali drops down onto the second one and flops out.

"Ahh! This feels nice."

I can only nod in agreement. "I haven't slept in . . . Pfft, I don't even know how long it's been at this point. I got the stardust, and then the next morning, everything began. It's been a *wild* ride."

"Indeed, it has." The door pops open, and Mr. Wang strides inside, a bright smile across his face. "And, thanks to you, the streets are now safer, another plan has been foiled, and the world is a bit better."

"Except for that shipment that got out," I point out. "According to Columbus—"

"We intercepted the shipment." Mr. Wang shakes his head. "As soon as the report came through, I used my considerable influence with the United Nations to freeze shipments of fast food all across the world. It wasn't hard to figure out which shipments were coming from the rift, since they were already cooked and that *very* clearly defies a great many FDA regulations. All the requisite food was destroyed, or is being destroyed at this very moment, and the world is safe! At least from that threat, I should say."

"Well, thank you." I nod to him. "Much appreciated."

"I couldn't handle things without you guys, and you couldn't handle them without me." Mr. Wang shrugs. "That's the arrangement we have, and I doubt it will change anytime soon. I'll have you back in a penthouse just as soon as possible, and I'll have more jobs for you starting tomorrow."

"I'm looking forward to the work, but I don't need another penthouse." I shake my head. "Maybe a bunker, but nothing fancy."

"A bunker, eh?" Mr. Wang frowns in thought. I can already see the gears spinning, and I have to wonder just what I'm about to find myself living in next. "I'll see what I can do! The president of the United States owes me a favor or two, so I'll see what I can swing. In the meantime, you get some rest and leave the world-saving to other people for a few hours. Deal?"

"Deal." I nod.

Mr. Wang starts to turn away, then turns back. "Oh! One more thing. That little Rift Crystal you have?"

I roll my eyes. "You'd like it?"

"Absolutely. I've been thinking of branching into fast food for some time now, and I imagine that the concept of eating dinner *inside* a rift would appeal to a great many people." Mr. Wang shrugs. "I'll pay you a cool million for it."

"A billion, and you'll pay it to Ali for the assorted construction and good-works things she does." I flip the crystal to him, and he catches it.

"Done. Ali, you'll find the money in your bank account when you wake up." Mr. Wang folds his hands in front of himself and bows, then turns and marches out through the door once more. It claps shut with a *bang*, and I let out a long sigh.

"Well, now that that's all done, let's get some sleep." I yawn and stretch, flopping back on the bed.

"Well, as tired as I may be, I'm not sharing a bed." John chuckles and climbs to his feet. He flops onto the floor, making the whole building shake. "See you all in the morning."

"And what will you be doing then?" I ask him. "Off to save the streets again?"

"I'm not working for Mr. Wang." John shrugs. "But, as you seem to attract trouble like honey attracts flies, know that I'll be ready to help you beat down anything that comes your way. In fact, I look forward to it."

He yawns, and within seconds, he's snoring loudly. I chuckle, then sigh and stare up at the ceiling. Sleep is tugging at my eyelids, and my chat goes dark as my body registers the onset of sleep, but I don't quite pass out just yet.

"Jason?" Ali whispers softly. "You still awake?"

"Yeah," I murmur back. "What's up?"

"I'm just . . . thinking about Krak," Ali answers.

"Yeah. Me too." I nod. "I have to admit, the subtlety of it does sound like him. Sneaking a transformative poison into the population is clever, but it doesn't quite seem right."

"I know. Krak was trying to rise up in dungeon rank, not take over the world." Ali laughs slightly. "From what I could tell, he seemed more interested in fighting his fellow dungeon lords than fighting humans."

"I think that's pretty accurate," I confirm. "Which leaves us with only a few options. Option one: he's changed. Option two: it wasn't actually Krak. Option three: this was all part of some larger scheme that we won't fully see until later."

"Options two and three aren't mutually exclusive," Ali answers.

"Trust me, I'm well aware of that fact." I let out a long sigh. "I do think it's one or both of those, though. When all this business started, all I was hearing was that the dungeon lords were getting cleverer. They were getting *ideas*, and it was all because of Krak. This business with the food: it was clever, but it wasn't particularly *brilliant*. Krak, on the other hand, was brilliant. Is brilliant, wherever he is." I think for a few long moments, trying to get it all sorted in my head. "Let's assume for a moment that it *was* Krak. How does it help him advance? Maybe it shows his initiative to a larger power, this mysterious queen. Maybe it was all a cover for something else. Maybe he really needed the stardust for something entirely different, and the whole thing was a charade to get us off the scent." I shrug. "I don't have the faintest idea, and if we open up the door to it being someone other than Krak, the options become so convoluted and endless that we could be here for days just trying to sort through it."

"Yeah." Ali's voice is a mere whisper. "In that case, get some sleep. We'll talk in the morning, maybe after you've cleared a dungeon or two. Whatever's happening, I bet it'll come gunning for you quickly enough."

"Fair." I nod. "Goodnight, Ali."

Her only answer is a snore, and I chuckle. I spread out in the bed, and my eyes flutter closed. The bed is a bit lumpy, but it's really not bad as far as mattresses go, and I feel myself sinking into the foam, sinking into slumb—

"Level up." I sit bolt upright in bed. "I forgot to level up! Well, I'm leveled, I just need to get my rewards."

As I wake fully back up, my chat reappears.

[ChaosRider: Whoa! Glad I didn't log off yet. It's almost morning, Jason. What are you doing awake?]

[DarkCynic: Yeah, get some rest! We want you at the top of your game tomorrow!]

[FireStorm: Besides, you've earned it! You know that, right?]

"I'll get sleep, I'll get sleep." I wave my hand. "I just thought you all would want to see my new gear and equipment, eh?"

The chat goes wild, and I select the first of my four bonuses. There's a flash of light, and a new dagger appears in my hand.

[Weapon Acquired: Rainbow Dagger]

[Level: B]

[Details: Can rotate between Fire, Lightning, Ice, Water, and Acid damage. Unlock more damage types through use.]

"Now, that's cool!" I smile and give the dagger a few practice stabs. "I don't know exactly how useful it's going to be, but it looks *incredible*."

Indeed, the blade shimmers with all seven colors of the rainbow, rather like an oil slick, and as I twirl it in my hand, light seems to shimmer throughout the room. It's a flashy sort of weapon if nothing else, and I have to admit that I like it.

[RazorEdge: SO COOL!!! I can't wait to see you liven up the dungeons with that thing!]

[ViperQueen: Time to bring back the seventies! Tie dye all the way!]

[DarkCynic: It kinda hurts to look at, I think.]

I chuckle a bit, then stow away the weapon and turn to the next reward. This time I select a skill, and with a flash, it appears.

[Skill Acquired!]

[Duplicate: One of your pets will be duplicated for a period of 60 seconds.]

"Also quite useful." I start to grin as the possibilities flash through my mind. There are a great many of them, no doubt about that.

[ShadowDancer: Ahh, yeah! We could see two Bjorns tag-teaming a boss!]

[LunarEclipse: Or two Blubs. Can you imagine *two* Living Bombs?]

[GoldenShield: Or two *Burnies!* They could light a place up, no doubt about that!]

I laugh as I imagine the possibilities, then think for a moment as I ponder my next reward. After a long pause, I select another weapon. I know, it seems like I'm wavering, but I can't really keep track of my long list of skills, and I *can* keep track of my cool weapons. There's a flash of light, and yet another dagger appears in my hands. This one, though, is a good bit longer than some of the others. Honestly, it's almost a cross between a sword and a dagger, and it has a hook on the end that, if swung backward, could probably deal quite a lot of painful damage.

[Weapon Acquired: Enlarged Dagger]

[Level: C]

There are no details with it. It's *just* a weapon, with no

particular magic associated with it, which is odd. Still, it looks like a nice weapon, and if I'm being honest, sometimes it's nice not to have a long list of magical properties to keep track of. I add that one to my inventory as well, then let out a long breath. There's only one option I haven't taken yet, and with a nod, I choose the new pet.

There's a pause, and for a moment, I wonder if the system is broken. Then, with a flash of light, a figure appears in front of me.

Not a beast. A figure.

I blink in surprise as I find myself looking up at an elf. He's a wood elf by the looks of it, dressed in flowing green clothing. A bow is strung across his back, and several daggers hang at his waist. He bows low as I stare, dumbfounded, his golden locks of hair falling all about. When he straightens back up, he slowly claps a hand over his chest.

"Allow me to introduce myself. My name is Elrith, and I will be your servant."

I slowly bite my lip and lift a finger. "Elrith? You're—"

"Not a beast. I know you're surprised, but you shouldn't be. Your skills work on sentient creatures as well as beasts." Elrith shrugs, then leans forward. "And, in my case, I didn't need a skill to convince me to join you."

I draw out my new Rainbow Dagger and point it at him. "I had someone try that trick on me already. It didn't work then, and it won't work now."

Elrith simply bows his head. "I understand your concern, but I am no dungeon boss. I am . . . Well, there will be time for my story. Allow me to excuse myself, and we will speak in the morning when you're more rested."

My pocket dimension flares open, and Elrith slips inside. A moment later, I'm alone once more and left staring, somewhat dumbfounded. This has been a day of surprises, to be certain, and they apparently didn't end once we left the rift. In any event, though, that's the last of my level rewards, and I yawn and flop back on the bed.

"Well, then. If that's all that there is, I'm going to get some—"

Master?

Bjorn's voice echoes through my head, and I sit up. The portal to the pocket dimension didn't close after Elrith's passage, and my Frost Wolf slowly steps out and pads up before my bed. I reach out and scratch him behind the ears. Astrid emerges a moment later, standing right next to him. I should note that there's so little space in this bedroom that we're all crammed inside *very* tightly, but we manage somehow.

"What is it?" I scratch Astrid as well, and I feel a smile spread across my face. "Let me guess. The two of you are getting married?"

Bjorn and Astrid glance at each other, and I suddenly wonder if my joke was more on point than I suspected. This is confirmed an instant later as a puppy, almost two feet tall, comes bounding out. His feet are huge compared to the rest of his body, and his fur is a lovely salt and pepper color.

This is Balder. He's our son.

"Well, congratulations!" I pet the two animals a bit more, then bend down and let Balder lick my hands. He lets out a small yap, then turns and bounds back through to the pocket dimension. I watch him go, and Bjorn lets out a soft woof.

He won't be ready for combat for a little bit, but we'll let you know.

"Well, given the rapidity of his growth thus far, I doubt I'll be disappointed." I smile. "You've done well. Now go get some rest yourselves."

The two wolves turn and slink back inside the pocket dimension as well, and I sigh and fall back on the bed one final time. This time nothing comes to mind, and nothing interrupts me. My chat disconnects for real this time, and my eyelids flutter closed. Almost instantly, I fall deeply asleep, sucked down into that wonderful, refreshing void.

Frankly, I don't know how long I'm asleep for. I'm as dead to the world as a doorknob, and my body isn't going to change that fact for anything.

Except maybe a dungeon.

BZZZZZZZZZZZZZZZZT!

The noise jars me out of a wonderful dream about fighting my way through a dungeon of cotton candy, and I sit bolt upright in bed.

I'm still in the same room, but it's not quite the same. Ali is gone. John is gone. And, of course, there's a massive, horizontal portal forming underneath the bed. I don't even have time to stand up before the whole thing falls through, sheets and all, and I plummet into the portal.

It isn't quite the wakeup call that I was expecting, but in this new world, unexpected is the norm. Lightning flares around me, and I grab for my weapons. Whatever's about to happen, I know I'll be able to fight my way through.

And then, once I've conquered that, I'll just keep fighting, and I'm not going to stop until I find this mysterious queen and knock the crown right off her head.

ABOUT THE AUTHOR

Kaz Hunter is the author of the Apocalypse Reincarnation, System Bound, and Rise of the Strongest Sovereign series. A graduate of Texas A&M University (go, Aggies!), he started writing on Wuxiaworld and Webnovel. He has since moved on.

Podium

DISCOVER
STORIES UNBOUND

PodiumAudio.com

www.ingramcontent.com/pod-product-compliance
Lightning Source LLC
Chambersburg PA
CBHW020650120726
47906CB00001B/208